Praise for *First B*

'Will Dean writes a mean thriller, with a keen ear for what scares us. The streets of New York shine off the page, and the action rarely lets up. Highly recommended'
Sarah Hilary

'Original, imaginative, thrilling!'
Marian Keyes

'This taut, twisted thriller kept me guessing until the very last page. Clever, compelling and utterly thrilling'
Lisa Jewell

'Rather special short, sharp shocker'
Sunday Times Crime Club, Star Pick

'Highly accomplished, dark and dazzling. *First Born* twists and deceives, and cements Will Dean's status as a truly rare talent. Pure brilliance'
Christ Whitaker

'Tiptoes into Highsmith territory here. Pacy, exhilarating and jaw-dropping, it's a meditation on identity and loneliness as well as a bloody good pageturner. New York buffets the characters about its ruthless streets, just as the reader is propelled from one twist to the next'
Erin Kelly

'Will Dean manages to accomplish the rare blend of excellent writing and intriguing, ingenious plotting'
Liz Nugent

'One of the most twisty-turny and, ultimately, satisfying stories of the year'
On Magazine

'A superb page-turner'
Steve Cavanagh

‘Taut, suspenseful, chilling and surprising’
Gilly Macmillan

‘Spine-chilling’
Irish Independent

‘Great pace, great twists, a perfect psychological thriller’
B.A. Paris

‘This psychological thriller is a masterpiece’
The Crime Review

‘The storyline is truly original, with one of those brilliant endings only a great thriller writer can dream up’
The Press Association

‘A clever and sophisticated construction . . .A jolly good read’
SHOTS

‘Powerful . . . Dean takes on issues of personal identity and familial responsibility’
The Financial Times

‘Equal parts murder mystery and psychological thriller, Will Dean dazzles with *First Born*. A tense, taut plot that blows through unexpected twists and turns, you won’t be able to look away until the final, shattering page’
Julie Clark

‘Dean has plenty of surprises for the unwary reader’
The Observer

‘This thriller promises to be unforgettable’
The Sun

‘The talented Mr Ripley would have enjoyed every moment of its tortuous plot. There is no higher praise’
Daily Mail

Also by Will Dean

The Last Thing to Burn

Published by Oneworld

Dark Pines
Red Snow
Black River
Bad Apples

WILL DEAN

First Born

HODDER

First published in Great Britain in 2022 by Hodder & Stoughton
An Hachette UK company

This paperback edition published in 2023

1

A CIP catalogue record for this title is available from the British Library

Paperback ISBN 978 1 529 30718 4

Typeset in Plantin Light by Hewer Text UK Ltd, Edinburgh
Printed and bound in Great Britain by Clays Ltd, Elcograf S.p.A.

Hodder & Stoughton policy is to use papers that are natural, renewable and recyclable products and made from wood grown in sustainable forests. The logging and manufacturing processes are expected to conform to the environmental regulations of the country of origin.

Hodder & Stoughton Ltd
Carmelite House
50 Victoria Embankment
London EC4Y 0DZ

www.hodder.co.uk

To all the nurses, hospital cleaners, pharmacists, doctors, paramedics, carers. We owe you all so much. Thank you.

1

I am half a person.

The darkest half. The half that isn't quite fifty per cent.

My fire alarm doesn't look as pristine as it should, so I stand up on my mattress and press the test button. It bleeps. I test it again because I read on Quora one time – a comment embedded deep inside a thread – that it's possible to get a false positive.

Sometimes I feel like I am a false positive.

Not sometimes. For at least eighteen of the past twenty-two years. Since I was four years old. That's when I realised two important things in life. First: there are no such things as identical twins. Second: the universe conspires to trip you up.

I test the alarm again and it bleeps.

I lie back down on the bed and the four baby-safe pillows compress under the weight of my head. Pillows made with air holes. Breathable pillow slips. It's rare that a full-grown adult woman suffocates from lying face-down in her sleep, but it is not impossible. There was a reported case in South Korea last year.

On my bedside table rests a knife with a three-inch blade. It's legal because it does not lock and the blade is short, but I made sure to order the toughest knife available. It's a balance of risks. Being incarcerated, even short-term, even just being questioned by the police, versus the risk of being violently attacked in my own home.

My entire existence is made up of balancing risks. KT, my twin, has never felt the need.

I want to move to the kitchen to make a cup of tea, but I will not leave while my phone is charging. Reddit taught me better. A retired firefighter shared his three top tips for avoiding house fires. This wasn't his opinion; it was his conclusion after years of experience. First: avoid electric bed blankets. Second: avoid cheap Christmas lights. Third: never leave your phone charging on a flammable surface. I don't watch my phone the whole time it's charging, I'm not insane, but I do lie or sit next to it, within arm's reach of my fire extinguisher and emergency fire blanket. There's another pair of extinguishers in the far corner of the room. Another pair in every other room of my small Camden Town apartment. I believe in forward planning.

Camden may not be known as the safest area of London but, again, there is a balance to be found. Most people look at crime statistics and property prices and then they make their decision. I need to avoid crime and I need to avoid bankruptcy, both serious risks living here. I'm also mindful of other pertinent factors. My estate agent was more than a little surprised when I asked for the exact elevation above the River Thames. Like he hadn't heard about rising sea levels. Like he hadn't watched the documentary by a Dutch scientist on YouTube about how the Thames Flood Barrier is already outdated and how if we suffer a once-in-a-century storm surge much of London will end up underwater.

When I calculate my budget, I always try to keep some money back for Mum in case she ever needs it again. Five years ago Dad's business almost went under. Mum has no job, no qualifications, no income. He doesn't want her to work. I don't feel comfortable with that set-up, that lack of autonomy, so I try to save a few pounds each month in case she ever needs it.

Next to my phone is a photo of them both. My parents: Paul and Elizabeth Raven. Good people. Caring and straightforward and down-to-earth. Honest, mostly. Mum is, at least. Next to that is a photo of me, Molly Raven, and my monozygotic twin, Katie, or, as I call her, KT. I don't use the term 'identical twin' because it's a blatant lie. A travesty. Our base DNA is identical, sure, but that's about all that is.

We were once one person.

We are not any more.

The photograph was taken last year before KT moved to the USA. She had already broken the news to me and I can see that loss in my expression. The trauma of it.

We are not identical; she is prettier and funnier and she doesn't need to constantly assess threats. 'I'll try anything once,' is what she always says. Why would you do that? And why would you be proud of it? Back in our three-bedroom Nottinghamshire house growing up, she'd be the one trying ice-skating for the first time while I sat in the café with Mum, watching. She'd be the one volunteering for things in class, whereas I never volunteered for anything unless it made one or both of us safer.

If I look closely at the photo I can see the scar in her eyebrow from when she fell on a Cornwall beach when we were seven. I was the awkward one even back then. The anxious one. KT was the adventurous one, always rock-pooling and fishing crabs and wanting to swim. I was left on the beach within my windbreaks, slathered in sun block. Always safe. That day, when blood was dripping down into her eye, Mum and Dad trying to wash the wound from a bottle of water, I walked away. I couldn't deal with the drama. The stares from other beachgoers. Or the fact that we looked so completely different in that moment. Mum and Dad worked hard to make sure I could handle everyday life, to ease my anxieties. But, in that moment, they were so focused on KT that they forgot about me. I walked off to sit on some rocks and nobody noticed. Mum and Dad were comforting KT, and in that instant they looked like a perfect family.

But she is my twin. That's precious. She is the closest person to me in the whole world. We are not like other people. We were an egg cell – a singular, beautiful egg cell – that split *in utero*.

KT took half of me and I took half of KT. I don't own pets because I can't afford pets and because my landlord will not allow pets and because – and please feel free to research this for yourself – there are an estimated four thousand incidents recorded each year in Europe alone of dogs and cats killing or seriously maiming their owners. That's one worry I can live without.

In the other corner of my room is a fireproof safe. In there I store my unused passport and my unused driving licence and my unused credit cards. I keep my documents up to date in case I need them for ID, or in case there's a war and I need to flee. Ordinarily, I have no interest in international travel, even with all the insurance in the world. I will not drive because according to the Office for National Statistics driving is the second most dangerous everyday travel activity after motorcycling.

I'm curious to check my phone's battery status but I will not be tempted to touch the screen. Never touch a phone that is being charged from a mains socket unless it's to disconnect the plug. Never take that unnecessary risk. I read somewhere online that to touch a connecting phone that is charging increases the already heightened electrocution risk by up to three per cent. The charger will need to be replaced next week, it's already a month old; the wires inside will be degrading.

My sister wouldn't think twice about it. She's so spontaneous and carefree that she manages to live life for the both of us. Has done since we were young girls. These days she's so addicted to her phone, her likes and retweets. She told me last year she once took it with her into her bathroom using a fifteen-feet-long electrical extension cable. I could hardly breathe when she said that. And this was in New York City, half a world away, and I told her, I said 'KT you must swear never to do that again. You must swear it to me.'

She did swear.

I'm sitting on the bed, putting on hand cream, when my phone rings.

It vibrates, and the vibrations make it slither slowly across my bedside table.

I check the screen. A number I don't recognise.

A siren rings out in the distance but I can't see flashing lights through my window. The noise grows. It intensifies and then I notice the police car speed by.

The phone vibrates in my hand.

I take a deep breath and then I accept the call. 'Molly Raven speaking.'

There's silence on the line, and then the sound of someone sniffing.

'Who is this?'

'Oh, Molly. It's . . .'

'Mum? What's wrong?' Mum never cries. She is a composed person. Methodical and calm.

'Molly, it's . . .' And then the sound of a cry.

My stomach pulls tight in my abdomen. 'Mum, what is it? Are you safe? Talk to me.'

But now it's Dad's voice on the phone. Soothing. His usual kind and patient tone. 'Your mum, she's . . .'

'Dad, you're scaring me.'

'Moll, I don't know how to tell you this.' He pauses. 'Oh, God. It's . . . it's your sister. I'm so sorry.'

I hear Mum sobbing in the background and my body turns to stone.

'She's gone, Moll.'

2

'What do you mean, *she's gone*?'

There's a pause on the line. My head knows what he's saying but my body and my soul are failing me.

'I'm . . .' says Dad, his voice small. Trembling. 'I'm so sorry, Moll.'

'Where has KT gone? Dad, please. Is she missing in New York?'

There's a longer pause. The sound of Mum crying in the background.

'She's dead, Molly. She's gone.'

My blood coagulates in my veins. Even though I knew what he meant, the words are too much. I sit on the bed.

'We want you to come right here if you can. I know it's really difficult for you to travel, but . . .'

'How?' I say. 'I don't understand, Dad. It's a mistake. How is she gone?'

I hear him swallow. 'The police don't know for sure yet. We found her in her apartment. She looked so peaceful, Moll.'

My mother screams.

'Are you sure it was her, though? One hundred per cent certain?'

'Yes, Moll, I'm sure. Katie is gone.' He sniffs again. 'The police here are investigating. Your mother and me, we want you here in New York with us. We need to be together.'

I look at my reflection in the window and my head is shaking by itself, willing all this away.

'Are you OK, Molly? Is there anyone you can be with until you fly over here?'

There is nobody. 'Fly over there? Dad, I . . .' I can hear sirens from outside their Manhattan hotel room. Pulsing sirens. 'What is that?'

'Fire truck,' says Dad. 'It's nothing. What did you want to say?'

'I'll come,' I say. 'Of course I'll come. Is there a fast ship to New York?'

He says, 'No, sweetie,' in the soothing tone he's used ever since I was a young girl. 'We've checked. But the plane is safe. It's completely safe.'

I swallow audibly. 'I know it is,' I say. 'Statistically. I know it.' One in a million. *Less* than one in a million. 'I'll be there as soon as I can. I'll do it somehow. I . . .'

'You have your breathing exercises, Molly. You'll be OK.'

'It's just . . .'

'What is it?'

'I always thought I'd know, you know? I always thought if this ever happened I'd feel it somehow. Sense it.'

'We didn't sense it either, Moll.'

'But you're not twins. It's totally different.'

'I know. I'm sorry. Do you need help booking a flight?'

I take a deep breath. 'I can do it.'

'She looked so perfect.' My father sniffs again but he does not cry.

'But how? How did it happen? This cannot be.'

'We don't know yet, Moll. But the people here say she wasn't in any pain at the end.'

Those two words shake me.

The.

End.

After we say goodbye I place my phone down on the bedside table and push my hands down into the mattress and ball my fists. I'm shaking, but I'm not crying.

Time passes. I feel numb. Detached.

When I get any news – good or bad – I tell my sister straight away. And she tells me her news too. That's what we do. If I choose a paint colour for a wall or I find a new soup at my favourite café then I tell her. Every little thing I do, I tell her. This is the kind of thing I would tell her immediately. She is the other half of me.

Was the other half of me.

My God.

The world doesn't feel right.

I walk through into my kitchenette and stare into the stainless steel sink. Her reflection stares back at me. I blink hard and take a pen and a piece of notepaper and sit down at the table.

My hand is shaking. I watch the pen, and the rollerball tip is waving around in the air. I put it down and pick it up again.

I write the word *List*. A well-known coping strategy. Order from chaos.

I write *New York*. I can't bring myself to write *Flight tickets*.

She's gone. She's really gone.

Pack case. Usually this would take me a week or more.

How will Mum cope with this?

Passport.

How will *I* cope?

Money.

I will never see my sister again.

Tell boss.

I take my phone and Google 'Katie Raven' but I just get links to her Twitter and her Instagram and her Facebook. Then I find articles written by her for the *Columbia Daily Spectator*, and an article about her volunteering at the Morningside Heights Homeless Shelter. I search entries from the past twenty-four hours but find nothing.

I check her Instagram.

The last photo on the grid is from three days ago. Central Park, October sun washing over one side of her face, highlighting the scar in her eyebrow. She looks so relaxed. I start to tear up but I continue to focus on her face, her hair, her smile as the image distorts through a saline lens. I wipe my thumb over the wet phone screen and her face shrinks. I release my thumb and it grows again to fill the screen. What do I do now?

An hour later I feel different.

Composed, but also empty.

More alone than you could ever realistically imagine. I entered this life with my twin sister and part of me thought I'd leave with her as well. Now I'm here all alone. A singular half.

The best thing I can do right now is be practical. Get things done. Mum and Dad need my support. I'll tick off the items on my list and then once that's in order I can let myself feel the pain. I can give in to the grief.

I Google 'safest airline in the world' and start researching. I narrow my options to five airlines that fly daily from London to New York. I need to take this more seriously than ever before because if my parents lose me now then they will have lost everything.

I always felt she would outlive me. She was nicer. In many ways she was a better version of me. She deserved a long life.

My bank balance is low but I can manage. I don't know the full picture but from what Mum tells me their financial situation is far worse than mine so I need to cover the costs of this nightmare trip on my own. Economy tickets with British Airways leaving at 15.50.

I have a framed picture of my sister by my lap, resting on its own breathable pillow.

My poor sister.

Up until we were seven years old, Mum dressed us both the same, although I think that was Dad's idea. In the photo we have pigtails and matching outfits and matching shoes. Little KT's socks look odd. One pulled high, the other down by her ankle. She did that on purpose. We used to go everywhere together. We even created an elaborate secret language, much to the chagrin of our parents.

It's dark outside.

I receive the flight confirmation email in my inbox and then I make a mug of tea. I make it strong and add an extra teaspoon of sugar. Most people would have opened the gin but there is no gin. Never has been. Now, more than ever before, I need to make zero mistakes and I need to stay clear-headed and in control of the situation. There is no longer anyone to help me when I stumble.

After writing out my full itinerary and double-checking luggage restrictions I monitor the weather forecast. Multiple forecasts. Still nothing on the news.

I Google *flight to New York checklist*. I need something called an ESTA visa waiver or else I won't be allowed into the United States. If I don't get granted one I won't be allowed to board my flight. I need to be with my parents. To talk to the police. I find the intimidating ESTA website. One question is 'What will be your temporary address in the United States' and I text Dad and he replies immediately: *The Bedfordshire Midtown Hotel, West 44th Street*. I enter that information and pay the fourteen dollars. I glance at KT's face in the photo and rub my eyes.

My breathing feels wrong. Am I going to have a heart attack? Am I going into shock?

More tea.

I research travel insurance. After reading horror stories of hundred-thousand-dollar hospital bills I decide to cover myself by purchasing two policies from two separate insurers headquartered in two separate continents. It's important to have insurance for your insurance.

As the bird outside my locked windows starts to sing I fall asleep on my bed with the photo of my twin next to me on its own pillow.

* * *

I wake up and immediately check Google but there's still no news about KT. I'm craving details: timelines, forensic evidence, medical reports, suspects in custody. I want to know the specifics. The ESTA was granted, thank goodness. I take a screenshot of the confirmation and send that to my back-up email.

Strong coffee. I cross-reference my lists and pack my checked bag and my hand luggage and then I repack them both. I research *can you take a parachute on a jet plane* and discover that you can but they do not increase your chances of surviving a serious incident.

I unplug all appliances except for the fridge, and then I leave the apartment. I secure all three locks on the door and climb into the minicab. The company knows me. They have on file that I insist on a Volvo and an experienced driver with no points on their licence.

My phone's lock screen shows my sister's face. *My* face. An Instagram photo from Central Park. My lock screen used to show a photo of her walking on Hampstead Heath, down by the swimming ponds, one of our favourite places in the world. I'm better with wildlife than I am with people.

I see glimpses of Buckingham Palace and Hyde Park on the way to the M4 motorway. At Heathrow the driver takes the Terminal 5 exit and I see there are armed police close to the terminal. I count four.

I pull on my backpack and thank the driver and retract the handle on my suitcase and then I sprint as fast as I can, dragging my bag in my wake. I've read on forums how unsecure landside areas before check-in are among the most risky places to linger in the modern world.

At security I'm told to take off my shoes and remove all liquids from my bag. I walk through and I do not set off the metal detector. My vigilance is total. I am constantly aware of those around me.

My bag gets searched and the agent looks quizzically at some of my hand baggage contents but then she lets me pass. I press the light green *quite satisfied* button as I walk away.

As I pass through the wine and spirits area I inhale a faint scent of Armani Mania and suddenly I cannot breathe. The familiarity of the fragrance. I stop and rest with my back against the wall and I squeeze my eyes shut to stop myself crying. I try to walk on but have to steady myself against the baggage trolleys.

I reach the gate a full two hours and forty minutes before take-off because I cannot miss this plane. My parents need me and I need them. We need each other to make it through this catastrophic loss. To make sense of it all.

My group, group five, is the last to board. I locate my seat and place my bag down by my feet and the flight attendant tells me it must be placed in the overhead locker. I am not happy about this. The bag contains the things I need to make it through this flight; that's why I packed them. I take my essential items from the bag and stuff them down into my deep coat pockets. When I sit down again, my security items and Pret sandwich bulge so much that the person in the middle seat grunts his disapproval.

'Something wrong?' I say.

He just shakes his head and looks out of the window.

Fool.

Fool in a middle seat.

Before take-off I listen carefully to all the in-flight safety announcements. I diligently read the instructions written around the emergency exit door and then I count how many rows of seats exist between me and the other exits.

We had always planned to be together in New York one day, just not like this. Never like this. Flying was unthinkable – it would have been an economy berth on the *Queen Mary II* ocean liner. A six-day voyage, with a back-up life vest and all the survival gear that could be squeezed into bags. She and I would have planned activities in Manhattan, walking in Little Italy and Chinatown, visiting Long island and New Hampshire if we'd had time.

All of a sudden I am tired. Weighed down by loss.

I tighten my seatbelt to the point where it's almost painful, and the guy next to me inserts earplugs and pops a tablet from a blister pack. Is that a sleeping tablet? What kind of idiot, honestly. We accelerate and take off and it's noisy but the flight is smooth once we're up in the air. I watch as London shrinks in the emergency door window. My heart shrinks with it. Leaving all this and flying to my dead twin.

People in other rows start putting on eye masks and ordering drinks from the attendants.

This doesn't feel real. We're above cloud level now, flying over the southwest tip of England, the area where we used to holiday as kids. They were good times. The four of us: a normal, reasonably functional family from the Midlands. Dad was fun and Mum was caring and busy. I knew back then that identical twins weren't identical. Not really.

Most of the passengers around me watch movies on their head-rest screens. Some are reading and some are already asleep.

The flight attendant approaches me. She smiles broadly and then there's a bang. A woman yells and the plane starts to nosedive.

3

The *fasten seatbelt* sign illuminates and the woman in front of me starts to pray.

Is this turbulence? We've barely reached the Atlantic. I look out of the window and the wing is still attached but it's shaking violently. What are the engineering tolerances of this aircraft?

The plane settles and levels out. The man beside me is no longer dozing. He looks over at me, confused.

'Turbulence has never brought down a jet aeroplane,' I tell him.

He frowns at me.

'I'd tighten your belt, though. Dozens of people break bones each year from leaping up out of their seats.'

He adjusts his belt.

People go back to their movies and the sleeping pill guy eventually goes back to sleep, his head resting on the person by the emergency exit door.

I imagine how this looks. A cross-section through earth's atmosphere, the layers as described to me in a geography class ten years ago. The ocean and then thirty-seven thousand feet of air and then an aluminium can with wings crammed full of jet fuel flying at five hundred miles per hour, the rivets and bolts and seatbelts and cockpit safety systems all procured years ago from the lowest bidder.

Passengers settle back into their entertainment systems. There's a woman sitting diagonally across from me watching a Christmas movie even though it's only October. My sister would have given me side-eye if she'd been sitting next to me on this plane.

Ideally I'd assemble my anti-hijack devices in private but needs must.

I locate the para cord in my deep pocket. It's military-grade string really, the type used for parachutes, and the YouTubers I've watched swear by it. I take five one-pound coins from my other pocket and start to weave a monkey-fist knot around the coins. You can make it without coins in the centre but it won't be as effective. I do all of this underneath a British Airways complimentary blanket. My seatbelt is as tight as it will go and my hands are at work and you'd never even know it. Monkey fists are illegal in many places in the world owing to their inherent power, but if you learn to weave one yourself, and you practise enough, train in the dark, then you can make one on board a plane in ten minutes flat. When it's done I place it in my right pocket and pull out a pair of socks. I take one and fill it with the remaining fifteen pound coins and place that makeshift weapon in my left pocket.

There's only a minuscule chance I'll need them, but not *as* minuscule as you might imagine. I'm a five-foot-five-inch-tall, twenty-two-year-old, seven-stone-two woman flying alone to the USA. It's not just hijackers I need to be watchful of, it's also troubled people who decide they'll open an emergency exit door mid-air, and people who go berserk for any one of a thousand different reasons owing to the stress and anxiety of long-haul flying. Not everyone is as level-headed as I am.

My sister was as level-headed as I am. The woman is still watching her Christmas movie. That's something I'll never again celebrate with her. We used to hang up our stockings together. We used to wrap presents together while listening to Christmas carols on the radio. That's all over now. I'll never take her to a casual pre-vetted pizza restaurant and spend the night laughing about the stupid things she did when we were kids.

The guy next to me starts snoring so I move around in my seat and cough and eventually he stirs and turns the other way.

I am alone in the world. Trapped on a plane, and my twin is gone. What is a remaining twin called? A survivor? I don't even know. But I do know that statistically most identical twins die within two years of each other.

The woman in front of me reclines her seat, and that makes me want to smack her with my monkey fist.

I worry about Mum. She's aged since Grandma died last year and I'm not sure how she'll deal with all this. For your mother and your daughter to die in the same year is too much for anyone to bear.

I pull my knitting needles out of my sock but keep them under my blanket. I take a folded piece of duct tape from my jeans pocket and tape the needles together – honestly, I was stunned when I found out they're permitted in the cabin – and then I push them back down into my sock. I'm not a hero or a brave person; I just believe that preparation and mindfulness can skew unexpected risks in your favour.

We fly over the white vastness of Greenland. Imagine crash-landing here. If you survived the impact and the probable fireball you'd have to cope with extreme hypothermia and famished polar bears with razor-sharp teeth. I'd rather crash somewhere else. Almost anywhere else. Our plane is heading towards Canada. That means grizzly bears and packs of wolves. My knitting needles won't help much in that kind of environment.

The flight attendants take away empty food trays and wine bottles, and then they start their next drinks service.

We enter US air spacc and fly over the dark, endless forests of Maine. We approach JFK. My entire body is stiff, and I am holding my seat armrests so hard the tendons in my forearms ache.

The wheels touch down on the runway.

I walk off the plane and start to feel queasy. I need food and hydration and I need rest. I need a hug from my broken parents. They'll need one back from me.

The airport is different from Heathrow. The accents of the officials and the people making public announcements. The signs and the fonts. The type of carpets here in the United States of America.

I reach Immigration and the police officers all carry guns. I found this sight reassuring at Heathrow, but here they seem dangerous. Menacing. I know they're here to keep order inside the terminal, and protect regular people like me, but I am ill at ease.

'US citizens queue over there,' says a woman. 'If you've

been to the United States before on your ESTA, then queue over there.'

Then a man shouts, 'First time visiting the United States, you need to be over here.' He points to a long queue and I join it. I am gripping my pristine passport so hard it's starting to bend, and my palms are sweating.

When I reach the front of the line I say, 'Hello.'

The man says, 'Passport, ma'am.'

I hand it over.

He looks at me, taking in my features, my unwashed brown hair and my narrow face and my green eyes. 'Business or pleasure?'

My twin is dead. No one seems to know what happened to her.

'Pleasure.'

Far from pleasure. The furthest thing from it.

'Place your thumb here.'

I do as he says.

'Stick it in further, follow the diagram.'

I do it.

'Fingers.'

I do it.

'Other thumb.'

I do it.

'Fingers.'

He looks at me and at my passport one last time then he stamps it and hands it back.

'Thank you,' I say.

'Yeah,' he says. 'Have a nice day.'

4

I run to the restroom and break down. Tears and dry-heaving. *Have a nice day*. I doubt I'll ever have another nice day in my lifetime. A kind woman from the next stall asks in a thick Spanish accent if I'm OK. I rub my eyes. Afterwards I douse my hands and arms and face in alcohol sanitiser gel.

The bags aren't on the carousel yet so I choose a position, my back to a wall, to wait for my suitcase to show up. People stare at my red eyes. I still can't comprehend that she's gone. Permanently gone. Not around for me to call on a Sunday, or play Monopoly with at our parents' house outside Nottingham each New Year's Day. I'll never discuss Dolly Parton songs or Shirley MacLaine movies with her again, nor share the small everyday irrelevancies of life.

In a way, in many ways, this city came between us.

I compose myself and take a deep breath, and then I walk calmly through the 'Nothing to Declare' channel.

When I pass through I'm greeted by emotional strangers with their arms held out wide. One man's in front of me holding a red balloon and a rose. He's almost crying. There's a family of six waiting for an elderly relative, all of them sporting home-made name placards.

I break into a run.

People stare.

I run outside and continue jogging towards the cab rank, and my bag twists on the kerb, and my wrist turns the wrong way. I correct my grip and a black Suburban SUV drives past so close the wing mirror grazes my shoulder. 'Uber?' he shouts. I retreat and join the queue for an official yellow cab.

No New York skyline out here. No Brooklyn Bridge. No sign of the Empire State Building.

Drizzle and a cool, gentle breeze.

A friendly guy with a scar on his cheek beckons me over to his taxi and places my suitcase in his trunk. I opt to keep my hand baggage with me in the back seat.

'Could you take me to the corner of West 44th Street and the Avenue of the Americas, please?'

'44th and Sixth, yeah, no problem.'

'No, the Avenue of the Americas, please,' I repeat firmly.

He ignores me and starts talking to someone on his phone through an earpiece and mic. I think he's Senegalese because there's a miniature Senegal flag hanging from his rear-view mirror, along with a Black Sabbath album cover and a Greenpeace placard. He's laughing and chuckling on the phone as he drives out of JFK. I'd rather he focused on the traffic but I don't say anything.

This is nothing like I expected it to be. I check my phone and the GPS map tells me I'm in Queens. Low-built houses with small yards and barking dogs. Homes stuffed into small lots; American equivalents of the family house where my sister and I grew up. I drive past one place with a tarp secured over its porch roof.

The driver cackles in the front seat and I study the map some more. We are heading in the right direction. I am comforted by my GPS. I reference it at every turn, every intersection.

'Could we take a bridge to Manhattan Island instead of an underground tunnel, please?'

He checks me in his rear-view mirror. 'What is it, lady?'

'Bridge, please. I don't like tunnels.'

'Sure, no problem. Queensboro. First time in New York, yeah?'

'Yes,' I say. 'First time. Thank you.'

He returns to his call and I see the beginnings of a skyline. It's part-eclipsed by industrial terminals and warehouses but I can see the tips of skyscrapers and the reflection of the East River. My heart is beating so hard in my chest and I cannot believe I am here in New York City on the saddest week of my life.

We cross over to Roosevelt Island and Manhattan reveals itself. My goodness. It looks exactly like a movie. Low sun streaming through grids of buildings; headlights shining like fallen stars. The city is pulsing. London has a rhythm all of its own, but this place is something else.

My twin sister lies somewhere in all this. Cold. Lifeless, in a stainless steel drawer or on a slab. She travelled to this city, this epicentre, and now she is dead. It's perverse, but I can't shake from my head the notion that I am somehow replacing her. I'm not, of course, not in any sense, but our base DNA is one hundred per cent identical. It's almost as if this city lost that specific DNA and now that loss has been corrected. The deoxyribonucleic acid, each miraculous double helix, has been replaced by a clone. A perfect spare. On a cosmic level there is something beautiful and monstrous about that. It's as if I shouldn't be here at all.

The Chrysler Building. The UN. The Empire State Building. We drive closer to Grand Central Station and I ask the driver, 'Are we about ten minutes away?' and he replies with a shake of his hand.

I frown at this and he says, 'This time of day.'

I call Dad and let it ring three rings and then end the call. He calls back almost immediately, three rings, and then ends the call. That's how my family communicates. Free of charge.

It feels all the more horrendous that my sister should die when our parents are in America visiting her for the first time. It's normal to feel safer than ever when your parents are close by.

We pass the MetLife Building and then the New York Public Library, and it is imposing. I hear sirens from across the street and instinctively I pull my seatbelt tighter. I realise my hands are balled into tight fists and my fingernails are digging into my palms. The in-cab TV plays a commercial for pain-relief medicine.

The driver makes a few turns and pulls up on a street corner. 'Bedfordshire Midtown Hostel,' he says.

'Thank you,' I say, looking up at the sign. He's right. It says Hostel, not Hotel.

No sign of Mum or Dad so I get out of the cab and the noise is everywhere. More sirens and horns and engines and people shouting into their phones. A gargantuan ants' nest of a city.

He hands me my bags and I hand him sixty-five dollars and he says, 'Enjoy New York.'

If only he knew.

I pull my bags close to my body and the door of the hostel opens and Mum steps out. She has aged a decade since I last saw her.

She smiles, but then she shakes her head and she weeps. Dad's right behind her but she's blocking the doorway. I drag my bags to her and I start to cry again. The pain in her eyes. At losing a daughter but also at seeing her live right in front of you, a reminder too exact to be any kind of comfort. If I were just a sister or a brother I'd have been reassurance. Straightforward support. But she looks at me and she sees KT.

She puts her palms to my cheeks and they are dry and cool. I shake my head and the air leaves my lungs and she says, 'I know, Molly. I know. Oh, my God,' and we squeeze each other and she falls to her knees and I fall with her. Half in and half out of the hostel. Me on the street and her just inside. Dad behind. We collapse in a heap and I cry quietly into the familiar crease of her neck and she wails. I smell Nivea skin cream.

Dad bends down and rubs my back. He says, 'Oh, Moll,' and he rubs both our backs and then he says, 'Best come inside, both of you.'

We stagger over the threshold and I see the reception area through tears. 'Are you OK?' I ask Mum.

She nods and bites her lip and then shakes her head and says, 'Not really, but I'm so pleased you're here, Molly.'

'We're both pleased,' says Dad. 'We've got your room ready – right next to ours, it is. A safe spot.'

The hostel reception still says 'Bedfordshire Midtown Hotel' so I'm not sure if this place is transitioning upmarket or downmarket or if it's stuck somewhere in the middle. The décor is more hostel than hotel.

'You two go up in the elevator,' says Dad. 'Won't fit all of us. I'll take the stairs.' Sounds strange to hear him say *elevator*.

Mum and I squeeze in with my cases and the doors slide shut.

'Where is she? I have to see her, Mum.'

My mother wipes her eyes and sniffs. 'I know, sweetie. We'll talk to the policeman again. It's complicated. Things work differently here.'

The doors open and we step out. Third floor. They have picked it for me. Safe enough at this elevation from street-level disturbances but not too high to be impossible to exit during a catastrophic fire.

'What are the police telling you?'

Mum shakes her head and Dad arrives and he says, 'This is home, for now.' He unlocks the hotel room door with a brass key. 'We're just next door, Moll. We're right here.'

'What do the police say?' I ask again.

Mum says, 'We don't know what's happening for sure yet, sweetie.'

Dad turns to Mum and says, 'For God's sake. It wasn't an accident, Elizabeth. We know it wasn't self-inflicted, and it wasn't some kind of freak illness.'

Mum sobs into her hands.

'What happened to her?'

'Police aren't saying concrete anything yet, Moll,' says Dad. 'It's hard to get any clear information out of them. But we think Katie was murdered.'

5

Murdered?

Why would anyone want to murder KT?

She was a sweet person. When I look at most people I see secrets and guilt: lies, deceit and self-loathing. But everyone knew KT was thoroughly decent.

The room is about the size of a double bed. I sit on my single bed: a wooden bench with a thin mattress and space underneath for my suitcase. A wire runs at the end of the bed from one wall to the other and from it dangles a single hanger with a small white towel. The bedsheets look thin and clean. The pillow is fine, though it's not a breathable baby pillow like the one back in London. There is no private bathroom. The lock on the door looks inadequate for the job. There is no air-conditioning but there is a fan. That'll work fine this time of year. It's a thirty-dollar room my parents have probably paid sixty dollars for.

It hits me like one wave crashing on a pebble shore, followed by the next. Tiredness, fear, loss, confusion, jet lag, hunger, nausea. We should have met here properly next year – brought together by a long ship journey, with all the right safety equipment, with proper planning. Time for us to reconnect and just be. Forgive each other for all of the harsh words. Laugh about it. I've daydreamed of the walks we'd take in Central Park. The chats we'd have in the apartment over bowls of cereal with cold milk, just the way we used to chat as teenagers. And now none of that will happen.

Mum is crying in the next room. The partition wall is far from soundproof.

They've given me twenty minutes to freshen up and change clothes before we go out for food. I can't face the communal bathroom yet so I change my clothes and take a drink of water. My room is taller than it is long. A dingy shoebox standing on its end.

Dad knocks gently on the door. I recognise the cadence of his knuckle taps from home, from back when my sister and I were tiny, sharing a room, sharing everything.

'You ready, Moll?'

I step outside and he takes me a little way down the corridor and says, 'Your mum's not handling this so well.' He looks exhausted. Broken. 'She puts on a brave face, but she's very tired.'

'I know.'

He closes his eyes and sets his jaw and then he breathes out and kisses my forehead.

'Ready?' asks Mum, appearing from their room.

We head downstairs. Mum's gripping her handbag so tight I think she might destroy the leather. Like it's an anchor point for her. A safety harness.

'Is there a Pret nearby?' I ask.

Mum looks at Dad and Dad looks at me. 'Maybe, but we haven't seen one yet. We go to the nice diner round the corner. They're kind in there and the food's good. Not too expensive.'

'You've been there a few times?' I ask.

Mum says, 'It's clean, sweetie. It's a safe place, I promise.'

'I don't think I can eat.'

Dad opens the door and lets us both walk out into the manic Midtown street-life. The pavements are alive with pedestrians, and there are yellow cabs, and a fire truck in the distance with a Stars and Stripes flag hanging from its rear end. We walk round the corner and the air smells of weed.

'There it is,' says Dad.

I want to press them for details about what exactly happened to KT and about whether they think her death was in any way linked to them being here in the city to visit her. I need the specifics. All the available information. But I also need to consider their wellbeing. They're both thirty years older than I am. They're even more out of their depth arriving here from their sleepy blue-collar village outside Nottingham. I need to help take care of them. They think I'm here so they can protect me, but in reality it's the other way around.

The diner has large glass windows and it looks modern, not retro. There's a menu board inside the glass.

We walk in.

Quiet conversations and efficient servers. A semi-open kitchen, which I always say is a good sign of cleanliness and transparency. The booths or banquettes are small. Imitation leather. On each table sits a ceramic pot containing packets of sugar and Sweet'n Low, and a small vase with an artificial flower. We are seated. One laminated menu each.

'The toast is pretty good,' says Mum. I guess I inherited my wild adventurous side from her.

'I think I'll have pancakes,' says Dad. 'With maple syrup.'

We both look at him. He looks back as if to say *What*? Mum mouths the word *Paul* at him. Our expressions are too complex to unravel but translate roughly as *How can you think of eating pancakes tonight*? Simple toast is somehow acceptable in these circumstances but pancakes, with syrup, contrary to any logical reasoning, are judged, by us both, in this instant, to constitute some sort of hideous betrayal.

'I might just have toast,' says Dad. 'I'm not so hungry really.'

We order toast. Two teas and an americano. The server is a Puerto Rican woman in her forties. She has a gentle smile and she doesn't rush us. Maybe she sees we're lost in the shock end of the grief spectrum, or maybe she treats all of her customers like this, because who doesn't need quiet kindness, especially in a hectic city like this one?

'I need to buy a few things,' I say.

'It's too late tonight for that, sweetie,' says Mum. 'You need rest after your flight. You know how you get if you're too tired. We can find you the things early in the morning, before we visit the police station.'

'Police *precinct*,' says Dad.

'You know exactly what I meant, Paul,' says Mum. I stare at them both. She puts her hand on his and says, 'I'm sorry, I'm just exhausted.'

I reach over to put my hand on top of theirs but the server arrives with our drinks.

'Two teas, one americano. Your toast is coming.'

We all thank her.

It's quiet in here. Calm.

'What . . . what happened?' I ask. 'I need to know what happened to KT.'

Mum hands Dad two packets of sugar. Her hand is trembling.

'They're not telling us much yet, Moll,' says Dad, stirring his coffee. 'We wish we knew more but the police have been so busy trying to catch whoever did this, we don't know details yet. They're still trying to piece together the puzzle, so they tell us.'

'Tell her about that evening, Paul,' says Mum. 'She deserves to know.'

He looks at her, and then he takes a sip of coffee and shakes his head and swallows.

'Your mother and I had planned to meet Katie at an Italian restaurant in the Upper West Side, out near Central Park. We'd been here for six days and we knew her neighbourhood a little. Back then we were staying at the Best Western, part of our travel package. It was our last night with your sister and we wanted to make the most of it, have some nice pasta. But she never turned up, Moll, and you know Katie, she's never late, she's always very punctual.'

'She always was,' says Mum, looking down into her tea.

'So we waited and waited and called and called.'

'We went to her apartment in the end,' says Mum. 'Your father was getting worried. We tried her buzzer, but nothing. So we tried the neighbour and eventually a young man came out of the basement; his mother owns the whole building.'

The toast arrives and Dad takes over. 'We ask him to let us in and he says he can't, he needs to call his boss.'

'The lad's mother,' corrects my mum.

'Right. So he calls her, I talk to his mother for a few seconds, she tells him to let us in straight away. He finds a key and he lets us in.'

Mum rubs her face with her palms. Then she shakes her head.

'Everything seemed normal at first,' says Dad, swallowing hard. 'No signs of a forced entry, no broken windows or doors. No . . . blood.'

Mum scrunches up her eyes.

'But she was there on her bed, Moll.' He places his hand on Mum's and squeezes it. 'Ever so peaceful, she was. Your sister looked like she was fast asleep. I promise you, she looked like she was asleep.'

'The police say there was no pain,' says Mum, biting her lip for a split-second. 'Katie wasn't in any kind of pain at the end. The policeman gave me his word.'

Dad nods his head.

'But what killed her?' I ask. 'How did she die?'

A man in the adjacent booth stares at me through a pot plant so I lean in closer to Mum and Dad over the Formica table.

'We don't know anything for sure until the . . .' Dad pauses and glances at Mum and then he mouths the word *autopsy* to me. 'We'll know a lot more tomorrow, I hope. Now, please, eat your toast, both of you. It's going to be a long week. You need to eat.'

I butter my toast and eat it. I'm hungrier than I realised and my belly rumbles in the diner. The toast tastes different from London toast. It's still comforting, still good. Just different. Mum picks at hers and Dad's already finished his, smothered in peanut butter and jam. Or *jelly*, as it says on the diner menu.

'You want anything else?' he asks.

Mum looks like she might keel over and die from a broken heart at any moment. I've never seen her like this. I mean, I must appear utterly atrocious right now: sunken, tired transatlantic eyes and crumpled clothes. But Mum looks haunted.

Her eyes are focused just above my head. Dad looks at whatever she's staring at. Their jaws drop. I turn my head.

It's KT's face on the TV news.

6

Mum stands up and Dad calls out for the waitress to increase the volume but the story has already ended and now it's the weather forecast on screen instead. Some kind of storm warning.

'What did they say?' asks Mum.

I check my phone and scroll through my newsfeeds and notifications.

'Have then arrested someone?' asks Dad. 'Charged anyone?'

I Google 'Katie Raven' and check under the news tab and there it is.

I show them my phone.

'Her beautiful face,' says Mum, her hands in tight fists, her lips pursed.

I read it out. '*NYPD are investigating the suspected homicide of a young British woman now named as Katie Elizabeth Raven. The victim was found in her apartment in Morningside Heights on the evening of . . .*'

'That's it?' says Dad. 'No arrests? No suspects in custody?'

'That's all there is, Dad. If they'd had a suspect in custody they would have let us know first, surely.'

'We'll find out much more tomorrow,' says Mum.

'They have to arrest whoever did this to Katie, and lock him up forever so he rots in a cell.'

Dad pays the bill. The guy opposite tracks me with his gaze as we leave the diner. He has bright blue eyes and a moustache. He's a pig if he thinks we're his free evening entertainment.

Mum shivers as we step out into the street, and Dad gives her his scarf. A couple pass us by and they look enraptured with each other. Like the two of them are the only people in Manhattan.

'Let's try to get some sleep,' says Dad. 'Moll, you must be exhausted. It's the middle of the night for you.'

'I'm OK.'

'We have to rest,' says Dad. 'At least try. The police will need our help tomorrow.'

We walk, Mum and me in front, our arms linked together in a way we haven't done since I was nine years old, always with my sister on the other side. This feels unbalanced. Dangerously out of kilter. Dad is behind us. He's got a strong protective instinct, always vigilant; maybe that's where I inherited it from. He always taught us girls self-defence at home during the summer holidays. Basic punches and kicks and evasive techniques. He wanted us both to be safe.

I say goodnight outside our rooms and Mum rests her head on my shoulder and she whispers, 'Why?'

Dad makes sure I'm secure in my room and then he goes to bed.

I want to unpack my bag as quietly as I can but there's nowhere to put anything. No bathroom for my toiletries and no wardrobe for my clothes. I start to unpack items on to the ground but the carpet is stained so I abandon the unpacking and check my coat instead. I have the monkey fist and I have the weighted sock. One makeshift weapon in each pocket.

I leave my room as quietly as I can, and click the door shut. I linger outside my parents' room but all is silent. The floorboards creak but I make it out and then I'm loose in New York City after eleven p.m. This is a classic Molly Raven risk-reward situation. One of the YouTubers I subscribe to explained the formula years ago, and I think it's a sensible thing to heed. The risk of me staying here in this Midtown hostel with no means of adequately defending myself – besides the aeroplane-approved methods – versus the risk of a very cautious, calculated form of late-night shopping.

I don't want to go out but I must.

I pass by a 7-Eleven and make a mental note to visit this place on the way back. I need water bottles and basic food supplies in case of a hurricane or dirty bomb. Unfortunately this is the wrong time of year to visit New York. If something like Storm Sandy hits again I need to be well prepared. For my sake and for the sake of my parents.

There's a food cart on the corner of each intersection. I go up to it and talk to the guy.

'Anywhere around here I can buy a baseball bat, please?'

'You want a smoothie?'

'A bat.'

'A bat?'

I nod.

'I dunno anything about no bats. The sports shop on 42nd is closed by now but maybe try the twenty-four-hour hardware store down on Broadway – you might get lucky.'

We exchange pleasantries, and I compliment him on his mango display. He asks me where I'm from. My name. I tell him I'm an admin assistant. He tells me he grew up in Kabul. We chat more. He tries to sell me a fruit salad.

'Thank you, sir, but no thank you.'

'You're welcome.'

Nice guy.

I walk down Sixth Avenue and try to stay away from the bright lights of Times Square. I don't need that kind of craziness. There's a souvenir shop across the street so I check around me and walk inside. It's a deep cave of a place lined with *I heart NY* caps and shirts, FDNY car plates, and models of the Statue of Liberty in every size you could wish for. I buy a bunch of things including a hat and a novelty lighter and a multi-tool with the Brooklyn Bridge engraved on it.

At the hardware store I buy a miniature water filter that screens bacteria. I pick up a bottle of extra-strong hornet and wasp spray, the kind that shoots a stream of foam, and I choose a rape whistle. For Mum and Dad I get a dozen wire hangers, and then a half-dozen more for me. Two small tarpaulins and three mousetraps and one small powder fire extinguisher. I ask the guy behind the counter if he sells baseball bats and he looks at the items I'm buying and he says, 'There something happening I should know about, is there?'

'What do you mean?'

He shrugs and sells me an 18oz Big Barrel Louisville slugger.

I walk back up Sixth Avenue with the bags, the handles straining and cutting into my hands. The lights are mesmerising. Like I'm floating through a fever dream.

When I pass the familiar smoothie cart on the corner the man says, 'Be careful who you brain with that bat, lady. I don't wanna be an accomplice after the fact.'

'Before the fact,' I say.

He smiles. 'Goodnight, English.'

I buy as many water bottles and nutrition bars as I can carry from the 7-Eleven.

No noise from Mum and Dad's room. If they manage to get a few hours of sleep then I'm pleased for them.

I place the bags down as quietly as I can on the end of my single bed, and then I unfold a tarpaulin and place it on the carpet under the bed frame. Just knowing I have a clean surface to store things on lifts my spirits. I stock the water in the corner and set the traps. The bat will rest by my pillow and the knife will sit in my coat, itself hanging from the door handle right by my head.

It's not a lot but it is something. I'm protecting myself in this room and I'll be ready if anything happens next door. Mum and Dad won't be surprised by my purchases. They know what I would say: you can't anticipate events in a high-density city like this one. It's like London on steroids. There could be a level five storm system; I'd say it's not that unlikely. That could then lead to crane collapses, or maybe the windows of surrounding skyscrapers would blow out, shattering jagged shards of glass all over the streets. If we had martial law and curfews for a night or two that could help, but it could also anger the local population. Before you know it you've got serious civil unrest in the five boroughs. I don't have enough food and water to wait out that kind of event, but I will have by tomorrow night.

My twin was killed. My monozygotic twin. We have the exact same face, save for a few minor scars and blemishes. The same body. Everyone knows there are killers who get a kick out of reliving their crimes in every detail. Everyone knows that.

I walk unsteadily down the hostel hall carrying my wash bag.

Nobody around.

The bathroom is small but clean. There's a shower over a bathtub and there's a basin and toilet. What kind of person would soak in a bath in a communal bathroom?

I wash my face and clean my teeth and feel more human. The face in the mirror is a ghost of a woman. I return to my room and change into my pyjamas and climb into bed. Bat on my left, knife on my right, hornet spray tucked underneath.

But my eyes will not close. I check my phone one last time: the Instagram photos on KT's grid, photos of her with her boyfriend Scott, and her with Violet, her best friend. KT looked happy. She looked well last week and now she is gone.

I place my phone on the window sill and charge it. The extinguisher's right there next to it.

I turn off the light.

Voices from the next-door room.

I hear my dad's voice but I can't make out his words. His voice is too deep. It's muffled.

And then Mum says, 'We have to tell her the truth, Paul.'

7

I wake to a knocking on my door.

My hand reaches down for the bat but it's sunk between my body and the side of the bed.

I scramble to pull it loose.

Heavy breathing from out in the hallway.

Someone trying the handle.

I drag out my bat.

'Just me, Moll,' says Dad. 'It's only me.'

I breathe again.

'Wait a sec.' I pull on my sweater and check the peephole. 'What time is it?' I ask, opening the door.

'Nine-thirty, sweetheart. Your mother wanted you to sleep.'

I clear the corners of my eyes and recall the words I overheard last night. Must have taken me hours to get to sleep after hearing that.

We have to tell her the truth, Paul.

'Mum managed to find you a Pret a Manger. Turns out there are lots of them here.' He hands me a paper bag turning transparent from grease. 'Chocolate croissant.' He hands me a cardboard cup. 'And a latte with one sugar.'

I smile and thank him and take them. He follows me into my room but there is no space in here. Not enough air. I retreat to the window and try to open it but it'll only budge an inch or so.

'We already ate breakfast,' he says. 'Your mum's not sleeping much. We thought we'd get off at ten sharp. That OK?'

'Of course,' I say, sipping the coffee. 'Thanks again for this, Dad.'

He smiles a flat, empty smile, and goes back to his room.

I'm starving, so I devour the croissant and the coffee and then I take a hot shower. The communal bathroom is already wet, steamy, soaked, but at least I don't have to queue. I fix my make-up in my room with a small mirror and then I check the contents of my handbag. We leave the hostel.

'Your father likes to take the subway, makes him feel like a New Yorker instead of a tourist, but we'll get a cab today, Molly. You don't want to try the subway, do you?'

'No, Mum. I don't.'

'We'll just hail a cab, then.'

Dad heads off across Sixth Avenue towards the overwhelming giant neon screens advertising Broadway shows and sneaker brands. Mum and I wait outside the hostel.

'Did you get some sleep, Mum?'

'A little. On and off, really. You?'

'Took me a while but then I did.'

'Good. You need it,' she says, taking a deep breath, then coughing. 'We all need to keep our strength up so we can help the police. Get justice for your sister.'

'The hostel walls are paper-thin, though,' I say.

'They really are.'

'I heard you and Dad talking late last night.'

She looks at me.

'What do you need to tell me, Mum? What's the truth you need to share with me?'

She looks down at the pavement and then fixes her hair and looks back up at me with a pained expression. 'It's not the right time, sweetie.' She rubs my shoulder reassuringly. 'Your father can talk to you about it.'

Dad yells from across the street and we join him and jump in the yellow cab.

'26th Police Precinct,' says Dad to the driver. We're all squeezed into the back seat.

'Where?' says the driver.

'Near Columbia University. Morningside Heights.'

'Wrong way,' says the driver, pulling out into traffic. We drive south and then he makes a turn and we start heading north. 'Street?' asks the driver. He's an Eastern European guy with thin fair hair.

Dad checks his phone and says, 'Amsterdam and 126th Street.'

The driver nods.

'Dad, what do you need to tell me?'

He looks over at me, then at Mum. He's wearing a tie today; he almost never wears a tie. He gestures to Mum and she nods.

'Not now, Molly. We can talk about it later after we've spoken to the police. We need to focus.'

He turns to look out of the window and Mum stares straight ahead. We're cramped together and awkward as hell. This is where KT would have told us one of her travelling stories or cracked a lame joke to cut the tension. I know everyone found me hard work as a kid. It took extra effort to ensure nothing upset me too much. Whereas KT was easy. If someone wronged her she'd address the problem swiftly and move on. Right now, in the back of a cab, this is where she would have saved us from ourselves.

According to my phone GPS we pass close to the Ed Sullivan Theater and Carnegie Hall, and head on up the west side of Central Park. I Google 'Katie Raven' again, and check Twitter for news or hashtags. She's everywhere. The *Mail Online* have a collage of her Instagram selfies, and they have some soundbite from Violet, her best friend. Strong New York accent. Mum watches the clip with me. Violet says how stunned she is. How KT was a brilliant scholar and their whole class are devastated by the news.

'You should look up from your phone once in a while and see the park, it's picturesque this time of year,' says Dad. 'Look at those leaves.'

Mum taps my knee in a way that says, *Forgive your father, he isn't thinking.*

The buildings become more stunted and normal-looking. Fewer skyscrapers. No giant neon signs or heaving tribes of tourists.

'Whatever the police ask you, just answer clearly and honestly to the best of your recollection,' says Dad.

'What else would I do?' I say.

'He didn't mean it like that,' says Mum. 'The police here talk differently from the ones back home. They're more direct. Just take your time with them, that's all. Think about your answers.'

'NYPD,' says Dad. 'They'll find out who hurt our Katie. Detective Martinez has been very helpful so far, and very kind to your mother. I have full confidence in the NYPD.'

I scan the faces on the street. 'Whoever did this could be walking past us right now.'

'Or he could be in Mexico already,' says Dad. 'But I hope to God he's still here. He needs to be brought to justice. He needs a—'

'This is close to where your sister lived, Molly,' says Mum, cutting him off. 'A few blocks from here.'

I look at the buildings and the windows. I can see her thriving in this neighbourhood. Jogging to the park or meeting friends for Japanese food. A shiver runs down from my neck to the base of my spine. This was her area. She walked these pavements. She lived right here.

'Can I see her place?' I ask.

'We'll check with the police,' says Mum.

She doesn't start to cry but I can tell she's doing her best to hold it together.

The cab pulls over. A two-storey police building with marked police cars parked outside on the diagonal. I pay the fare. There's a lone policeman outside the front entrance standing in front of a giant shield.

'Here we are, 26th Precinct,' says Dad. 'You ready?'

We both nod, but he's the one who doesn't look ready. His face is ashen.

As we approach, the policeman on guard stares right at me, as if he's seen a ghost. And in a way he has. No doubt he's watched KT on the TV news, or else maybe there's a photograph of her pinned up on a noticeboard. And now he sees me. A replica. He watches me walk inside the building.

Bolted-down chairs and an out-of-order vending machine. Posters and leaflets and a large water dispenser. Two people in here waiting their turn. We approach the desk and a plain-clothes cop comes over to greet us. He looks at my parents and says, 'Elizabeth, Paul.' And then he looks at me and says, 'Hi, Molly. I'm Detective Martinez, please follow me.'

He lets us through a few locked doors and into a large room full of cubicles and no natural light.

'I want to reiterate how sorry I am for your loss. We're going to do everything we can to find out who did this and bring them to justice.'

Dad says, 'Thank you, detective.'

Mum takes a tissue from her pocket.

'I'd like to ask you some questions one by one, if that's OK. Standard procedure. My colleague, Detective Ramirez, will talk to you, Elizabeth, in Room B, while I talk to you, Molly. Paul, if you could just wait right here, we'll come to you as soon as we're done.'

Dad swallows and blinks twice.

'Is that OK, Paul?'

Dad nods.

'Can he come in with me while I talk to your colleague?' asks Mum.

'Afraid not, ma'am. We always do it this way. Paul . . .' He looks at Dad but Dad doesn't look back, he just shifts in his chair. 'Mr Raven, sir. Can we get you a coffee or water while you wait?'

'No, I'm fine, thank you.'

Detective Martinez nods and leads me into Room A.

Two green chairs on one side of a desk. Two green chairs on the other side. A pad of paper. Three empty paper cups. A mirror on the wall.

'Coffee, tea, water?' he asks.

I'm thirsty, but I have no idea about the state of the kitchen here. 'No, thanks.'

'Take a seat, Molly.'

He has a thick file under his arm and he opens it on the desk.

'I need to ask you questions about your twin sister and her life here in New York. We want to piece together all the fragments so we can investigate deeper into what happened and charge whoever did this, OK?'

I nod.

'Some of my questions might be uncomfortable, or you might think them irrelevant, but I need to ask them, all right? I'll be as quick as I can. I don't want to keep you here from your parents for a minute longer than necessary.'

'What happened to her? Who could have—?'

'I need to ask some questions first, Molly,' he says, interrupting me. 'That OK?'

I nod.

'You live in London, England. Is that right?'

'Yes.'

'When was the last time you talked to Katie?'

'It was about five days ago. FaceTime.'

'What was it you talked about, Molly?'

My throat closes at the memory. Us chatting less than a week ago. Not as easily as we used to, but still. Chatting as though we'd have the chance to chat a thousand more times in the years ahead. Saying nothing profound to each other whatsoever. No chance to say goodbye or express love or anything of the sort.

'About Mum and Dad, mainly. She was frustrated at them. They're here visiting KT for a week or so. Holiday of a lifetime. Well, they've extended their trip now because of . . . It's their first time to America as well. We haven't travelled much, not like KT.'

'Frustrated, you say?'

'Nothing serious – KT was just venting. We're twins. Three minutes age gap. We talk about nearly everything. Stupid stuff, everyday stuff. It's not like two sisters or two best friends. We just offload on each other. It's like a reflex.'

'Why was she frustrated, Molly?'

'I need to know what happened to my twin.'

'Why was Katie frustrated, do you think?'

'I don't know, really. Dad being Dad, I guess. He's annoying sometimes.' I break out into an unexpected smile. 'He can get overexcited in new places. And he's been very excited to visit New York, railroading Mum into things he wants to do without really consulting her or thinking about her. Dad likes to spend money and Mum worries a lot. And then he'd talk her into a whole day at the Intrepid Sea, Air and Space Museum, and she'll just do it even though she has no interest in that. Normal marriage drama, I guess. KT wanted Mum to stick up for herself more, do what she wanted to do.'

'Was Katie unhappy or anxious? What mood was she in?'

I take a minute.

'She seemed normal. I don't know, I wasn't analysing it in the moment. Maybe a little tired? She'd spent the night at her boyfriend's place.'

The detective makes a note. 'Identity of her boyfriend?'

'Scott Sbarra. I've never met him.'

The detective writes down the name but I can tell from his demeanour he already knows it. Maybe he's already interviewed Scott. Maybe he's a suspect.

'Back to that last phone call for a second. The FaceTime call. Did Katie mention she was scared about anything or anyone? Do you know if she had any arguments recently? Any enemies?'

'KT? No, not her style. Everyone loved her. She was the easygoing, fun-loving, smiley twin.'

He looks confused.

'We're identical, but we're not identical.'

'I think I get what you mean.'

'It's weird to be here and she's not with us, you know. Especially with Mum and Dad; it feels like we're going to go and pick her up and go see a movie. Mum and Dad found her in her apartment. They've seen her and they've been able to say a real goodbye. They're grieving, but I can't believe she's really gone. I can't get a grip on it.'

'I understand. We have people who can talk to you about that if you like. Help you through until the burial.'

'Will that be here or in England? How soon can we have her back?'

He frowns for a moment. 'Let me look into that for you. Listen, you sure you don't want a water or a coffee?'

I do not want to get caught out in this place needing a toilet. 'No, I'm good.'

'I asked you about enemies Katie may have made.'

'Honestly I can't think of anyone.'

'Did she have a good relationship with her boyfriend? She ever mention anything less than positive about Sbarra?'

'They've only been together since spring. I think they were OK. She liked him.'

'She never talked about arguments or fights or anything of that nature?'

'No, I don't think so. Why? Do you know she had a fight with someone? Did she die in a fight?'

'Who were her other schoolfriends?'

'From Columbia?'

'Right.'

I adjust my posture. 'Violet.'

'Violet Roseberry?'

'Yes. They were really good friends. Hung out a lot. She was KT's tour guide her first semester. She's a native New Yorker and she helped KT out. She trusted her.'

The CCTV camera in the corner of the room flashes.

'Did she mention other people in her life here? Her tutor? Any other boyfriends before Scott Sbarra? Any neighbours? Classmates?'

'Not really.'

'Don't take this the wrong way, but did Katie have any vices you know of?'

'Vices?'

'You know: gambling, narcotics, anything she might hide from you.'

I smile. 'No, not KT. She would try things once maybe but I wouldn't say she had any vices. Maybe being too nice, if that's a vice? Too gullible and friendly to strangers. Not on her guard enough. She was a little naïve about the risks of modern life, but that's hardly a vice.'

I answer more questions about her friends back home, and her hobbies, and her ex-boyfriends in London, and then I remember Mum's words. *We have to tell her the truth, Paul.*

I ask, 'What happened to her?'

'We're treating your sister's death as suspected homicide, Molly. But it's complicated. There were no signs of a forced entry. Few indications of a fight, no scratches or blood or skin under her fingernails.'

'So it could have been an accident?'

'We're working on the assumption it wasn't an accident, pending further investigation and medical reports. We have trace evidence collected from the scene. Fingerprints and hair samples, things of that nature. And your sister had some bruising to her face.'

My palms fly up to my own face instinctively. 'Bruising?'

'We'll be able to tell you much more soon. I'm sorry, it's early in the investigation.' He glances at the mirror on the wall, takes a deep breath, then looks back at me. 'Did you know your sister took out a life insurance policy recently?'

'She did?'

'Do you know what prompted that decision?'

'No, I had no idea. Life insurance? That makes no sense. What was she afraid of? You have to find out who did this to her.'

Martinez says, 'We will, Molly. Listen, I really appreciate you talking to me.' He hands over his card. 'If you think of anything else, you call me or text me on that number. Do not hesitate.'

'OK.'

'Now I'm going to talk to your father.'

8

When all the interviews are over, we step outside the precinct building. Mum's been crying. Her eyes are puffy. Dad looks restless.

'So, what are we supposed to do now?' I say.

Dad looks down the street then back the other way. 'I think we need to talk,' he says.

We walk in silence past the St John the Divine Cathedral and into the northernmost end of Central Park. There are joggers with headphones and old people with small dogs. Children play in the West 110th Street playground. The air is crisp.

'It's the company,' says Dad. 'I did everything I could but it wasn't enough. We've lost the business.'

'I'm sorry.' This is not a complete shock to me. I'll do what little I can to help Mum. To help both of them.

Dad scratches his nose. 'Twenty years down the drain. Creditors could have given me more time. Wouldn't have killed them to be flexible. Anyway, it seems trivial now, but we wanted you to know. The important thing right now is to find out what happened to Katie.'

It feels like we're talking properly. Out here in the fresh air. Everything out in the open.

'I want to know how she died,' I say. 'Martinez said that

there was no sign of a fight. Could she have done this to herself? Could she have fallen and then poisoned herself with painkillers? Had a heart attack or something?'

'Police say it's suspected homicide,' says Dad. 'That's what they're treating this as. No suspicious toxins or narcotics found at the scene. And our Katie would never have killed herself. There's no way she would have even thought about it.'

I've thought about it.

More than once.

'I think she was poisoned,' says Mum. 'She definitely wasn't shot or stabbed, and I didn't see any marks on her neck so she wasn't strangled either. I think someone drugged her and hit her.'

'Oh, God,' I say.

'I know,' says Mum.

Dad says, 'Hang on, Liz. We don't know anything yet. Martinez told me he couldn't go into details as the medical examiner or the coroner was still working on her conclusions, but he understood we needed to know more and he said he'd call me as soon as possible.'

He places both hands over his mouth and sighs, and then the three of us stare ahead blankly for a full minute.

Sirens in the distance.

'Martinez told me we can go to the apartment today after twelve-thirty,' says Dad. 'He said the landlady would let us inside. Apparently all the crime scene work has been done already. We're not to take any items away just yet, but we can visit if we want to.'

'I want to,' I say. 'I need to see where she lived.'

Dad checks his watch.

Mum says, 'I'm not sure I can go inside there again. I'm not sure I can handle it, sweetie.'

'Dad?' I say.

'Wait,' says Mum, squeezing her eyes tight, taking a breath. 'Maybe I'll come and wait outside. Or a little way down the street. Of course you need to see her place, Molly. To say goodbye.'

'I can't say goodbye until I've seen *her*,' I say.

A sycamore leaf floats down from above and lands by my foot.

'I asked about that as well,' says Dad. 'First priority is to catch the scum that did this, but then I want to know exactly when they'll release her to us so we can go back to England and give her a proper church funeral. I told him how Grandad was a lay preacher and how I wanted her buried close to us. How our family home isn't too far from the parish church.'

'What was his answer?' I say.

'That he'll let me know the details. Not his area. That they don't want to delay things for us a minute more than necessary.'

We walk from the park to the apartment along the streets she would have jogged on, and pass the people she would have smiled to. I don't smile. I grit my teeth.

'That's her dry-cleaners,' says Mum. 'And over there is the corner shop where Katie bought coffee and bread and milk.'

'The *bodega*,' says Dad.

'That's what they call a corner shop here,' says Mum.

We trudge on.

A middle-aged woman in an ankle-length coat looks at me with a horrified expression. We pass each other and I look back at her and she's still staring at me, her head turned, her eyes wide.

'This is the street,' says Dad.

'Oh, Paul,' says Mum, shaking her head.

'You want to stay here, Liz? You want me to find you a little café or something?'

She looks at Dad and then at me and says, 'No, I'll come with you both. I'll do my best.'

The building is smart. Brown brick. Four storeys with a tiny yard out front with climbing shrubs concealing the ground-floor windows. It's a whole world away from KT's old flatshare in London.

Dad buzzes the owner's apartment bell and she comes down wearing a cashmere wraparound dress and a pair of beige Uggs.

'How are you all bearing up?' she asks, with an over-caring expression, and then she sees me and she says, 'Oh.'

I can't meet her eyes. She's visually scanning me, comparing every physical detail to KT.

'You must be the twin,' she says. 'I'm Victoria.'

'Molly.'

She pauses for a moment, still gazing at me, then says, 'I'm sorry. Come in, please. Do come in.'

She opens the ground-floor apartment door. There is no crime scene tape. No chalk outline, or piles of disposable CSI latex gloves. There is only order.

A kitchenette with fancy coffee machine and smoothie-maker. A bathroom with proper deep bath and separate shower. I can see the lipstick on the bathroom mirror shelf, the lipstick that was KT's present for her birthday back in June. For *our* birthday back in June.

Mum sits on one of the two kitchen chairs and wipes her eyes with a tissue.

The room still smells of KT, and in a way it smells of me. I can hardly breathe. The blankets are folded the exact same way I fold blankets. The tea towels are draped over the oven door handle the way I would do it. The *exact* same way.

'She had a good time in this place,' says Dad, looking around the living room. 'I'm glad she got to experience the life she dreamed of.'

He says that even though it killed her. There is no malice in his voice but I can tell that Victoria, the building owner, still standing in the doorway, is deeply uncomfortable.

I push the door into the bedroom.

Double bed.

An expensive-looking mattress, but all the bedding has been removed.

A rug from Laura Ashley. The exact same rug was in her London apartment during the final year of her undergraduate course at King's College. I remember us texting back and forth for weeks because of the price.

'She was right there,' says Dad, pointing at the bed. 'They've taken the sheets and pillows, but she was right there. Like she was asleep.'

Opposite the bed is a photo collage. There's a picture of Mum and Dad outside Nottingham Castle, and a picture of them in her London flat from last year. Then there's a bunch of Polaroid photos. One of her outside the Bronx Zoo, taken from down by her waist. Another of her with Scott Sbarra, her boyfriend; he looks like a classic jock in a TV series. Square jaw, short hair and a dimple in his chin. There's a photo of her class at Columbia, including Violet, her friend. She has a Yankee cap on but I can see her red hair underneath. Then there's a Polaroid from on board a small plane, holding a glass of champagne. There's another woman in the shot. One final photo of her with a young guy wearing a T-shirt with a clenched fist on it above the words *End Chad.*

'Mum, I'll be back tomorrow,' says a voice from the other room.

I step out into the living room and Mum and Dad are with Victoria and someone else I can't quite see until he steps out from behind her.

'Molly Raven, this is my son, Shawn. He lives downstairs, you might recognise him from the internet, or . . .'

'Hi,' he says, looking me up and down.

His bomber jacket isn't zipped up.

The T-shirt he's wearing underneath is the same one in the photo on the wall. The one with the fist and *End Chad.*

9

'Say hello to the Ravens properly, Shawn,' says the landlady.

Shawn introduces himself again without making eye-contact. 'Hi, I'm Shawn.'

I walk up to him. 'Hi, I'm KT's twin.'

He looks uncomfortable. Maybe because it's obvious I'm her twin, or maybe he's just ill at ease. I'd be ill at ease if my mum treated me like a little kid. He keeps wiping his hands up and down his trousers. This guy looks around my age. Veins popping out of his neck and his hands, but he's not a bodybuilder type, he's just ultra-lean. Like a marathon runner, or an actor who has trained long and hard for a shirtless scene.

Shawn does not meet my eyes. When he talks, he focuses on the floor, or the wall or just above my head.

'Really sucks what happened to your sister.'

Sucks? It more than sucks, Shawn.

'Did you see anything that day?' I ask.

His mother looks uncomfortable. 'Oh, the house was totally empty,' she says. 'We only let out this ground-floor apartment. Shawn and I were both out. We've explained it all to the police. I wish we had been here to call the authorities.'

Dad says, 'She's in heaven now. In a better place.'

The landlady crosses herself and says, 'I need to take a call. Shawn can you look after the Ravens for ten minutes?'

He looks at her like a teenager who's been asked to tidy his bedroom.

'You live downstairs?' asks Dad.

'I have the basement studio,' he says, straightening his back, managing to look at my dad for a second. 'I run my business down there and I pay market rent,' he adds. 'It's not like I'm living in my mom's basement.'

Well, it kind of is like that, Shawn.

'Katie loved this flat,' says Mum. 'She used to FaceTime me back in Nottingham – that's where we're from – showing me all the original features and the old windows. She was very happy living here.'

'Shawn. Do you have any idea what might have happened to my sister?'

He doesn't say anything, he just looks down at his Nikes and shakes his head in an exaggerated movement from side to side.

'KT have any arguments in here, or out on the street?' I ask. 'You know if anyone ever threatened her or yelled at her, anything like that?'

'No,' he says, looking at her bed. 'Nope, zip. I'm sorry.'

I walk slowly to her bed and catch her subtle scent once more and it makes me stop and I lose my breath again.

'Molly?' asks Mum. 'Are you sure you're all right in here?'

I smile at her gently. 'Are *you* OK in here?'

She nods and looks at Dad.

'If you do think of anyone,' I say to Shawn, 'any little detail, can you let Detective Martinez know, please. He's at the 24th Precinct.'

'26th Precinct, Moll.'

'Sure, no problem,' says Shawn.

The noise of a siren half a street away. Car horns and raised voices.

The landlady returns. 'That was an enquiry about this actual apartment – you see, we get a lot of demand being so close to the campus. I told them it's not available right now, but I'll need to keep them updated. I know it's a difficult time, but if you'd let me know if you want to keep the place I would be obliged. Katie paid, or rather her sponsorship paid up until the end of next month, but from December first you'll need to pay rent or else I'll give it to a new tenant. I hope you don't think it's crass of me to talk like this.'

'We won't need it,' says Dad in a defeated voice.

Mum stands up and says, 'Let us just think about it, would you, Mrs Bagby? It's all very . . . new, all this. We just need a few days to deal with it all. If that's OK.'

Victoria nods and says, 'Sure, take a few days, get back to me when you've discussed it.' She looks at Dad with an expression that says, *Let me know as soon as you can.* And then she turns to her son and says, 'Shawn, would you stay with the Ravens and let them out? I need to go meet a business associate downtown.'

'But I gotta go upload,' says Shawn.

'Can that wait half an hour, dear?'

He grunts something and she leaves. Two minutes later he grunts something else to us and says he'll be back in ten minutes.

'We'll organise for her things to come back to Nottingham,' says Mum. 'I can sort it out. Get it all shipped and put back in your bedroom. We still keep your bedroom, Molly.'

'I know you do, Mum.' I stayed there last Christmas, along with my sister. Two single beds separated by a strip of no man's land. Two small desks. Two single wardrobes.

'We'll get shipping quotes,' says Dad, more to himself than to us. 'It might be expensive. I'll ask Detective Martinez if we can take back some personal items in our checked baggage next week.'

'I'd like some of her things,' I say. 'I want to fly back with them. Her shawl, maybe.' I walk to the shawl folded over her sofa armrest. I pick it up and hold it to my face and something unlocks inside me. Facing a sofa, facing a wall, the scent in the shawl, it breaks me. Armani Mania. I buckle. My tears soak the loose-weave fabric and I hold it tight to my face and I cry. I'm aware of Mum crying behind me, Dad holding her, saying, 'Let her, Elizabeth. Just let her.'

The convulsing stops. I sit down on the sofa, the shawl still tight to my eyes. She was my other half. Spouses say that but it's never true. We *were* each other's other half. If we had ever had children they would have been cousins but they would also have been genetic half-siblings, we were that closely connected. We entered this life together. And now she's gone.

'I gotta leave soon, so . . .' says Shawn from the doorway. 'I need to lock this place up, Mom told me.'

'Just five minutes, lad,' says Dad.

'Sure, no worries. That's cool,' says Shawn.

I wipe my eyes on the shawl and take some deep breaths.

'She loved you so very much,' says Mum.

And the truth is that Mum is being kind here but she has no real idea how much she loved me and how much I loved her. Our relationship was deeper than she could know. It was something that existed just between us. A private thing. Mum loved us both but she cannot understand the depths of our relationship. Nobody can.

That photo pops into my head. Shawn and KT together.

'How well did you know my sister?' I ask him.

He points to his own chest. 'Wait, what?'

'There's a photo of you together on the board in her bedroom.'

'Molly,' says Dad.

'You guys went out or something?' I ask. 'What the hell happened to her?'

'No, wait. Nothing, I mean . . .'

'You dated her? You *wanted* to date her?'

'No. There's a photo up?'

I point to the photo pinboard. To the Polaroid. To the T-shirt.

'Oh, that,' he says, laughing uncomfortably. 'No, you see, that was a night when her friends were here and I came upstairs for a minute, no big deal, they were playing music. Her boyfriend was here too, so no. Scott was here then. It was nothing, I swear.'

Some alarm goes off on Shawn's phone.

'You know KT's boyfriend?' I say.

'I don't know him, I just met him a coupla times, he was always hanging around. He smokes so I'd see him outside, you know. No smoking in the building, Mom's rules.'

'Do you like Scott, Shawn? He a good guy? He ever hurt KT in any way?'

'What? No. Not that I heard about. Listen, this isn't anything to do with me. I just live here, man. Sbarra's one of those guys, you know the kind. Like a ladies' man, seems like he never had any problems, no obstacles, just cruising through life and all the doors opening, you know? Like a car driving through green light after green light. Listen, I gotta go now. It's work, I'm sorry. I gotta lock this place up.'

'Was Scott up here the day KT died, Shawn?'

Shawn looks at the bed, then at the window.

'Listen. I gotta go, it's—'

'Was he here?'

'Scott Sbarra? Six foot four, blue eyes, two-twenty? Yeah. Scott was here. Hard to miss the guy.'

10

Leaving KT's apartment feels permanent. Like closing the book on her life. I get a knot in my stomach just thinking about it.

Mum and I linger on the building steps while Dad tries to hail a cab.

'How do you feel?' asks Mum.

How do I feel? *How do I feel?* Lost, angry, terrified, alone. Desperately sad. Like my twin was stolen from me by this neighbourhood, this mass of people. I feel like flying straight back to London and locking myself inside my apartment to decompress.

'I think it helped just a little,' I say to Mum. 'To make sense of things. Seeing her life here.'

Mum gives me a hug and her earring catches on mine. 'Sorry,' she says pulling away. 'It's never been easy for you to let your emotions out – you have your father to blame for that. Katie had the opposite problem. My fault, I suppose.' Mum starts crying and laughing at the same time. Dad gestures that he has a cab waiting.

'The detective kept asking questions about jealous boys and money problems,' says Mum. 'Did Katie mention Scott's jealousy to you?'

I shake my head. 'I didn't even get to ask many questions. The detective did all the asking. He said she had some bruising to her face.'

Mum holds my hand. 'We saw that,' she says. 'It was very faint, sweetie.'

I watch the fringe of Central Park fly by. We pass by the Lincoln Center: hundreds of carefree tourists taking selfies in front of the fountains.

The scent of her stays with me. That shawl. And in this taxi, squashed into one side of the back seat, I vow to avenge all that has happened. Everything is out of kilter. Skewed. I need to seek out those who are responsible for the pain in her life and help put the world back into balance. She'd have done the same. This cannot go unpunished.

We reach our hotel and there's vomit outside my parents' door. A man is cleaning it up best he can with a mop and bucket but it's already soaked into the carpet tiles. He apologises and Mum says, 'It's not your fault, dear.'

They want to take a nap. I explain how I'll go out for a while. Explore the city. Get some air and stick to the safe, touristy areas. Mum looks so much older all of a sudden. Twenty years older. I'm lucky to have her. Always selfless and reliable. The family rock.

I check Scott Sbarra on my phone. He's not a difficult person to find on the internet. Not like me. From his LinkedIn page I can glean where he interned last summer. On Facebook I find a string of ex-girlfriends or ex-flings; most of them look something like KT – something like me. He's done charitable work in Kenya, building some kind of school, and he's made damn sure we all know about it. He lifts weights. Scott Sbarra takes good care of himself and he rows for the Columbia heavyweight squad. I'm a competent researcher. I get results. I check the rowing team website. Location of the training grounds. Their boathouse. I check their schedule and their coach's details. He should be finishing a session soon. I look up bus routes and timetables because I refuse to take a subway.

The hostel is quiet when I sneak out.

A substantial part of me wants to return to the relative safety of my room. To quit. But a larger part needs answers. Needs to dig deeper. To interrogate this man.

The Midtown lunch rush has ended but not much changes. It seems to always be a rush out here. People walk even faster than they do in central London. Phones fixed to ears, small backpacks: urban confidence.

Unfortunately the bus I've researched leaves from Times Square.

I find the right place with help from my friendly local street vendor. He tries to sell me a smoothie but I politely turn down his offer and promise I'll buy one later on.

The bus is OK. I have my monkey fist and my knitting needles and my sock stuffed with pound coins. I feel like I can handle this journey if it means I get to judge KT's boyfriend, to look into his eyes.

I step off the bus at West 218th Street. This is not Midtown, not even close. This isn't even Harlem any more; this is the northernmost tip of Manhattan island. North of Fort George and Washington Heights. This is Inwood. The streets are dangerous in a different way up here. Not so many pedestrians, lower terrorism risk, but also fewer recognisable chain stores that offer some kind of sanctuary, real or imagined.

I follow signs to the Columbia boathouse. One new structure built next to an old building, a concrete slipway leading down into the Harlem River, the tangled trees and burnt foliage of Inwood Hill Park in the background, and the Henry Hudson Bridge beyond that.

I can't see anyone in the water.

Eventually a tall guy my age walks out of the new boathouse in track pants and a T-shirt.

'Excuse me,' I say, smiling, exaggerating my English accent. 'Is Scott Sbarra here today?'

'Don't I know you?' he says, narrowing his eyes, his lip curling on one side. 'Julia's party, right? Katy, is it? No. Kirsty? Sorry. How you doing?'

How does he not know about KT? I'd imagined everyone on campus would have been talking about her. Especially Scott and his teammates.

'Is Scott here?'

'Sure, Scottie's here. I just saw him in his boat. Probably in the showers now. He'll be out in a minute. Hey, you going to the thing at Alisha's tonight?'

I shake my head.

'See you around, then,' he says, walking away, placing his earphones in.

Somehow I knew Scott would be here training but it's still a shock.

A trio of guys walk out five minutes later. One of them, the stockiest of the three, stares at me, smiles, then his face changes. His expression drops. He frowns. When they're further down the street all three turn to look back at me.

Scott comes out on his own, a backpack on his chest as well as one on his back.

He stops dead in his tracks when he spots me.

He doesn't faint or throw up or cry or anything like that but he stops. He is completely still. Paralysed by the sight of me.

'Scott Sbarra?'

His face drops.

'I'm Molly.'

He walks slowly towards me.

'I didn't know you were in the city,' he says. 'I mean, I'm really sorry about your sister. We're all in total shock here.'

Not in so much shock that you missed rowing practice.

'Can we talk?' I say.

'Of course,' he says. 'When did you get here? How did you know I would be here?'

'Arrived last night.'

He sighs and adjusts the straps on his backpacks. 'Katie always talked about you,' he says, giving me a double-take just to make sure he's not talking to his dead girlfriend because not only do we look almost identical but we sound almost identical as well.

'I can't believe she's gone,' I say. 'It's a nightmare.'

'Tell me about it.' He looks tired all of a sudden.

'There somewhere around here we can sit and talk?'

'Yeah, there's a coffee house a block or two away, that OK?'

I like walking around here with Scott. He's three or four inches taller than Dad and his shoulders are twice the breadth of mine. He has long muscles: the physique of a tall swimmer rather than a bodybuilder.

'She was a great girl,' he says. 'A great person, I mean.'

'I know.'

'We'd only been dating a few months but she was really special, you know? I liked her a lot.'

'She told me.'

'She did?'

'Of course. We're twins. We tell each other absolutely everything.'

He looks at me with an expression more of fear than of warmth. Like maybe I know something I shouldn't.

He opens the door to the coffee house and I walk in. The heat of the room, and the coffee aroma, instantly put me at ease. That and the familiarity of the place: wood floors, takeout cups, beat-up leather armchairs. I could almost be back in London.

'Triple-shot espresso with a dash of almond milk,' he orders.

'Just a cappuccino, please.'

'Name?'

'Scottie.'

We sit down near the window.

I look right into his eyes as he blows into his espresso. *Do you know who killed my sister?* I want to ask. *Do you know what happened to the person I entered this life with? Did you ever do something to hurt her?*

'I don't know what to say, really,' he mumbles.

He doesn't look sad or distraught. His eyes are clear and white.

'You must be hurting,' I say.

'Very much,' he says. 'Yeah. When they catch the guy who did this I'll . . .'

He sets his jaw and I see the muscles on the sides of his face bulge.

'Did you see her on the day she died, Scott?'

'No.'

'No? Someone told me different.'

'I mean, just early in the morning. Before my run. Briefly.'

'Did she seem OK?'

'I left when she was still asleep. We studied at Butler the night before. Katie slept in later than me.'

'Tell me about her life here. I can't stay in New York for long and I want to give the police some help if I can. Someone out there knows who did this. They have to be stopped.'

'Katie? Easygoing fun-loving girl. I guess you're the same.'

We were never the same.

Not even close.

'She made friends real quick at school. Lots of guys wanted her, you know, but she was picky. English, I guess. She was tight with Vi Roseberry – you talked with her?'

'Not yet.'

'Can be a piece of work sometimes to be honest but she's cool and they were close, you know, like soulmates.'

I find it troubling that he disregards both himself and me as my sister's soulmate. Surely I'd be first candidate and him the runner-up, not Violet Roseberry.

'Was KT ever stalked on campus, as far as you know? Ever threatened or anything like that?'

'Her neighbour from downstairs was a creep. Just a Class A loser. But he seemed harmless. If Katie had been stalked properly then I'd have fixed it – just look at me.'

I look at him. 'I guess.'

'I would never let anyone hurt her.'

'Someone killed her, Scott.'

There's a pause and it feels like the whole coffee house is listening to our conversation, but they're not. They're checking likes and follows, tracking their subscriber counts and their LinkedIn profile views.

'But there was nothing I could do about that.' He sighs. 'She wasn't easy sometimes, your sister. She travelled to all kinds of places without me, abroad, and she went out with friends. She had other guy friends. I tried to be relaxed about it, but I couldn't protect her when she was out with some other guy, could I?'

'I guess not.'

He fixes me with a cold stare, then looks out of the window and drains his coffee. 'Some bullshit with her tutor, Prof Groot, old dude with a beard. I'm not in his class. It was nothing specific but she was always weird around him. Some misunderstanding but she'd never explain it to me.'

'Professor Groot?

'Eugene Groot, Lit Hum.'

I make a note. 'What is Lit Hum?'

'Literature and Humanities.' He checks his watch. 'I'm sorry, Molly, I gotta get to class.'

'Is there any other detail, even something small? Something I can take to Martinez?'

'To who?'

'Detective Martinez, Homicide. He hasn't talked to you yet?'

He looks uneasy. 'No. Some other cop. Different name.'

'Help me. We need to find out what happened.'

'You think I don't know that? I want this guy on Death Row by next week.'

'Death Row? In New York?'

'You know what I mean.'

I write my phone number down on a paper napkin. 'Call me. With information, but also just to chat about KT. I want to keep talking about her. I want to keep her alive for a while longer.'

Scott looks at me like I'm disturbed and then he places the napkin in his pocket and puts on both rucksacks. 'I gotta go now. I'm real sorry about your sister.'

He leaves.

11

I'm tempted to hail a cab but I can't afford the fare right now. I mean, I can cover it, but who knows what my expenses are going to look like in the days ahead. I walk down Broadway and realise what an incredibly long street it is. The buildings either side are single-storey. Mechanics' shops and delis and convenience stores. A no-win, no-fee attorney's office. I find a bus stop and try to make sense of the timetable.

'You a tourist? Tourist, are you? You from out of town?' The woman has her granddaughter with her and she's dragging a shopping bag on wheels.

'Yes,' I say. 'Sorry, I'm trying to get back to Midtown.'

She scrunches her nose, then licks her teeth. 'Best take the subway, honey.'

'I don't like being underground.'

She shakes that away. 'Oh, it ain't nothing. Millions of people take it every day. Just don't look at the rats. Or the perverts. Course, there's less of both than back in my day. The subway ain't what it used to be and I mean that in a good way – course back when Koch was mayor . . .'

'Could I get a bus from around here?' I interrupt.

'A bus? A bus, I guess you could, would take you longer though, I'm just tellin' you the truth. Traffic. Walk down two blocks and get the . . . I don't remember the number but you'll see it, from opposite the Albanian drugstore, it's run by the Albanians now, nice family, used to be Dominican owners but they moved on, big green cross in the window.'

'Thank you.'

'Don't mention it, sweetheart. Have yourself a nice trip. Take care now.'

I walk down to the bus stop and figure out which route I need.

The sign says I'm still in Inwood and according to the map my best option is a bus down to Grand Central Station and then walk west from there.

I lean against a cool brick wall and a car pulls up and the driver shouts, 'You Susan? You going to Port Authority? Susan Bryers?' and I shake my head.

On the bus I manage to get a seat next to a gaunt man with patchy stubble.

The buildings grow in stature: two storeys, five storeys, seven. The skyline is an uneven concrete wedge growing towards Midtown and beyond.

I dig deeper into the social media accounts of Scott Sbarra. His Instagram is locked but his Twitter is public. The guy next to me takes a call and says, 'I'm still in Inwood. Well, you're gonna have to wait,' and then ends the call. Scott follows the people most other people seem to follow: Obama, Trump, Elon Musk, comedians, Oprah, a few astronauts and public speakers. I find videos of him rowing, and an official Columbia University video with a short clip of him talking about the heavyweight row team and their training trip to

Canal 54 in Florida. He's handsome in an obvious, almost cartoonish way, I guess.

We pass through Sugar Hill and into Hamilton Heights, and it feels safe enough from inside the bus, as though I'm watching it all on a TV screen. It's not so different from London but it's also totally different. The bus smells of weed and breath mints and leather, and some of the buildings outside have wooden water towers atop their roofs. London does not have these water towers.

I check for KT's name on the news and the stories are building. There are pieces about her death on Fox News, CNN, the BBC, but also 4Chan. There's a whole thread about her on Reddit. And then I see it. Someone has written that KT's identical twin has arrived from London.

I look around the bus, self-conscious, even more self-conscious than I usually am. I take out the monkey fist from my pocket and hold the heavy end in my palm. The paracord weave isn't as perfect as I would like it to be but it'd still hold up as a weapon.

I find Professor's Groot's office on the Columbia website, and I call it. I leave a message with my number asking him to call me back. I say it's urgent.

The guy next to me disembarks in the Upper East Side and, unfortunately, a less than ideal passenger replaces him. She's ninety, or at least she looks ninety. She tells me all about her father and how he died riding the Cyclone at Coney Island. I listen politely but, when she talks about going to meet her grandfather now in the park to pick native raspberries, I turn my head to look forward. It's not that I'm being rude, I just don't want to encourage her. She says, 'You heading down to Times Square?

Phew-ee, the things I could tell you about that intersection, and 42nd Street – course that was in the time before, and things have long since changed, all different now in the modern day, I ain't sayin' it's better, just changed is all. Back then the Square was a Wild West kind of a place. A friend of my grandaddy got hit in the eye by a cooked egg back in '82, cracked him right in the socket, hard-boiled – well, he never did journey back to Manhattan, that man. Now what was his name?'

I get off at Grand Central Station and it feels good to be in Midtown again. The verticality of the place is overwhelming but at least I can identify familiar shops and cafés. At least the grid system makes sense down here. It's almost impossible to get lost in Midtown Manhattan so long as you can count.

I glance up at the MetLife Building, and head west towards Madison Avenue, hungry, and grimy from the air.

There's a guy I notice in a shop window. He has a thick moustache and a baseball cap. I keep on walking and wait for the green man and then cross Madison. He crosses fifty feet behind so I take a left and head south. Past the Park Avenue Liquor Shop. He doesn't follow me. I go into a Starbucks. Slow, deep breaths. I scan the street through the window as I eat a sandwich. It makes me feel a whole lot more human. When I exit I see the moustache guy across the road looking at his phone. So I go back into Starbucks and head out of a side exit. No sign of the guy. I walk back towards Grand Central. If he's really following me then I'll know soon enough. Can't see him. I turn away and head to Fifth Avenue, close to the New York

Public Library. I see him tracking me, photographing the library with his phone, trying to look like a tourist, so I duck into a Muji store. He doesn't come inside. After five minutes I walk out, monkey fist in hand, and head back to Grand Central two blocks away. No sign of him. My heart is racing. I enter Grand Central Station and walk down the steps and look back and he's right there and then I really panic. I start running, my coins jangling in my pocket. I sprint down to the concourse area and scan the place for him and for help. There's an oyster restaurant. I stand with my back to the restaurant and then from behind me, from inside the restaurant itself comes a voice into my ear. 'Molly Raven, do not be afraid.'

I turn and bring my monkey fist up and show him the weapon and he backs off a few paces. Nobody else seems to notice us.

'Why are you following me? Who are you?'

He holds out his palms in a calming manner and then a cop approaches and says, 'Everything OK here? This man bothering you?'

The man says, 'Bogart DeLuca, private investigator, I used to work out of the three four.'

The cop ignores him. 'You OK, ma'am? You need any help?'

I look at moustache guy.

Moustache guy repeats, this time to me, 'My name is Bogart DeLuca. I'm a licensed private investigator here in New York City. I've been hired by Columbia to look into your sister's case. I want to help is all.'

'Anyone you want me to call, ma'am?' says the cop.

'No,' I say. 'I'm OK. Thank you, officer.'

He looks at me for a few seconds and then he looks at DeLuca. 'I'll be right over there.' He points to the stairs overlooking the restaurant area.

'I'm sorry I scared you,' says DeLuca. 'I'm a klutz sometimes.'

'Mind if I see some ID? A badge?'

'Sure, sure.' He hands me a small ID card.

'No badge?'

'I'm not a cop any more, Molly.'

'How come?'

'Long story. Can we sit down somewhere and talk? I have a bad leg and it's giving me fucking shooting pains.'

I wince.

'You OK?'

'I don't like cursing,' I say.

'You don't like cursing?' he says. 'This is New York, Molly – it isn't a case of liking or not liking. Listen, I'm sorry about your sister. I'm gonna help get to the bottom of it. I'm real good at my job.'

We sit outside Shake Shack and he buys two milkshakes. The cop's still watching.

'Columbia hired you?'

'Well, not exactly, not precisely, you know. I was hired by a private foundation, affiliated with Columbia, to look into the case. The foundation's connected to the school – philanthropy, that kind of thing. It's complicated.'

'A foundation?'

'The folk that sponsored Katie through her schooling.'

'The scholarship?'

'Well, yeah, kinda – more of a sponsorship than a scholarship. They want to help find out what happened to her. The board of the foundation. So they called me.'

'What's the name of the foundation?'

'They're very private, Molly. I'm paid by an attorney out in Grand Cayman, several steps removed. I'm not even sure of the foundation's name myself, truth be told. Some outfit in Europe.'

'I think I'd rather just talk to the police,' I say.

'You could do that,' he says, sucking milkshake through his straw. 'But I worked both sides of the fence and I know how to get efficient results. Trust me, the NYPD are the best in the world – I still have buddies there – but you put on that shield and you take on a shitload of cases, pardon my language. Katie's case is red-hot right now but soon there will be another dead girl and then another. If it isn't solved pretty quick it just becomes one of many. I hope I'm making sense. But, you talk to me, I'm working one case until I solve it. One. And that case is your twin sister.'

'You're just working on KT's case? Nothing else?'

'That's what I said. Also, the detective assigned to your case – Martinez is his name in the two six, good man, or so I'm told, never dealt with him personally but we know the same people – he won't receive a cash bonus if he solves the case.'

'But you do?'

'Oh, yeah, I do. I have an incentives plan. Contractual performance-related incentives.'

'So why follow me? Why not send an email? What do you need with me, DeLuca?'

'Bogart, call me Bogart.'

'What are you doing following me, Bogart? You scared me.'

'Sorry. I need to ask you some questions about the case is all. Time-sensitive questions. I heard from a little bird you have a return ticket flying on a British Airways triple seven in five days and I wanted to touch base with you so we can work on this together. Nobody knew Katie like you did, am I right?'

I nod.

'See what I mean, then.'

'What do you want to know? Who she knew? Where she went?'

'Sure, but I have most of that already. You can help me because I suspect your gut works the same ways as hers did, if you get my meaning. What I'm trying to say is, Molly, what is your gut telling you right now about who killed Katie?'

I look around at the commuters with their earphones and paperbacks. 'My gut tells me it was someone who knew her well.'

He nods.

I remember Scott's calm manner. 'My gut tells me to look into the boyfriend.'

'Scott Sbarra – and?'

'The young guy who lives in her basement.'

'YouTuber named Shawn Alexander Bagby. Oh, yeah, that kid's on my radar all right.'

'And her friend Violet. Maybe. Probably not. I don't know. I haven't met her yet.'

'Go on.'

'We've never spoken, but KT once mentioned she came on a little strong sometimes. Like an obsessive friend, a little too clingy. It was never sexual – she never came on to KT in that way, never propositioned her – but as a friend she was very intense. Needy.'

He makes a note of this in a small pad with a pencil.

'This is useful. You got a surname?'

'Roseberry. Violet Roseberry. I think she had some mental health problems a while back. KT told me she was in a secure hospital for a while. Some place in the Catskills.'

'Nuthouse in the Catskills?' he says. 'Interesting.'

'Hospital,' I say, glaring at him.

He makes a note.

'Anything else, Molly? I guarantee you I will work night and day to crack this case. I will not rest until I help bring Katie's killer to justice. Is there anything else? Anything bothering you, maybe?'

'I want to talk to her professor at Columbia. I left a message, told him it was urgent.'

'Professor Crabtree? Philip Crabtree?'

'No, I don't know that one. I mean Professor Groot. Eugene Groot.'

'OK, rings a bell. Why are you interested in Groot?'

I think back to Scott's expression when he mentioned the professor. 'KT said something in passing a few months back. That he'd been very friendly with her, very interested in her work. They had dinner out in some place called Nolita one time.'

'Did they now?'

'I remember because I'd never heard of Nolita before and it made me think of *Lolita*. By Vladimir Nabokov.'

'Nolita's down between the Bowery and Little Italy,' he says.

'I know. I looked it up.'

He glances down at his pad. 'Scottie Sbarra, Shawn Bagby, Violet Roseberry, Professor Eugene Groot. You have a feeling in your gut about anyone else? Even just an inkling?'

I consider telling him about Dad. How he hasn't really reacted or cried about KT. How something feels off. How he sometimes acts like he's on vacation rather than in mourning.

'No,' I say. 'Just those four.'

12

Bogart DeLuca gives me his card. It has a kind of a shield on the back, like he hasn't quite given up his police career just yet.

It's cold on the walk back to West 44th Street and my hostel. I get a text from Mum as I open the door from the street. *Where are you?* I reply *Here.*

South African students pass me by in single file.

I knock on their door and Mum looks worried. She also looks like she might be taking sleeping pills again. She did this after Grandma died and Dad had to take control of her medication for a while, rationing it out, giving her a tablet before bed each night so she wouldn't take three all at once to knock herself out.

'Where have you been, sweetie?'

'I met KT's boyfriend.'

Dad stiffens and straightens at the mention of Scott Sbarra. 'What did he have to say for himself? He hasn't had the decency to introduce himself to your mother or me yet, or even so much as send a card.'

'How would he even find you?'

'Well,' says Dad, flustered. 'Did he give *you* a message to pass on to us? Anything?'

'No, but that doesn't mean he didn't care about her,' I

say. 'It's not like they were married, Dad. Maybe we should cut him some slack.'

'I'll cut him something,' says Dad.

'Paul,' says Mum.

'I just want to hear his side of the story, that's all.'

'I heard it,' I say. 'They studied together the night before at the Butler Library at Columbia. He stayed over and left early the next morning.'

Dad snorts.

Mum says, 'Did he seem like a nice boy, Molly?'

I shrug. 'I guess.'

'Molly has better taste,' says Dad.

What he means is that I'm a twenty-two-year-old virgin who has never even been on a proper date. I have carefully drafted profiles on three dating apps, one of which Mum even paid the subscription for as a birthday present, and I've never matched well enough to meet anyone in person.

'He seems all right, Dad. He's a rower.'

Dad stands up a little taller.

'And I met a private investigator looking into KT's case.'

'A what?' says Mum. 'How did you meet him?'

'What did he tell you, this private investigator?' asks Dad.

'He's been hired by Columbia – or not by them, but indirectly, I think he said. Paid for by the foundation that funds KT's scholarship.'

'He's paid by them?' says Dad. 'Why?'

'I guess they've invested a lot of money into KT and now they're annoyed they won't get a long-term return. I don't know, Dad. It all happened in the heat of the moment. He asked me who KT would hang out with, same kinds of questions Martinez asked us all. This investigator used to be a policeman, apparently.'

'Used to be?' says Mum.

Dad takes a call from his bank manager and marches down the hall.

'He's going stir-crazy in this tiny room,' says Mum.

I look inside their room and it's only about forty per cent larger than mine.

'You should have stayed in the Best Western,' I say.

'I wish we could have.'

I look up at the stained ceiling.

'Your father's trying to negotiate a voluntary liquidation agreement with creditors. Some kind of payment plan. We shouldn't even be here in the first place. He's under a lot of stress, your dad.'

'Not just him – you as well.'

'We're tougher, though,' she says.

We hug. The carpet smells of bleach, and the silhouette of Dad backlit by the hall light grows as we hold each other tight.

'I just want her killer caught,' she whispers. 'Locked away forever.'

'Me too.'

'Violet Roseberry emailed me asking for your contact details,' she says. 'She found us through the company website. I think she wants to get in touch. She said she has some of Katie's things for you. I gave her your details, I hope that's OK.'

'Sure. I'll take ten minutes and reply to her now.'

'We'll see you down in the diner. Want us to order for you?'

'No, I might need a little more time so don't wait for me.'

'Of course we'll wait for you, Molly,' says Mum. 'We'll have tea until you get there. You take as much time as you need.'

I go into my room. Baseball bat, hornet spray, knife.

Three new emails. Two spam. One from Violet Roseberry asking if we can meet. Giving me her number and Scott's number in case I need help while I'm in the city. I reply suggesting we meet late this afternoon. She says five p.m. outside the West Side YMCA, next to the park. I say OK, see you there.

And then I search in my folder for old messages from KT.

4,773 emails.

Usually we texted or FaceTimed, but we often forwarded articles and links to each other. Sometimes we didn't even stop to think if the other twin would want to read the piece; we just automatically forwarded it. We were two sides of the same double helix. I don't know how many times we emailed the same article to each other at the exact same time. What I find interesting she usually finds interesting. *Found* interesting.

One message isn't from her Gmail or her King's College account or her Columbia account. It's a single email from *katie999@fortressmail.tv*. The message dates from last year and it's blank. It doesn't even say *test*. I can see I replied to it with, 'This you, KT?' and she never responded so I assumed it was spam or phishing. But

999 was her favourite number, so maybe it was a spare account.

I Google *FortressMail.* Still exists. Operates out of Panama. They talk a lot on the site FAQs about end-to-end encryption and open source and VPN technology and how there are no records or IP logs kept. I try to log in with her username. I use *mollyraven* as a password and it fails. Apparently I have four more attempts. I try *katiemolly* and *mollykatie* but they both fail. Two more attempts. We had a language as kids – not a very sophisticated one, but aged six or seven we used to use opposites or sometimes drop the first letter from each word. KT and I could talk at normal speed, or, eventually, even faster, and our parents could never keep up. I try *atie.* Incorrect. One attempt remaining. I try *olly.*

It works.

This inbox has 774 emails, 773 of which have been read.

Her sent items folder has 592 emails.

Her deleted folder is empty.

Her drafts folder has one email.

I open the draft. It's dated from nine days ago and it's written to *OPO64@fortressmail.tv.* An email from my sister that was never sent. The subject line is *Her.* The email reads *I'm sorry to bother you with this, I know you're busy with work, but V is driving me batshit crazy. She will not get it. I'm afraid she'll do something serious to herself. Once she told me her dad has a pistol in his bedside drawer and her mum has enough codeine pills to kill a baseball team. She's obsessed and I don't like it xx*

V must be Violet Roseberry, KT's best friend, the woman I'm meeting in just over an hour. But she's a woman in her early twenties; just how dangerous could she really be? Who did KT think about sending this message to? *OPO64*. That doesn't ring any bells. And this person, a he or a she, is busy with *work*. Why did KT never send the email? I Google *OPO64* and I get a bunch of acronyms and technical specifications, and then, on page seventeen of the search results, I find something relevant.

The department of Literature Humanities at Columbia University, New York.

Building OPO.

Room 64.

Professor Eugene Groot.

I take the business card from my pocket and think about forwarding the draft email to Bogart DeLuca. Surely Martinez would be the better choice? But I'd have to admit I hacked my dead sister's email. Maybe I could say I knew her address. I could tell him I already had the password.

There's a noise behind my shoulder. I reach for the bat and my door starts to shake on its hinges. Someone's trying to pick the lock, probing the keyhole with a metal implement. I swallow hard, my heart thumping double-speed, and then I stand up slowly and adopt a defensive stance: one foot forward, knees flexed. I could scream, but a competent attacker would stifle that in a second or less. I raise the Louisville Slugger above my head and the door opens and it's a little old lady with a hairnet.

'Oh, God, I'm sorry! Don't hurt me!'

I lower my bat and say, 'I thought you were breaking in!'

'Don't hit me. Oh, God. Please, lady.'

'It's OK.'

'No, no. I work here. I just checking each room make sure everything OK. I do rounds once every other day. I work here four years.'

'Everything's OK,' I say. 'Sorry I scared you.'

'OK, lady.'

She walks away and I vow to improve my security somehow. I need to be protected but I also need to stay legal. One risk is me getting attacked, the other is me getting into trouble with the NYPD. That's the line I must negotiate.

I pack my small rucksack with the knife and sixty dollars cash and the hornet spray. I lock my door and head outside.

The air is heady with the smell of roasting nuts mixed with petrol fumes. Two men are arguing outside the office building opposite, and a one-legged pigeon is fighting to pull a french fry out of the drainage gulley.

I head over to the food cart on the corner, the guy who helped me find the hardware store.

'You again. How are you doing, Molly?'

'You remembered my name.'

He smiles. 'One day you're gonna be my new best customer.'

'What's yours?'

'My what?' He breaks off to serve two cups of bubble tea to a couple. 'What's my what?' he says.

'Name.'

'Jimmy.'

'Your real name.'

'My name is Mahmud Nadir. You can call me Jimmy. I'm Jimmy.'

'OK, Jimmy. I read you won an award for your smoothies.'

He holds up some folded cardboard certificates. 'I got three prizes. Two for hygiene and one for my fruit salad.'

There's a US flag and a small Afghan flag and a photo of his family behind the counter.

'Could I have a smoothie?'

'No problem.'

'Mango and raspberry, please.'

'You got it.'

He hands over the smoothie and I hand over five dollars and my backpack.

'Wait, what is this?' He backs up and holds his hands up. 'Whatever it is, I do not want it. No way. No, thank you.'

'It's a go-bag,' I say, smiling.

'It's a *what* bag?'

'A go-bag, Jimmy.'

'Where you goin'?'

'Exactly.'

'Girl, you speakin' in riddles.'

'How long have you been in New York, Jimmy?'

He still won't take the bag from me. 'Eighteen years, why?'

'You know how sometimes things can go wrong. A big storm or a financial crisis. Maybe an explosion or a bus crash or mass shooting, that kind of thing.'

He looks at me suspiciously, his hands still far away from my backpack.

'I always like to keep a few important items away from my hotel room when I travel. Sometimes I use a left luggage locker in a train station. I wondered if I could leave this bag with you. I'm going back to England soon so it's just for a few days. You can look inside: there are no bombs or body parts.'

'I can't take it.'

'Please, Jimmy. It's a family emergency and I can't afford a locker right now. You can look inside the bag if you like.'

He narrows his eyes. 'What's in there?'

'A little cash, some water, some bug spray, spare clothes, a multi-tool, some Tampax . . .'

'All right, all right, that's enough. I'll keep it for you. But I'm not taking responsibility, you hear? If it goes missing or someone takes it, then that's your sorry luck for leaving it with me.'

'Deal.'

'You're a crazy English girl.'

'I know. Now, can you tell me where I can find pepper spray or bear spray?'

'No bears in New York City.'

I raise my eyebrows.

'Place downtown near 14th Street I heard about a way back, not sure if it's still there though. Sell all kinds of martial arts karate weapons. Flying stars and the like. You be careful what you do with those things, Molly. You been on a course?'

'Thanks, Jimmy. See you soon.'

He disappears from view muttering as he hides my backpack away inside the cart.

I pass the diner and tell Mum and Dad where I'm going. I guess they gave up waiting as both are eating chicken pot pie with french fries. Mum apologises, and I take a napkin full of fries with me and go.

Yellow cab up to the YMCA in the Upper West Side takes ten minutes.

She's waiting outside.

Short red hair. Blue jeans. Thick black coat: the kind a construction worker might wear.

Violet watches me get out of the cab.

And then she collapses to the ground like she's been shot in the head.

13

I run over and help up the woman Scott called KT's soulmate. Nobody else seems to notice her on the ground.

'I'm fine, really, I'm fine. My knees went weak, I need food, I guess. I'm good. Jesus, I'm an idiot.' She stares directly into my eyes as she gets back to her feet.

'Hey, miss. Your fare!' yells the cab driver.

'Pay the man,' says Violet. 'I'm OK now.'

I pay him and he looks at me like I tried to rip him off.

'It's more of a shock than I expected. To see you, I mean. Jesus,' says Violet. 'God, I'm sorry. I'm Violet, Vi, Katie's friend.'

'I know.'

'I know you know, I'm just saying. Fuck, you look just like her, I mean obviously, duh, you're twins, but you look just fucking like her. Like nothing's even changed – you even frown like she did.'

I shrug.

'I'm sorry about what happened,' she says.

'Thank you.'

'No, I mean it. I'm real sorry. That it happened here in New York. It's horrific.'

'It's not your fault.'

She says, 'Can I give you a hug? I'm not coping with this very well. Is a hug too weird? Maybe I shouldn't. Or? That OK? I figure we both need it.'

'I'm not sure.' KT was the hugger, not me.

'Come on.'

We share an awkward hug outside the entrance to the YMCA and it's only broken when a Japanese guy comes outside, wheeling his bike.

'Can't you see we're right here?' Violet tells him. 'We're both invisible to you? You couldn't have waited one second, dude?'

He apologises even though he really has nothing to apologise for, and Violet says, 'Fuck. Let's go into the park.'

We cross the road and enter Central Park south of Dalehead Arch. There are locals with small dogs on leashes, and there are tourists in bad denim. One young woman passes us, talking about how she might scrape the grades for UCLA.

'Do the cops have any leads?' she says. 'I still can't believe Katie's gone. Cannot fathom it. They tell you anything yet?'

'Not really.'

'In her own fucking apartment. I told her to live on campus but did she listen? I survived in this damn city my whole life and she didn't listen to me.'

'You're from here?'

'Mom's from Brooklyn, Dad's from Queens, though I haven't seen him since I was a little girl. I study the same program as Katie. Up to my eyeballs in debt and working two jobs in Williamsburg just to pay bills.'

Violet seems flustered. Maybe she's still in shock.

'KT said she had a lot of fun with you, said you were a great friend.'

'She said that? That's sweet. We've only known each other a year but we were real close, you know. We had some wonderful times together. Those parties last year. I guess with you being in London and all she needed someone here in the city.'

'KT and I weren't in touch so much this past year.'

'I know, sweetheart. I'm sorry. Katie told me you didn't take the news well. Her studying over here.'

I clench my teeth. 'We'd always lived in the same place, the two of us.'

'It's hard with sisters; I got five of them,' she says, her expression softening. 'Trust me, I know.'

'Totally different with a twin, though.'

Violet looks at me and says, 'Let's sit down over there, come on.'

We walk into a baseball field and sit on the green-painted spectator benches. There's no one playing. It's empty.

'How are you coping, with the news, with the adjustment? How are you holding up inside here?' She taps the side of her head.

'It's still a shock. Doesn't feel real. Maybe I'll come to terms with it after the funeral. Maybe then it'll make more sense.'

'Will that be here in the city or in England?'

'In our village near Nottingham, in the Midlands. Dad's going to talk to airlines about it.'

'That's too bad,' says Violet. 'I would have liked to be there to say my goodbyes.'

'You can't fly over?'

'I can hardly make rent this month, Molly. In fact, truth be told, I can't make rent this month.' She starts to frown and then she taps her temple with her finger. 'But I'll be there with you guys in spirit. I swear on my life I'll be there in England in spirit.'

We both stare forward at the rust tone of the trees and she says, 'Smoke?' I shake my head and she shrugs and lights up a cigarette. 'You two were real close until she moved over here, eh?'

'As close as two people can be.'

She turns to me and shakes her head. 'You look just like her. It's weird, but it's nice, you know what I mean? I don't mean to be disrespectful, it's just a comfort in a way to see you. It's like I still have a piece of my Katie here, you know.'

Your KT?

Three boys approach with a mitt and a bat and a ball. All three are wearing baseball caps.

'Ballpark's closed, kids,' says Violet. 'Come on, it's October already.'

The smallest kid says, 'My uncle said we could play here.'

Violet sniffs and says, 'Your uncle? The park's closed. What, you want to argue with me some more about this? Can't you see we're talking here, me and my friend? Jesus. Can't you see we're talking?'

They wander off, dragging their bat along the ground.

'Upper West Side brats.'

'How can you tell?'

'Oh, I can tell. It's easy.'

'What do you think happened to KT, Violet?'

She takes a long drag on her cigarette and then blows smoke out of her nostrils. 'Only God knows, but she had some people in her life I'd say might have been . . . how should I put this? Toxic, maybe. Problematic.'

'Who? Scott Sbarra?'

'Scottie? Nah, Scottie's a sweetheart. He doesn't have a vicious bone in his body, that one. Never messed her around too much, always treated her nice as far as I heard, and that's a rare thing – you find me another guy like that at our school, especially a jock.'

'Who, then?'

Violet looks at me. 'She ever mention any of her teachers, her professors?'

'Professor Groot?'

'Yeah, exactly. Professor Eugene Groot. Everyone knows you have to keep your eye on him.'

'Why?'

She stumps out her cigarette and lights another. ''Cos he's a leery silverfox motherfucker, that's why.'

I cringe at the language.

'What? You OK?'

'I'm just not used to cursing.'

'Get outta here. Truly?'

I nod.

'You're not shitting me?'

I shake my head.

'Fuck, Molly. Your sister swore like a sailor. I need watch my mouth around you, really?'

'It's OK. I think I'm getting used to it.'

'So you two look the same except for an eyebrow scar and your dress sense, but you're pretty much fundamentally different, huh?'

'KT was much more outgoing than me. We used to joke that she took all the extrovert genes and I took all the introvert genes. What were you saying about Eugene Groot?'

'Like I said, he's a lech. Pretends to be an upstanding family man – his wife's a bigwig human rights lawyer always on CNN, always representing some hacker or whistle-blower or freedom-fighter. But Eugene Groot isn't quite as upstanding as he makes out. We can tell, see. Most of the women in my class understood him before he even opened his mouth. Knew he was the type to profess church and family values while he stares at your shirt the whole damn class. The type to have photos of his kids on his desk while he's asking you out for a drink.'

'He did that with you?'

'Not with me, Molly. He did it with your sister.'

'I remember something about that. What happened?'

She looks at me. 'I told her not to go through with it.'

'But she did?'

'She said this kind of thing happens in London as well, and it's normal there. It's nothing, all consenting adults. But the man played some strange games.'

'What do you mean?'

She flicks ash from the end of her cigarette. 'It's weird talking to you about this. It doesn't feel right.'

'I need to know, Violet. I can't live with her killer on the loose.'

She looks up at the clouds, and with her head tilted that way, she says, 'I've already been through all this with the police. They went out.' She moves her head to look at me. 'Your sister and Groot. They slept together.'

14

We walk diagonally across the park towards Fifth Avenue and the Plaza Hotel.

My head is full of my sister.

'Feeling OK?' asks Violet, studying my face.

'You mind if we stick to the grass or the small paths?'

'Small paths?' she says. 'Why?'

'I just don't like these major paths through the park. I feel exposed. It doesn't feel too safe.'

'What, you'll get attacked by a pigeon or a tour guide, what is it?'

'If someone came driving through at speed? You know. It's New York.'

She screws up her face.

I mouth the word *terrorists* and she blows a raspberry and says, 'Let them fucking try.'

'You're not scared?'

'If I thought like that I'd never get out of bed, Molly. Shit, we just have to get on with it, same as you guys in London, no? Am I wrong?'

'Seems more threatening here.'

'We have sugar lumps all around the park, and we got New York's finest all over the goddamn place, you don't even see them but they see you. Cameras. FBI listening in to phone calls. Tech we're not even aware of. Molly, they see you right now.'

'Sugar lumps?'

'The concrete blocks the city puts everywhere. They stop cars and trucks driving where they shouldn't be driving. Barriers, you know.'

We keep walking.

'That why you carry a slungshot, is it?' she says.

I tense up. 'I don't carry a slingshot.'

'I said *slungshot*, Molly. That ball of rope hanging out of your pocket, that why you carry it, is it, to stop terrorists?'

I push the monkey fist deeper into my pocket. 'Self-defence,' I say.

'Yeah, whatever. You know they're illegal in the city, right? All weapons are basically illegal here. Other states you can walk around with an open-carry AR15, but here we're defenceless. But we're all defenceless together, that make sense?'

'If you had a twin, and she was killed in her bed, you'd carry something.'

She thinks about that. 'I'm sorry. Of course you're scared, it's understandable. I'm sorry. Shit, Molly, my big mouth. I'm real sorry.'

'It's fine. Tell me more about the professor.'

'There was some kind of investigation a few years ago, some kind of sit-down. I wasn't involved but people talked. He kept his job, I guess, but most of the female students gave him a wide berth. Your sister liked him, that's the thing – she genuinely really fucking liked him. Very smart guy, Groot, probably the best in his field.

Brain like a supercomputer. Not as smart as me, but he gets pretty close.'

I smile.

'I'm not even kidding.'

'What's his field?'

'Contemporary civilisation. World authority on Hobbes. You know, *Leviathan*, the social contract, nominalism.'

'And you think he was having an affair with my sister? How serious was it?'

'Don't *think*, Molly. *Know*. There were a couple of months back in the spring when she talked of nothing else. Infatuated. Every time we met for a slice of pizza it was Eugene this and Eugene that. She started going away with him upstate, think they went to Albany one weekend, just to be more safe, walk around like a real couple for a few days instead of always hiding.'

'You think Groot hurt KT?'

'I don't know what to think, honey. But I do know things were heating up between those two.'

'Heating up?'

A squirrel runs across the ball field.

'After summer Katie was talking about giving Groot an ultimatum because he had discussed leaving his wife and kids, usual douchebag bullshit. Predictably, he decides not to go through with it, for the sake of the family and all that, even talked about *doing the decent thing instead of the enjoyable thing*, what the fuck, you believe that?'

'I wish she'd talked to me about all this.'

'She would have done if you'd been here in the States, I'm sure. I wasn't a replacement, Molly I was just a stand-in, you know, short-term.'

'Maybe I could have helped her through it.'

'She also told me your dad was acting kind of peculiar on the trip here. Not being himself. She tell you that?'

'Dad?'

'Yeah.'

'He's under a lot of pressure. Finance stuff.'

'Yeah, Maybe that was it, then.'

Sirens erupt all around us and a police car swerves up on to the grass. I drag Violet into the bushes for cover and then an ambulance stops by the police car. Someone in the park was taken sick. Some kind of manic episode. We watch as they get helped into the ambulance. No cuffs or guns drawn.

'The hell you pull me into a shrub for? It's just a fucking ambulance.'

'Sorry.'

'Come on, my shift starts soon. What are you doing now? I know I said the city's safe but you can't stay in the park at night, you know, not even with a slungshot, it's not OK for you here in the night-time. I'm dead serious about that, Molly.'

'I'm heading back to my hostel to read emails.'

'You're staying on West 44th, right? I'll walk you to your door?'

A shiver runs down my neck. 'How did you know I was on West 44th?'

'I don't know, maybe your mom told me or something? I thought to myself, fuck, why would you stay in fucking Midtown of all places?'

'Where would you have stayed?'

'Pretty much anyplace that's not Midtown, but whatever.'

We walk along a street by the park, backtracking towards the YMCA, and in the shade of the trees is a line of horse-drawn wagons.

'Can we take another route?'

'Terrorists here too?'

'Horses.'

'Horses? Come on, we'll take Billionaires' Row.'

'Huh?'

'West 57th. Rich freaks who pay to live well above the likes of you and me, Molly Raven.'

I walk past a grille down in the road, and steam billows out of it and gets pushed away by the breeze. I hold my breath to avoid any potential Legionnaires' disease particles.

'Why all the steam?' I say when I'm safely past it.

'This city's powered by steam, some of it anyhow. Laundries, parts of NYU, heating systems, the lot. Not just Marilyn Monroe getting her panties damp, you know.'

'I thought that was breeze from the subway.'

'Same difference.'

'Did you visit KT much in her apartment?'

'Yeah, now and then. We studied there together a few times when Butler was too busy, you know.'

'The Butler Library?'

She nods. 'Katie tried to cook for me one time but that didn't turn out so good so we ended up in the Village after midnight eating tacos with two Korean guys. But yeah, we hung out in her place on and off. I helped her install the AC unit on her back window.'

'Did you see her downstairs neighbour?'

'Skinny kid who won't look at you? Yeah. I've seen him there, and he even came to school one time.' She frowns. 'Maybe I should've told the cops about him, come to think about it.'

'He came to Columbia?'

'We found him on the steps, the famous ones. If you've ever seen a New York movie, trust me, you'd recognise the steps. Said he was filming some YouTube video or something, had permission, but it was pretty damn clear he was there for your sister. Practically stalked her the first month she moved in. Of course, back then he was a skinny dude with acne scars and no eye-contact. Now he's a muscly dude with lasered cheeks and no eye-contact. Spent all that money on himself and still can't look you straight in the eye. You think he's a suspect?'

'I get a strange vibe from him.'

'The cops tell you how Katie actually died? I apologise if that's an insensitive question, only they don't say much on the news.'

'We don't even know all the details yet. Mum thinks she was drugged or poisoned.'

She looks pale. 'My God.'

We walk on.

'This is me,' I say, pointing at the Bedfordshire Midtown Hostel sign.

'Take good care of yourself, Molly. I loved your sister very much, I want you to know that.' She doesn't cry, but there's a tremble in her lower lip. 'And I'm so sorry she's gone.'

'Me too. Can I call you if I have more questions before I go?'

'You can call me any time day or night, sweetheart.'

I go upstairs. Mum and Dad are out. I find Detective Martinez's card and email asking him to look into Professor Eugene Groot and Shawn Bagby. I explain why. Then I find Bogart DeLuca's card and call him.

'DeLuca Investigations.'

'I need you to look into Professor Groot some more.'

'Hey, Molly. I was gonna call you. He's on my radar already, on the wall chart. I'm looking at it right now. You got specifics? Anything new or actionable?'

'Just that he may have had an inappropriate relationship with KT. Can you find out what he was doing the day she died? Where he was? Alibis and that kind of thing?'

'Already on my list but I'll bump it to the top. Leave it with me. You OK?'

'I'm OK.'

'You ever feel uncomfortable or followed, call the police. Do not hesitate. Don't call me, even. I'll help you if I can, always, but if you're worried go straight to the cops.'

'OK.'

'Call you back.'

He ends the call and I hear noises coming from next door. 'Mum,' I say, opening the door. She doesn't say anything back; she just hugs me and I feel her shoulders through her coat. She needs to eat more. She needs to rest.

Mum takes a deep breath in and says, 'We need to talk about your sister's body.'

15

We huddle outside the doors to our respective rooms because there isn't enough space in either one of them for all three of us to stand together. The carpet tiles are stained pale pink from the bleach.

'They told you how she died? What happened?' I look at Mum and then at Dad.

'They can't tell us more yet, Moll.'

'Why not?'

'The autopsy results. They'll let us know as soon as they can. Your father pressed them on it.'

'Said they have some DNA samples they're working on,' says Dad. 'Working through fingerprints and CCTV from the area. And they're investigating her electronic footprint.'

Mum clamps her wrist to her mouth for a while, and when she removes it I can see the finger marks left on her skin.

'Sweetie, all we know is, they're treating it as murder. They have their reasons and we'll find out more tomorrow. Listen, we talked to a funeral director. We've been to talk with three of them.'

'OK.'

'About how to get Katie back to England.'

I look at Dad but he just shakes his head and looks down at the floor.

'You know I wanted us to all fly back home together,' says Mum, her voice cracking. 'When they release her to us. Wanted to fly home as a family.' Tears in her eyes. 'With the coffin. But, apparently, it's not that simple.'

'Why not? And why are we even talking about all this when her killer is still free?'

'Because she's our daughter,' says Dad sternly. 'We want to get her back home.'

'The problem is the cost,' says Mum. 'The cost of flying Katie back with us. It's a lot more than we can afford. Out credit cards are maxed out, they've all been understanding what with our horrendous experience this week, but we can't get her home with us that way.'

'So you do it by boat?' I say. 'By ship? I looked into travelling here by ship, remember? Maybe that's cheaper. Slower, but cheaper. I think it would be. I could ask for an advance from my boss.'

Mum shakes her head. 'It isn't cheap enough.' She looks up at Dad and says, 'God, I hate that a decision this important and personal comes down to money. We don't have friends or relatives we can ask. Most of them are worse off than we are. Why the hell . . . what's wrong with . . .?'

He looks down at the floor again. 'So – what? We just leave her here?'

'No, my love,' says Mum, swallowing hard. 'We can have a kind of a service here in New York.'

'We can't bury KT here, Mum. We can't leave her here on her own forever.'

'It's a crematorium service, Moll,' says Dad, putting his arm on Mum's shoulder. 'A cremation close to here near Brooklyn. Beautiful place called Fresh Pond – they explained it all to us. It's like a chapel. We can do things the right way, and then fly back with Katie, with the urn, her ashes. All four of us together, just like we wanted.'

'Cremation?'

'It's not what we talked about, I know that,' says Dad. 'We've always been buried in this family, on your mum's side and mine. But it's the only way.'

'Her ashes?'

'We can spread them in the garden at home, sweetie,' says Mum.

Dad coughs.

'Or, if we have to sell the house, then we'll spread them in the churchyard in the village. I'm sure the vicar would say a few words. He's always been very kind.'

I shake my head and say, 'It's a lot to take in, Mum.'

'I know. We've had a long day and we still don't know when the medical examiner will hand her back to us. We should get an update on that tomorrow and then we'll book a time for the crematorium.'

'The police don't want to keep her longer? For forensic tests?'

'I don't know, Molly. Paul, what did the detective say?'

'Martinez told me once the . . .' He lowers his voice. 'Once the autopsy is complete, cause of death established, we'll get her back with us soon. It won't take long. This week.'

'We'll have her back soon,' says Mum, a tear running down her cheek. 'I think I need a lie down. I don't feel well.'

They nap, and I take the time to scan news channels for any updates.

When Mum and Dad are ready we go eat soup and bread in the diner. The quiet pace of the room is comforting. We don't talk much; we just eat. Too much to process in one day.

They say goodnight and go to bed. I give them my Louisville Slugger. They're not surprised. They know me. Mum accepts it with a weary smile, probably just to appease me. Then I sneak out and buy a bubble tea from Jimmy and he says, 'I still got your bag, I haven't looked inside.'

'You can look inside if you want.'

'I don't want.'

I walk down Fifth Avenue past the New York Public Library, past the Empire State Building and past the Flatiron Building, until I reach Murray Hill Tactical.

There are no other women in the shop. From the sale section I buy a self-defence belt made from reinforced leather with a solid bronze buckle. A guy with a handlebar moustache says, 'Yeah, that'll break a car windshield with one swipe, so imagine what it'd do to a perp.'

I ask what else I can carry in New York City and he blows air through his teeth and says, 'There ain't much, truth be told. You can't have a firearm, obviously. I can sell you a mil-spec torch with a strobe at three thousand lumens – that'd temporarily blind a bad dude. How about that?'

I need to be able to defend myself. My parents. 'I'll take two.'

'I haven't told you the price yet.'

'How much?'

'Sixty bucks a pop.'

'I'll take one, then.'

'No law against walking round with a bat and a ball but you gotta have the ball, see. That's important. You haven't got a baseball on your person and you're in big trouble.'

'Pepper spray?'

'You go to a licensed pharmacy and get yourself a pocket-size bottle of capsicum self-defence spray. Not expensive.'

'I will.'

'Anything else?'

'How about this?'

He shows me a 140-decibel attack alarm. 'Only seven bucks on special.'

'I'll take three.'

He bags it all up and I walk back up Fifth Avenue. I buy a cup of tea and a pastrami sandwich for a homeless woman. I get three pepper spray canisters from Walgreens. There's a pipe sticking up out of the middle of the road near Madison Square Park and it has steam pumping out. A chimney from the bowels of the earth.

In bed I scroll through my notifications: weather, natural disasters, political strife, anything connected to the US east coast. Nothing too troubling. I take a deep breath and start looking through KT's secret emails.

Some of the messages are flirty and some of them are downright explicit. I read through a few dozen messages back and forth with several people who I assume are not Scott, before I come across one email from early May that does grab my attention.

It talks about helping to get rid of a neighbour from her apartment.

Then it goes on to the morning sex they had in the Park Hyatt, Chicago.

It talks about the breakfast they had in bed after, and how he was sorry.

It talks about the Little League game he had to leave for.

It talks about her term papers he had to grade.

16

Next morning I email Professor Eugene Groot PhD from the discomfort of my narrow hostel bed. I introduce myself politely and ask if I could have half an hour of his time. That seems reasonable after he ignored my first message. I tell him I can travel up to Columbia to meet him at his office.

Mum and Dad are talking urns and coffins and flower choices, and it feels too distant from reality for me to comprehend. They want a mahogany urn that they can get engraved back home in Nottingham. They think it'll be best to spread some of her ashes in the churchyard, probably just close family members in attendance, and then keep the rest in the urn to memorialise KT. I drift away and start imagining her autopsy scars, the rough Frankenstein stitches holding her lifeless body together, her skin cold and greying, and I have to physically shake the idea from my head. I'm nauseous. What kind of twisted mind do I have where I can visualise her like that? Visualise *myself* like that?

'We can go to Pret if you like, Moll?' says Dad.

'Sure.'

We sit in the window of the Pret on West 42nd Street. Mum picks at a granola and fruit salad, and Dad and I both have pastries. Three cups of good, strong coffee. I saw an influencer on YouTube say you should never countenance visiting a chain restaurant in New York City because the one-off authentic places are so incredible here. The finest in the world. But I'm not that person. Mum and Dad are not those people. We lack that adventurous spirit. When Mum's egg split into two, when it cleaved itself, all that bravery and spontaneity went to KT and left me like this.

Email notification. Eugene Groot apologises and says his schedule is busy until late February. Late February? He expresses his sincere condolences. I write back immediately that I have some important information relating to him and I'd like to discuss it, out of courtesy, before I take it to anyone else. I suggest Midtown or Columbia.

We gather our things together and head back out on to the street. Detective Martinez wants to talk with Mum again, just a formality, or so he says. Dad will take her there and wait outside.

Email notification. Groot says can I meet him at the Harvard Club on West 44th Street at six p.m. I reply that I will be there.

I do some shopping, then I walk alone to Central Park with my eyes peeled for anyone suspicious-looking. I have my hands inside my pockets because it's a cold, crisp October day, and the guy in front of me is talking to his friend about the upcoming New York marathon. About the inconvenience of it all. The extra street security. His friend says *You wait until Macy's Thanksgiving Day parade next month if you want to see inconvenience.*

Inside the park an old Chinese man plays some kind of stringed instrument and his music is unlike anything I have ever heard. It is sad and it is beautiful.

I find the rock monoliths close to Inscope Arch, and perch on top, but not too close to the edge.

All around me is life. Layers of activity and noise; impossibly narrow skyscrapers building up behind the treeline like stalagmites in a limestone cave.

I try to wrap my head around KT's death, and my new role as a surviving twin. How will I cope with that? How will it change my hopes and dreams? We will not have kids at the same age, the way we dreamed of. We will not marry in the same church the way we talked about. We will not holiday together with our husbands and our children in Cornwall as we always imagined we would do, drinking crisp white wine in some sleepy fishing harbour while our children devour their strawberry ice-creams.

My rocky perch overlooks the Wollman ice-rink and it is a menace. In most places this would be serene: skaters swirling and scraping round the ice, left alone for us to all admire. But here each strictly controlled skating session is preceded by a quarter hour of safety messages and legal disclaimers. All sorts of loudspeaker warnings and regulations about when to take photos and in what zone those photos can be taken.

My mind's a muddle, but being in this little corner of parkland is helping me to order my thoughts. My return flight is booked to leave in a few days. Me and Mum and Dad. And an urn full of ashes. In the meantime I will do everything I can to aid the police and aid Bogart DeLuca.

I'll update him as soon as my dinner with Groot is finished tonight.

I imagine KT sitting on this very rock eating a giant pretzel or flirting with Scott Sbarra. Or she might have even FaceTimed me from this spot before things became awkward. If I could go back in time and change things, I would.

Email notification. It's from Groot. It says there's a dress code: no jeans or leggings or T-shirts. I already know I'm going to hate the Harvard Club. If there's any mingling and small talk I will not perform well. *Where did you study?* they'll ask, and I'll answer that I didn't, and they'll ask *What do you do?* and I'll say I'm an admin assistant for a paint and wood stain manufacturer and then they'll smile and nod and move on. The truth is, we can't all be overachieving academics destined for the UN or a top law firm; some of us are meant to be normal, and there is no shame in that whatsoever.

Back at the hostel I shower and put on black trousers and a black shirt and black shoes.

'You look smart, dear,' says Mum.

'Thank you.'

I step closer to her. Put my hand on her shoulder. 'If you ever need to come and stay with me in London for a bit, Mum – for whatever reason – you can, you know. I don't make much, but my job's safe. If you need to—'

She places her fingertip to her lips for a moment, and then kisses me on my forehead and mouths *thank you*.

I leave without explaining about Groot because I worry they'll want to come as well and then I'll discover absolutely nothing of value. I want to see the professor for myself. Hold his gaze. Assess him.

The walk to the Harvard Club takes less than five minutes but the transformation is dramatic. From the manic Times Square end of Midtown to a string of clubs and expensive-looking hotels. The Algonquin, the Iroquois, the Sofitel. And then the red-brick Harvard Club with its flags, and a doorman in full uniform holding the door open for me.

'Good evening,' says the receptionist. 'Member or guest?'

'Er, guest. Of Eugene Groot.'

'Of course, please sign in just here.'

I sign in.

'Take a seat over there and I'll let Professor Groot know you've arrived.'

She walks away and I feel uncomfortable in this vast room with its serious portraits and plaques and bookcases.

'Ms Raven,' says a man an inch or two shorter than my father, a man with sparkly blue eyes, tan skin and a well-groomed grey beard. 'Groot. Eugene Groot, pleased to meet you.'

'Thanks for seeing me.'

He closes his eyes for a few seconds, and then leads me towards an ornate staircase and says, in a low, discreet tone, 'I'm so sorry for your loss, it's a dreadful tragedy. The whole department is in a state of shock.'

'Thank you.'

He leads me through to a grand hall. A soprano is singing, filling the double-height room with her voice.

'The Club's been here since 1888. Most of the architecture is McKim's work.' He sounds strained when he talks. A little nervous. Overcompensating. 'And yes, that elephant head is real.'

'Did KT ever come here?'

'Not that I know of,' says Groot.

We walk through dark-red-painted corridors to another staircase. The steps creak like you'd expect in an old English house, and then we arrive at the dining hall.

'Beautiful room,' I say.

'Isn't it?'

We sit and are presented with menus.

'It all looks very grand, but let me tell you the Harvard Club Foundation scholarship fund helps support numerous undergraduates through their studies. All this is a form of giving back.'

'KT talked about you,' I say.

He puts on his reading glasses. 'Your sister was an excellent student. An enquiring mind.'

'She was fond of you.'

He looks away and summons a waiter and asks for a bottle of still water at room temperature.

A *sommelier* comes over and Groot looks at me. 'Should we stick to water, perhaps, or should we make a more appropriate toast to Katie? Too soon? Please, you decide, Molly.'

'We can toast her. But I don't drink.'

'Not at all?'

'Not a drop.'

He turns to the *sommelier*. 'One glass of the Billecart rosé.'

Moments later he's presented with a tall flute of pink champagne.

'To the memory of your sister.'

'To KT.'

My tumbler chinks his flute and we drink.

'Did you know her well?' I ask.

'At postgraduate level every teacher knows their students to a much fuller extent than at undergraduate, so I'd say I knew her a little. I always wanted to see her go on to study for her PhD. Katie would have made an excellent doctorate student.'

He orders shrimps and crab cake. It sounds good, but I cannot risk food poisoning from improperly prepared or stored shellfish, so I order roasted heirloom beets because they sound safe. The professor lectures me on the history of Columbia, the theories of Hobbes, the future of the Ivy League. He orders a glass of Meursault for himself. Fifteen minutes later he orders another.

'Have any of your other students ever been awarded a scholarship from the same foundation?'

His porterhouse arrives along with a bottle of red wine, and my rib lamb chop arrives too, and he tells me he'd never heard of the foundation or the scholarship until KT was awarded it, but that he's gone on to suggest applications from several more of his students.

'Seems like a very generous scholarship,' I say.

'Generous!' he says, his voice slurring a little. 'It's more than generous, Molly. It's downright unprecedented. Fees paid and an apartment close to school and a living stipend. It's unheard of. I'd like to see very much more of it.'

'It's offered through your department, or through the main Columbia office?'

'Actually, it's nothing to do with Columbia. It's a private scholarship, or, sorry, rather it's a *sponsorship*. I am aware of similar sponsorships at other institutions around the world, of course; often student-specific, often tied to a religious order or sporting potential. If you don't mind my saying, Molly, it is very pleasant to meet you.'

'And you.'

'No, I mean, it's a cliché and all, but talking with you here, it brings back Katie one last time. It's as if I'm talking through you to her in some way. Forgive my appalling sentimentality – this Burgundy . . .'

He must be drunk. I'm sitting here with a mineral water, whereas KT would have skipped the main course and taken him to some underground bar.

'I don't mind.'

He chews his porterhouse and drinks his wine. The label on the bottle says Nuits-Saint-Georges. Groot's lips are darkening. He says, 'There are rooms upstairs for members, and their guests, and very well-appointed they are too.' He looks around.

'Did you ever meet KT's boyfriend?' I ask.

'I'm not sure. Name?'

'Scott Sbarra.'

'Doesn't ring any bells, I'm afraid. I did notice her together with a young student one time. Broad chap, possibly a lacrosse player?'

'That's Scott. He rows.'

'A worthwhile pastime. My wife used to row up at Dartmouth. She's set to be appointed a judge next year.'

He looks me up and down and drinks more wine. His teeth are dark red.

'KT told me you visited her apartment.'

'Well, I wouldn't say visited.' He puts down his knife and fork and dabs his lips with his napkin. There's a breadcrumb caught in his beard. 'But yes, I think I did walk that way one time with her, before heading on to a meeting. That must have been it.'

'She said you went inside with her. Into her bedroom.'

'Well,' he says, coughing slightly on his food, 'I'm not sure that's strictly correct.'

I think back to his email.

'She said you helped her get rid of her neighbour? Some guy harassing her?'

'Ah,' he says, looking relieved. 'Of course. How could I forget? Yes, there was one time when I helped remove a young man from her property. Glad to be of assistance. That was it.'

'Was he acting suspiciously? Violently?'

'He was borderline stalking your sister, as I recall.'

'Her neighbour? How do you stalk from the same building?'

'Harassing, then. Bagby, his name was. I've already shared this with the police. From what I can recall, he was obsessed with her. She shrugged it off, but he seemed to me to be dangerously obsessed.'

The cheeseboard arrives and he pours another glass of Nuits-Saint-Georges.

I don't want to confront him too directly about the affair. I can get more from this man with honey than with vinegar.

'KT mentioned a hotel in Chicago. Bumping into you, I guess. The Hilton, was it? The Park Hyatt?'

Groot looks me up and down.

'What happened between you and my sister, professor?'

The volume in the room is loud. Conversations and laughter.

Groot scratches his beard and leans towards me and says, 'You really are identical, aren't you?'

I nod.

'Physically, I mean.' His eyes scan my body. 'In all aspects. Physically identical.'

17

The walk back to my hotel is a detox: the washing away of Eugene Groot. The rain is heavy and it gusts with the wind, especially through the crosswalks where narrow streets meet broad avenues. I see a woman carrying a skeleton costume in see-through plastic wrap. It's almost Halloween and I'm relieved. I'll be back in London by then.

I understand how a young woman might have found Professor Groot attractive in the cold stone sober light of day at Columbia. He's esteemed in his field, a world-renowned expert within his niche, and he's handsome in a tweedy, self-knowing kind of way. But for him to proposition me . . . I mean, he didn't exactly do that, but he might as well have, his body language was unmistakable – and all when my sister's body is barely cold. It's unthinkable. What else could he be capable of?

I walk past the diner on the way to my hotel and pause for a moment. The windows are steamy and a family of four is sitting, the two girls drinking milkshakes, not twins, just standard sisters, and their parents look relaxed. They look like they're having a good trip. I open the door and walk inside.

'Welcome back,' says the waitress. 'Let me seat you.'

She does.

Corner table. She can probably tell I like to be seated here, a position where I can oversee the whole room and predict threats before they materialise. I'm safer here than I am in the hostel room. Plus this place serves toasted bagels with Nova Scotia lox and cream cheese.

I write notes on my phone, trying to remember exactly what Groot said, because I want to hand over a complete set of intel to both Detective Martinez and Bogart DeLuca before I fly home. In an ideal world I'll give them some concrete evidence, something only a monozygotic twin could glean, but this isn't an ideal world.

Not even close.

The waitress tears off three sheets from her order pad and puts it down on my table complete with a biro.

'Oh, thank you.'

'You're welcome. You writing a novel, sweetheart?'

I can't think of a witty retort. I'm too tired and I have seen too many things this week so I just shake my head and she smiles and walks away.

I scroll through KT's Instagram feed and Facebook page and make a note of every location she's checked into in the past twelve months. Mostly it's all Brooklyn vegan restaurants and some place called Wu + Nussbaum near Columbia, but also two yoga studios. Sporadically she'd visit locations further afield, just as Groot said she did. There's a trip last month to St Kitts and one in May to Monaco for the Grand Prix.

I dig deeper into the comments under her posts. If someone wanted to steal your identity I guess public profiles like hers is where they would start. You'd have her name, Katie Raven, and then her profile photo – does that give up valuable biometric retina data? Plus you have her birthday. *Our* birthday. Why would you want everyone to have access to all that sensitive information?

There's a guy tagged in one post, a post from Aspen last winter, and he has ninety-four thousand followers. He follows ten people. His profile photo is a man sitting in a sports car on the top of some mountain. His profile says he's a philanthropist and negroni enthusiast. His photos are mainly of vintage cars, old houses, him skiing, him kite-surfing, him in Japan. There are photos of a school he's involved with in Tanzania, and photos of him on safari. There's a picture of him at a Phillips vintage watch auction. There's a photo of him as a boy next to a propeller plane. His name is James Kandee.

I order a cup of camomile tea. Mum texts me asking where I am, so I tell her.

From their social media feeds I can see that KT and this Kandee guy were in the same place in the world at least five times during the past twelve months. They were in St Kitts, they were in Aspen, they were in Monaco, they were in Malibu, and they were in some place called Turbach, although the caption says Gstaad, Switzerland.

Turbach.

That word is written in a note I wrote while researching late last night.

The Turbach Foundation.

I Google the place and discover it's a small settlement close to the exclusive ski resort of Gstaad. I Google the Turbach Foundation and the website is more like an abandoned webpage. There's a 'Contact Us' page and a general 'About Us' page. The foundation was established back in 2014 to *make the world a better place.* I Google James Kandee and find his Wikipedia page. It's brief. Born in 1989 in Nairobi, Kenya, James is the current owner of a polo team in Argentina, a green energy company based out of London, and a real estate company in Hong Kong. He serves on the board of seven non-profits and charities. He is the only surviving child of Jemima and Freddy Kandee, owners and founders of the largest private cargo air fleet in continental Africa. They were tragically killed in a car crash in 2013. Google images offer a different side to James: hundreds of photos of him with young beautiful women. Where he is twenty, the women look about twenty. Now he's well over thirty the women still look about twenty. I scroll down the search results. A mix of philanthropic escapades and wild parties in the Caribbean. There's one photo, taken on the back of a yacht, on a semi-circular bench. The women are all looking out to sea; their faces aren't shown, just the backs of their bikini clad bodies. There is only one man in the picture, James Kandee, and he's looking straight at the camera. A small, delicate man.

I focus on the woman two places over from James. The back of her head. It's *my* head. My hair. A tan version of my neck.

I finish my tea.

All of the places, dates, names and pertinent information go down on the waitress pad. All of it. And then I photograph the pad.

There's an old blogpost on page eight of the Google search results, an interview with Kandee. He interned for two hedge funds, two non-profits, and a charity out of Moscow. It says he studied for one semester at NYU film school but I can't find any other mention of that. It says he took a suite at the Carlyle while he studied in New York. It says it was his family's suite.

I search KT's secret email account for specific words: St Kitts, Monaco, Grand Prix, Aspen, Gstaad, Turbach, Carlyle, Malibu.

I get several hits. All of them irrelevant.

Except one.

No pleasantries or salutations. The subject line of the email is Monaco. The email says: Teterb 9am.

That's all it says.

Mum and Dad walk into the diner and Mum looks more like Grandma now; her posture is shrinking. She is ageing a year each day. Dad still looks like Dad. He looks like he's holding it together for her sake. Like he isn't quite so affected.

I stand up and hug them both.

The waitress arrives and Mum mouths to me, *You OK?*

I nod.

They both order tea and muffins, and then they take off their coats.

'We went to talk to Detective Martinez again today,' says Mum. 'He asked about you. About how you're holding up.'

'I just want them to find out who hurt KT. And then I can spend the rest of my life figuring out how to live without her. That's how I'm holding up.'

'We have some news, Moll.'

'What is it?'

Mum puts her hand on the table and Dad places his hand on top of hers.

'First of all, the medical examiner is releasing Katie back to us as of nine a.m. tomorrow morning.'

I smile. 'That's good. That's good, right?'

'We'll talk to the crematorium tomorrow. They seem open to fitting us in as an emergency case. You can talk to them with us if you like.'

'OK.'

Dad squeezes his eyelids tight together and then he says, 'And the police told us what happened on the night Katie died. Information from the autopsy.'

I gesture for him to tell me. He bends closer to me and lowers his voice.

'They say it was homicidal asphyxiation, Molly. That's what happened – they know that for sure now.'

I put my hands up to my neck. 'Oh, no.'

Mum reaches over and takes my hand.

'She was strangled?' I say.

Mum shakes her head. 'The police say it was very quick, sweetie. They think it was a . . .' She looks to Dad then back to me. 'A pillow.'

'A pillow?'

'A pillow or a cushion. They found fibres,' says Dad. 'In her eyelid and inside her mouth.'

I think back to the baby pillow in London. How you can actually breathe through it.

The soups arrive and we pause our conversation.

'But how? KT was strong. A pillow on her face?'

'She had bruising on her cheeks but also on her torso and upper arms. We never saw those marks. She was pinned down in the bed, my love,' says Dad, and Mum is crying now. He puts his arm around her. Holds her tight. 'The police say it would have happened very fast. A few minutes from start to finish. Or less, even. Katie would have lost consciousness well before she died.'

I take a deep breath and focus on Mum.

'Her blood work came back clear,' says Mum. 'No drugs or poison. Your father was right – she didn't hurt herself. That might have been much slower, so that's something to be grateful for.'

I feel sick.

'At least we know now,' says Dad, looking tired. 'It's the worst thing that has ever happened to me, to any of us, but at least we know now.'

'Did they say anything else?' I say.

'They asked where your father and I went shopping that dreadful afternoon.'

'Where was that?'

'Your mum went to Macy's. I went to the Apple store. Just window-shopping.'

'Are they close to arresting someone yet?' I ask.

'Martinez couldn't tell us,' says Dad, picking up his muffin. 'He just said they were working on the assumption that the perpetrator knew Katie. There was no sign of a struggle and there were no reports of screaming or shouting. The doors and windows were secure and nobody heard any scuffles. It seems like Katie let the killer in. Or else the killer had a key to her apartment.'

'But why would she let a killer in? Why would she do that?'

Mum looks at me. 'Because she trusted them.'

18

Our morning hostel activity revolves around our two doors, and the hallway immediately outside. We make sure we hold the bathroom for each other so at least we protect that semblance of normality. Wet hair, thin H&M robes Mum bought on Fifth Avenue the night she moved here and realised the bathrooms were communal, wash-bags under arms, disposable slippers Mum brought from the Best Western.

From the outside we look like a normal family.

Mum and Dad have to pick an outfit for KT for her cremation tomorrow. Just saying these words inside my head is hideous. Picking her an outfit? How on earth did we get to this point? All her life, she was near us, she was safe. And then she moved to New York and all this happened.

I call Violet.

'Hey, Molly. I was just thinking about you. How are you holding up?'

Traffic noise in the background.

'Can we meet, please? For a quick coffee or something. I know you're busy but I need to ask about KT's sponsorship. I need to find a few more pieces of this puzzle before I fly back to England.'

'I got class now but I'm done by eleven. Meeting Scottie actually. You want to do a threesome?'

The phrase seems wholly inappropriate, especially as Scott was sleeping with someone identical to me.

'The three of us could have coffee? Sure. Then I can ask him some questions, too.'

'Or a dirty water hot dog? How about it? I'm hungover as fuck. You had a NYC dirty water hot dog yet, Molly?'

'I don't think it's for me.'

She laughs.

'Meet us on the corner of 72nd and Broadway. Eleven-fifteen.'

'I'll be there.'

I walk out to Jimmy's food cart. 'Morning.'

'Hey, Molly. Smoothie? Fresh papaya?'

'I'll take a coffee, please.'

He looks at me like *how do you take it*?

'Black with one sugar.'

'Coming up.'

'You miss home, Jimmy?'

He makes the coffee and talks over his shoulder. 'I miss my cousins and my nephews and I miss my old neighbours. But I'm a New Yorker now. I miss the food back there, and the heat. I miss some things, I guess.' He hands me the coffee. 'But this is my home. Best city on the planet.'

'I still find it scary here,' I say.

'The way I see it, Molly, you gonna die of something some time, you may as well just relax and make the most of the day you're in right now.'

'I wish I could do that.'

He starts rearranging the fruit out on display: guavas and mangos and oranges and kiwi. 'You will. Only way to survive in New York is to just let it happen. Face it all head-on and ride the wave. Wall Street guy once said to me, *Just turn up and do good shit every day.* Turn up and do it. Simple as that. Some people overthink these things but I don't reckon us New Yorkers got the time.'

I decide to walk up to 72nd Street because I'm starting to get my bearings, at least in this small area of Manhattan, and because walking helps me think. My favourite place in London is Hampstead Heath in September. Hyde Park is nice, but it's still in the centre of the city and the ground's too compacted. At least on Hampstead Heath the ground's soft in places. It's big enough and wild enough to almost feel like my childhood village, the one my parents will surely have to leave next year after the bank forecloses on their home. *Our* home. I thought I'd be more unsettled by the thought of it but it's nothing compared to what we've all been living through the past few days.

The area around Columbus Circle is pretty overwhelming: too much traffic and too many people. I cross and skirt the southwest corner of the park.

Mum and Dad seemed more settled this morning. I think it's because they finally know how KT died. We have the *how* but we do not have the *who* or the *why*. Meaning I have about thirty-six hours to come up with something I can give to Martinez and DeLuca.

I pass the YMCA where I met Violet that time, and head up towards Broadway.

The evidence suggests that the perpetrator knew KT. That she trusted him. It suggests the perpetrator is strong, enough brute force to pin her to her bed. KT was a swimmer. She had real upper body strength.

I think about Scott Sbarra and how he has the potential. Strong enough to push a pillow into his girlfriend's face and then just up and leave and act like nothing happened. Free to live his own privileged life, rowing competitively and winning trophies; ending up in some downtown city law firm, becoming an equity partner in his fifties married to some media executive, both of them clearing a million a year with stock options. I then consider Violet, although I don't think she's a likely suspect. She doesn't seem the type. KT trusted her, and why on earth would you smother your own best friend? I walk past the New York City Ballet. Might Groot have hurt KT? Might he have killed a young woman to save his own marriage? To silence her?

All I know is that I'd make a useless detective. Pathetic. I try to imagine the risks just here, in the core of the Upper West Side. I pass by an Apple store and a deli. This wouldn't be a key terrorist target because they'd hit high publicity areas like Wall Street or the Rockefeller Center. But I am aware of men with their hands in their pockets, and of overhead scaffolding that could theoretically buckle and crash on top of me at any second. Before I received that phone call from Mum and Dad in London I read about a man in Berlin who walked down the street minding his own business and stepped on a closed cellar door, the metal doors flush with the pavement. It fell in. He broke his neck. Paralysed.

69th Street. I keep on walking.

I make a pact with myself to work all night tonight. Rereading the emails and reanalysing KT's social media accounts. I will stay in the diner or in some 24/7 café and I will drink strong coffee and I will make much-needed progress.

Broadway and 72nd Street.

'Molly!' yells a voice from across the street. 'Molly, over here.'

I cross over to them. Violet Roseberry and Scott Sbarra. KT's best friend and her boyfriend. Violet's lipstick is smudged, and Scott's hair is a mess. He nods his greeting and Violet hugs me.

The suspicion that they've spent the night together crosses my mind, but I dismiss it. Not these two, surely. Not so soon after.

'Dogs,' she says.

I frown.

She points to the shop. 'Gray's Papaya. Best hot dogs in the whole of Manhattan.'

'I dunno,' says Scott.

'Cannot resist a dirty water hot dog,' she says. 'No one can.'

We walk inside and there's already a queue at eleven-fifteen. We order three hot dogs with sauerkraut, and three papaya drinks, and we get them to go.

'We eat them out on the street?' I say.

'Few blocks, come on.'

Violet leads us to a playground with trees and a basketball court. A group of young teenagers are skateboarding and flirting and smoking cigarettes. We sit on a low wall and my hot dog is probably the best I have ever eaten. It hasn't been boiled in filthy water; it's been cooked properly. Thoroughly.

'It's delicious,' I say.

'Told you,' she says.

Scott's thrown away his bun because he says he wants to stay in ketosis, whatever that is. A scrawny bird pecks at it and we sit three in a line watching the skateboarders and taking whatever sunbeams manage to slice between the buildings.

'I'm leaving tomorrow,' I say.

They both look at me.

'We're flying back with KT.'

'You're having a funeral back in Nottinghamshire?'

I don't want to complicate things by telling them about the cremation because I know they'll want to come, and Mum and Dad want family only, just the three of us, the four of us with KT, so I just nod. 'We'll have a service in Nottingham.'

'I wish I could make it,' says Violet. 'I wish I could afford to fly over for it, I really do. Maybe I can write a letter and you can place it in the hole with the casket or something.'

'Maybe.'

Scott doesn't say anything.

'I saw on the news about the pillow,' says Violet. 'I'm so sorry, Molly. Katie was such a great person.'

'Yeah, she was,' says Scott.

'It's on the news already?'

'Since last night. Caught it on NBC.'

'The police believe the perpetrator was someone KT trusted,' I say. 'They might need to interview you both again, I think. Did either of you have a key to her apartment?'

'I have a key,' says Violet. 'She had a few extras cut when she moved in, said she was terrible for losing them, and how her landlord in London charged her crazy dollars for changing the locks, or withheld her deposit or some bullshit. Wait, I've got it here.'

She shows me her keyring.

'I don't think I got a key,' says Scott.

'You don't think?' says Violet. 'Dude, you know if someone gives you a key to their place. It's the kind of thing you remember.'

'OK, OK, then I don't have one. No big deal. I don't have it. What about the douchebag living in the basement, the kid who followed her around? He'd have a key – why don't the cops talk to that guy?'

'I think they are,' I say.

'If he did it, I will kill him with my bare fucking hands,' says Scott. 'I will rip him—'

I cut him off. 'Do either of you guys know about KT's trips? To Monaco, to Aspen, to St Kitts?'

'It was through the school, I think,' says Violet.

'No, it wasn't,' says Scott sucking the last of his papaya juice through his straw. ''Cos we argued about it when she went to Aspen that time. It was part of her scholarship programme. They did a bunch of trips each year, her and the other students.'

'That when you put your fist through her wall, Scott?' says Violet.

'It didn't go *through* her wall.'

'What?' I say.

He crushes his plastic cup in his hand.

'I thought she came back from Monaco with a hickey. Any guy would freak out if he saw that on his girlfriend's neck.'

'Only it wasn't a hickey,' says Violet.

'A bruise or some shit,' says Scott.

'Where did the bruise come from?' I ask.

'I don't know,' he says. 'She said it was some kind of rash. Skin irritation.'

'So, not actually a bruise.'

'I wasn't on the trip, Molly. I don't know what happened out there. But I didn't like the people on that scheme,' says Scott.

'You meet any of them?' I ask. 'The organisers or students?'

He shakes his head. 'No. I just got a real bad vibe. Flying girls around, always girls, on a private plane. What the hell kind of academic scholarship do you call that?'

'One I'd sign up for in a fuckin' heartbeat,' says Violet.

'Ever hear the name James Kandee?'

'No,' says Scott.

'Maybe,' says Violet. 'Katie might have mentioned him.'

'I think he's behind the scholarship. Some kind of international party guy hiding behind a façade of philanthropy and green energy initiatives.'

'Sounds like a dick. Look, I have practice, I gotta go.' He stands up and looks at me. 'Molly, I just want to say again how sorry I am about Katie. We only went out for a few months, you know, but I really liked her. I'm sorry.'

We have a brief hug and he has the hardest chest and arms I have ever touched in my life. I feel shallow for noticing but I can't help it. His arms wrap around me effortlessly and he smells of sandalwood.

'Thank you,' I say. 'And thanks for showing KT around New York. She always had great things to say about you.'

That's not quite true: she mentioned once that he was cute but clingy, like a big puppy.

He leaves us.

'That was sweet of him to say,' I say.

'He's a stand-up guy,' says Violet.

'I guess,' I say. 'Is it true he punched a hole in KT's wall, though?'

She nods.

'He ever get into trouble? I think I remember KT saying something about him one time. About his past.'

She looks around.

'What?' I say. 'You can tell me. I was her twin, for God's sake.'

'There were some bullshit allegations from his boarding school, stuff that followed him here, but you send your kid to a mixed boarding school deep in the woods of Connecticut, what the hell do you expect?'

'What kind of allegations?'

'They were all dropped, Molly.'

'Come on. I won't tell a soul.'

'I should never have said anything.'

'What is it?'

'Honestly, you'll jump to the wrong conclusions. It's from years back.'

'KT must have known about it. So tell me.'

'Ancient history.'

I stare at her.

She sighs and taps her forehead and says, 'Two girls accused Scott of some rough play back in school. They were seventeen, he was sixteen. He'll talk about it openly if you ask him. The whole thing was dropped.'

'Rough play?'

'They were fooling around. Some choking game or whatever, not my scene. One of the girls was scared, some kind of misunderstanding, but they sorted it out amicably, Scottie's parents and her parents. All in the past now.'

19

I walk back through the lower third of Central Park, trying to analyse what Violet shared with me.

There's a skinny guy on a fold-out stool drawing a charcoal caricature of two young brothers. Not twins, just regular siblings. They clearly want to go play in the wide open spaces, kicking dry leaves and playing catch. Maybe twenty minutes ago they wanted their picture drawn but right now, in this moment, their parents are doing everything in their power to keep them sitting perched on the rock until the artist has finished his work.

After seeing them today, if anyone has a slightly obsessive vibe, an intensity that doesn't feel altogether healthy, I'd say it's Violet, not Scott. He's so laid-back it's like he doesn't have a care in the world.

I sit down on a bench, defeated. The cremation of my twin will take place tomorrow whether the police have someone in custody or not. The four of us – three living Ravens and one deceased – will fly back to England tomorrow night, come what may. And I worry that as soon as we've left United States air space the police here will slow their efforts, not out of any incompetence or lack of professionalism, but because relatives are no longer close by to hound them. There will be other homicide cases in New York; there are statistically around three hundred per annum. Many of those will have surviving relatives and communities in the Tri-state area. They'll be pushing, and we'll have fallen silent.

My parents need closure. We all need it.

Mum texts me to check I'm OK. I reply I'm fine and ask her if she's OK. She's a marvel, she really is. Grieving and out of her depth in this foreign metropolis, she is doing what she knows KT used to do. Until this year, KT and I would text and call and FaceTime every day. Oftentimes, all through the day. Sharing stupid meaningless pieces of information. Photos of dresses and jackets in changing rooms. Photos of celebrity haircuts from fashion magazines. I'd tell her what I ate for dinner and she'd tell me the same. If she sat down at a lunch and a friend told her a secret she'd text me from the toilets and tell me what she'd said. It's still a secret if you only tell your identical twin. It's like telling the other half of yourself.

From my park bench I call Detective Martinez, but the call goes straight through to his voicemail. I don't leave a message; I call Bogart DeLuca instead.

'DeLuca.'

'Hi, Bogart, it's Molly Raven.'

'I was just thinking about you, Molly.'

That seems creepy. I pause and he says, 'I've found some stuff. Can I show you some things I've dug up so I can get your reaction? That possible, you think?'

'I could come to your office?'

'You could, Molly, you could. But I'm based all the way down on the Lower East Side. Canal Street. Right now I'm at Hudson Yards – fancy place, you know it?'

'No.'

'OK, where are you right now?'

'Central Park.'

'OK, OK, you walk down Fifth Avenue, right, headed south. Past the boutiques, past the library, past the Empire State. Before you reach the Flatiron you'll see a small park called Madison Square Park, around 26th Street, you follow?'

'Madison Square Gardens?'

'Not the Garden, no. The Park. Madison Square Park.'

'I'll find it.'

If I didn't have my phone I'd be completely lost in this city.

'I'll walk across from here and we'll pray to the Almighty the heavens don't open till later like they're forecasting. Meet you at the park in about thirty minutes. You want a coffee?'

'Yes, please.'

'A frappuccino or something, pumpkin spice soya latte? What do you want, Molly?'

'Black with one sugar.'

'You got it.'

I make my way to the Plaza Hotel, and down Fifth Avenue, as he instructed. The strip of sky visible between the buildings looks ominous. Navy blue with a grey hue. When I reach Madison Square Park the wind's picking up but there's no rain. I pull my coat tight around my throat and look around for DeLuca.

'Molly,' he says, coming up behind me with a wool hat and two cardboard cups of coffee, his a tiny espresso cup. 'Black, one sugar. It's Ethiopian, tell me what you think.'

I try to sip it but it's too hot. 'Delicious,' I lie.

He nods, and gestures to a bench half-shaded by trees. Leaves are falling all around us. A well-fed squirrel sprints across the paving slabs.

'Do you know who killed KT?'

He sips his espresso and looks around conspiratorially. 'I worked lots of cases in my time, police and PI. I know when we're getting close.' He looks at me. 'We're getting real close, Molly.'

'I have some fresh information for you,' I say. 'Want to run it by you, see what you think.'

'Go ahead.'

'I heard something about Scott Sbarra today. Something disturbing.'

'What did you hear?'

'There was a complaint from his boarding school in Connecticut. Some kind of erotic asphyxiation game where the girl complained, not sure if it was to the police or the school, and then dropped the complaint. I'm going to tell Martinez about it.'

'He already knows.' DeLuca sips his coffee.

'He knows?'

'Yeah, we both know about Sbarra. That's what I wanted to talk to you about. Thing is, his old roommate told me, one of them, guy from his dorm, really intense guy who's now at MIT – told me Sbarra was with some redhead girl the evening of Katie's murder, but that was at least an hour after your parents found her. Roommate told me Scott was seeing her on and off, some redhead girl from Queens or someplace, some redhead Columbia student, friend of Katie's. Ring any bells?'

'He was with Violet?'

'Violet's from Brooklyn, but yeah, it could fit. Look at it this way. If they were seeing each other – and that's a big if – then they probably won't want to talk about it unless pressed by Homicide. 'Cos I'm guessing they both feel pretty lousy about it right now, especially with you and your mom and dad over here from England. I figure if they've both got alibis then it's each other. We'll need to match their story up against time of death.'

Earlier today when we went for hot dogs. I did think it was strange that they were together. Violet's lipstick smudged and his hair a mess.

'I don't know,' I say. 'Her friend and her boyfriend?'

'Just a working theory is all,' says DeLuca, draining the last of his coffee. 'It's like the scientific method. You come up with a hypothesis and then you test the shit out of it.'

I sip my coffee and blow and sip some more. 'I've talked to Groot,' I say. 'I think he may have had a long-running thing with KT, not just casual dates.'

'Oh, he did,' says DeLuca. 'That I do know for sure.'

'You know for sure?'

'Let's just say through the means available to me as a licensed private investigator in this great city, I became the short-term caretaker of sixteen bags of the Groot family's garbage.'

I raise my eyebrows.

'Dirty work, Molly. Someone's gotta do it. Ninety-five per cent of the contents were garbage, literally. But I did find some shredded papers and shredded receipts, and one shredded photograph.'

'A shredded photo?'

'Picture of Groot and your sister. Looked innocent enough, fully clothed, but he had his arm round her shoulder. Shredded, Molly.'

'You taped it together, or . . .?'

'I had my intern patch it together. About all he's good for, truth be told.'

'You think Groot could have hurt KT?'

'Too early to tell, but let's say I'm looking into him up close and personal. My gut tells me he's the kind of guy who likes to take students out to dinner and impress them. Maybe he sleeps with them. Maybe it's a sex thing or just a power play or maybe he didn't get any when he was a college kid himself. Thing is with Groot, I can tell he's his own worst enemy. He can't stop crossing the line with his students, but at the same time he's desperate to keep his fancy big house up near Greenwich and his two fancy cars and his wife's big-shot salary and their social circle and their kids at private schools and the whole nine yards.'

'But why would he hurt KT? I'm suspicious of him, just like you are, but it still seems out of character for a gentle academic sort.'

'If you'll pardon my saying, Molly, it was a gentle sort of murder, if there can even be such a thing. The pillow MO, sorry, *modus operandi*, well, that's a very quiet way to kill a person. Usually reserved for people putting their great aunt out of her misery at the nursing home, that kind of thing. This didn't look like a crime of passion. This was, in some sick way, a compassionate act, at least in the eyes of the killer. It's the way a parent might kill their child.'

'Jesus.'

'Any detective will tell you the same thing. I never worked homicide, I was always narcotics before I went private. If I need any specialist back-up I know the right people. I can assure you of that.'

'Good.'

'Groot doesn't have an alibi for the night of the murder far as I can tell, Molly. He's shredded five hotel receipts – you know, the printed A4 receipts they give you in an envelope when you check out. Three from the Hilton on Times Square, and two from smaller hotels, the Algonquin and the Iroquois.'

'I've seen those two hotels.'

'Famous old Midtown hotels,' says DeLuca. 'You've probably seen them in some movie or soda commercial. Beautiful façades.'

I turn to face Midtown and see three tourists all in transparent plastic ponchos, all photographing the Empire State Building.

'Those hotels are all close to the Harvard Club.'

'You got it, Molly. Guess he wouldn't stay in the Club with her. Too risky.'

'OK, but what about Shawn Bagby, the guy living in the basement?'

'Turns out he's a real nasty piece of work, that kid,' says DeLuca.

'Tell me more.'

'You ever hear about incels?'

'What?'

'Incels. Some kind of movement – my intern explained it all to me. Stands for *involuntarily celibate*. Can't get laid, basically. Course, in my day if you couldn't get a girl you just adjusted your standards, know what I mean, went for someone with a nice personality plus a lazy eye, that kinda thing. Kids these days get told to go to hell by a few supermodel types and they set up some internet forum and obsess over the rejection and come up with all these codes and they egg each other on, you know.'

'Shawn is an incel?'

'Was.'

'Was an incel?'

'Nowadays he's a wholesome YouTuber, over a hundred thousand subscribers, touching on one-fifty. Talks about intermittent fasting. How he transformed himself so fast. Lots of sponsored videos of him working out and preparing his avocado-egg white smoothies or whatever bullshit those kids drink. But a year ago it was a whole different story. He was a dumpy kid with bad skin and a worse attitude. He really hated women. You know, misog . . .' He trails off.

'Misogynistic?' I say.

'Yeah. I mean he hated women. Young women. There's a Reddit that was deleted a while back because incels were committing suicide, killing innocent people, but I gained access to it through my PI contacts and channels. Shawn Bagby was a moderator on a sub-forum. He talked about how attractive women played games, were responsible for all the evil in the world, responsible for three of his friends committing suicide, yadda yadda.'

A kid kicks his football over to us and I kick it back.

'Some of it mentioned your sister specifically.'

'What? What did he say?'

'Never mentioned her by name, but talked about his neighbour upstairs getting her apartment paid for by a charity because she's so good-looking. Talked about her being a Stacy, which is incel code for a woman who sleeps around, basically – no value judgement on your sister from me; that's what Bagby said. Boasted he used to follow her around. Also talked about what it would feel like to kill someone.'

My jaw drops.

'I'm still digging, Molly. I'll let you know my findings soon.'

'He wrote about what it would feel like to kill?' I feel dizzy.

'Never with his real name, you have to consider that. These guys thought they had anonymity. I mean, your own father or your priest could be active on one of these extreme forums and nobody would ever know, you see.'

'If it's anonymous, how do you know it's Bagby?'

'We have ways and means. His username contained three numbers. I traced other usernames on other forums, specifically chat forums around men and fasting and health. Eventually found a defunct YouTube channel started by Bagby two years ago. It's called Seeking Alpha and it's all about tips for lame-ass guys to talk to women. Ways to trick them into bed if you catch my meaning, all sorts of horseshit from the best shoe-risers to make them look taller, to vocal exercises to deepen their voices. Anyway, the contact email from that YouTube channel was a Gmail account and the email address contained the same three numbers. Then I cross-referenced the sentence structure Bagby uses when he writes long-form, on a Reddit or his own blog or in the descriptions of his videos. There's one word he routinely misspells. It's a dead giveaway. A tic, of sorts. Bagby was a toxic incel, all right. Not sure if he is any more, I think he's moved on, but he did talk online about how women like your sister don't deserve to live.'

'Does he have an alibi for that afternoon?'

'Not that I can tell.'

'How long before Martinez makes an arrest, do you think?'

'Won't be long, Molly. They'll be accruing evidence first, try to get a confession out of whoever did it. A solid case for the DA to work with. Don't think it'll be more than a few days. Last thing we need is this bastard walking around the streets of New York a day longer than necessary.'

20

I walk back to my hotel, leaning into the wind. Outside the New York Public Library, where brass plaques are sunk into the paving stones, a bearded man dragging a shopping cart full of plastic bags chants, 'The end is nigh, the skies will be falling upon us all.'

There are people walking out of 7-Elevens holding multipacks of water. Not just the odd customer. Every customer.

I head to Times Square instead of going straight to my room, and there are warnings displayed on the big TV screens, and on the moving messages that wrap around buildings. Newsreaders analysing Hurricane Teresa. The mayor of New York talking into a nest of microphones, saying something about Long Island and Staten Island. Warning of electrical issues downtown. Saying the subway system may have to be shut down from tomorrow night. Hopefully I'll have already left JFK clutching KT's ashes, flying away from the hurricane. I will not board the plane if the storm has already made landfall, if it intensifies. I will not face that kind of turbulence; I have a knot in my stomach just thinking about it.

Mum calls and we talk about what to do tonight, our last night here. She says, 'Your father wants us to have a special dinner, something to say goodbye to Katie, one of her favourite places.'

'I'm not sure we can afford that, Mum.'

'That's what I told him,' she says. 'Your father says we should mark the night, with tomorrow being tomorrow and all.'

She can't say the word *cremation*, just like she can't say the word *bankruptcy*. Mum can't face up to the fact that KT will be cremated in Brooklyn instead of buried in our village. The idea is too violent and too foreign for her to vocalise.

'KT loved diners, actually,' I say. 'We could go to our diner again?'

'That's what I told your father,' says Mum.

I hear Dad take the phone from her. 'Hi, Moll. Your sister thought our diner was a generic Midtown tourist trap – her words. What about Chinatown?'

'Sure, Dad. Sounds like her kind of thing.'

I go and get my coat and five water purification tablets from my hostel room. If the storm were to hit freakishly early, the number one priority will be drinkable water. Then I walk to the diner and it is steamy inside. I don't get my favourite table but I get the one next to it. Good view of the room. I try to order a bagel with cream cheese and lox, which is what they call smoked salmon here, but they've run out of bagels.

'What's a fountain soda?' I ask.

The waiter points to a drinks machine.

'I'll just have chocolate milk, please.'

Twenty-eight hours until I board the red-eye back to London. Twenty-eight hours to hand over something substantial to Martinez. Something concrete. A lead that he may not yet have found, something to push the case forward so it doesn't get forgotten about as soon as I leave American soil.

I research Shawn Bagby some more. If he hates women so much, then that could be motive in itself. Couldn't it? Couple that hatred with seeing my sister every day, maybe her rejecting his advances. That could drive some men to extreme violence.

Bagby has over one hundred and forty thousand subscribers. His videos are generally about exercise and diet, but also cover general mindset subjects with video titles like *I woke up at 4am for 4 weeks and this is what happened* and *How to talk slow so you never get ignored* and *5 tips to look taller* and *Beard shape tricks to bring out your inner alpha* and *How to turn a no into a yes every single time.*

The comments are toxic but I watch enough YouTube tutorials and vlogs to know that comments are usually toxic. Even on innocent-looking videos, the comments, for whatever reason, are horrific. His subscribers seem to be, almost exclusively, angry young men. Someone calls him a 'retired volcel' so I research what that means. A volcel is voluntarily celibate as opposed to an incel who would be involuntarily celibate. A sub-comment argues with this, saying Bagby is much worse, he's a fakecel now, someone who, although previously an incel or volcel, has worked so hard on his appearance, physique, manners etc that he is now more of a Chad than an incel. A Chad. I recall that word from Bagby's T-shirt the day we visited KT's apartment. Something like 'Destroy Chad' or 'Death to Chad'. I'd thought that was weird, having connected the word Chad to the country, not the male forename. I dig deeper. A Chad is a male version of a Stacey, an attractive woman. Apparently, a Chad is someone who is gifted – unfairly, in the eyes of incels – with all the classic attractive attributes of masculinity: a square jaw, confidence, strong posture, height, good hair, broad shoulders.

Maybe the simplest explanation is the most plausible one? Shawn had a key, or at least had access to a key. He could have monitored KT's comings and goings. He could have let himself in. Bagby knows the building layout, and the times when the only other resident, his mother, would be out at one of her meetings.

I re-read the emails from KT's FortressMail account. Nobody mentions names, but judging from the way the emails are written, and by the fact that well over half of the mails come from two accounts, it's obvious she used this account as her primary way of communicating with those two people. KT gave her secure address to them. It's not clear from the evidence whether the two individuals knew each other, or of each other. *OPO64@fortressmail.tv* writes very short messages that are unashamedly flirtatious. Asking how she feels. How she felt the night before. Asking for photos. Asking her to *do* things. That one's Groot. Emails from the other account are even more succinct. Numbers and street intersections. Co-ordinates. Telephone numbers and postal codes. Times and dates. Bank account details. Other numeric codes.

The flirtatious emailer, Groot, sent one message ten days ago which reads *Can't. Family stuff. Wait until after Thanksgiving.*

Mum and Dad appear at the window and they don't look as devastated as they have of late. Mum's eyes are still miserable but her mouth is smiling. Dad's wearing his hood tight around his face. They gesture for me to come out and then the waiter asks them to come in out of the rain and they look apologetic and Mum taps her watch.

The wind has intensified. A copy of the *New York Post* flaps around in the gutter before it's pushed flat against a mailbox.

'Chinatown is this way,' says Dad.

I know which way it is. I've acquainted myself with the map of Manhattan, at least from Central Park down to Wall Street. We walk past the Harvard Club with its doorman, who ignores me, if he even recognises me, and head down Fifth Avenue.

'Storm's brewing,' says Mum.

'We'll fly out before it reaches here,' says Dad. 'That's what the BBC says.'

We hail a cab for the rest of the journey to Chinatown. We're all drenched and cold. Dad finds a noodle place with a sign in the window saying it was reviewed or featured in *Time Out*. 'Katie would have loved it here,' says Mum, making a heroic effort to be positive.

'She'd have asked the chef to choose for her,' I say.

'She was an adventurer,' says Dad.

They order beer and I order water. We eat noodle dishes and the food is incredible. Fresh herbs. Deep, rich stock. Velvety noodles.

'Are you going to be OK tomorrow at the service?' asks Mum. 'It's not the way we wanted, not really, but we get to fly back together and that's the main thing.'

'She loved this country,' says Dad. 'I don't think she would have minded. In a strange kind of way I think she'd have approved.' He smiles and then laughs. 'She'd have thought a funeral in our sleepy little village would be too boring for her.'

'True,' I say. 'This is more KT.'

'She always asked about you,' says Mum. 'Even when you weren't talking properly these past months, she asked about you every day. Wanted to know about your job and how you were doing in London.'

'I know, Mum.'

'Until you were both about four I couldn't tell you apart,' says Dad. 'Most of the time I just guessed.'

We all smile and Dad sips his beer to hide the emotion on his face. This is one of the things he always says, one of his stories.

'Remember that time, just after your grandma died, when Grandad bought you a pair of ice-skates to use in Nottingham ice-rink, one pair between you. Do you remember that, Moll?'

I smile and nod. 'I remember, Dad. I was seven.'

'You two were both so angry. It was the first time you'd both realised there was a down side to being an identical twin.'

'He never made that mistake again,' says Mum.

We finish our noodles. The broth is spicy and my tongue is tingling but it's a pleasant sensation.

'Are you all packed yet, sweetie?' asks Mum. 'I've got some space if you need to put anything in my case. You can borrow Dad's case scales if you need to weigh.'

'I'll pack later,' I say. 'I need to research more.'

'You should rest as well, Moll,' says Dad. 'Big day tomorrow. Think we'll all need our strength. Need to be at the chapel by two-thirty sharp. And then we fly just after nine.'

'I know, Dad.'

'Your mum thinks we should take a cab to the crematorium with our luggage and ask them to store it there, and then go straight on to JFK airport.'

'It makes sense,' says Mum. 'We'll already be halfway there.'

'I say we leave our bags at the hotel.' He still calls it a hotel. 'And then come back and pick them up. Yellow cabs aren't too expensive, fixed price to JFK, and I don't want to arrive at Katie's . . . you know, I don't want to turn up with all our suitcases. It doesn't seem proper.'

'Saves money, though. I don't see how we can afford . . .'

'We can manage it,' says Dad, sternly. 'For God's sake, I'll work three jobs when we get back if I need to. Tomorrow has to be done right.'

'And the storm won't affect things?'

'No,' says Dad, softening. 'You should see the crematorium, Moll. It's beautiful, like a cathedral – rock-solid. It has a chapel and everything.'

'It's dignified,' says Mum.

'You said you were researching tonight,' says Dad. 'Researching the storm? The flight path? What?'

'The case,' I say. 'Suspects.'

Dad's brow furrows. 'Leave that to the cops, Moll. They know what they're doing.'

'Nobody knew KT like I did. I can add value.'

Mum puts her hand on mine. 'Your father means you need to take a break from it. Don't stay up too late, OK?'

We battle through the storm, the cab's wipers moving as fast as they'll go. Mum and Dad walk to their room to pack while I head back to the diner. It's open 24/7, says so on the window, and it is my favourite place in this intimidating city. It's warm and consistent and it manages to feel safe, somehow. Like the staff understand some of my worries and anxieties, and act accordingly.

I'm halfway through my first coffee, researching the Connecticut boarding school Scott Sbarra attended, scanning his Facebook friends for people I can make contact with, when my phone rings.

'Hey, Molly, it's Detective Martinez. Now a good time to talk?'

'Sure,' I say, placing down my cup. 'Thanks for calling back.'

'Sorry it took me so long. What can I do for you?'

'I was talking to Bogart DeLuca, the PI hired by Columbia. We were talking about the four people closest to KT in New York, and who had what motive. Alibis, opportunities, that kind of thing. I'm not sure if he's updated you on this yet. We wanted you to look deeper into Professor Eugene Groot. He was likely involved with my sister, romantically. Scott Sbarra, he has some previous allegations of erotic asphyxiation from his high school days. There's a chance he's in some kind of relationship with Violet Roseberry. I don't know if it's likely or not, but maybe they could have done this together, or maybe she covered it up for him? I don't know, I'm sorry, I'm rambling. The guy downstairs, the incel, Shawn Bagby. I don't trust him.'

'I can agree with you there, Molly. We've looked into Bagby's past. Multiple complaints from multiple women all around your age. No convictions to date.'

'Has DeLuca had a meeting with you yet?'

'Well, that's the thing that worries me, see, Molly. I've never heard of Bogart DeLuca, and with a name like that I'd be unlikely to forget him in a hurry. I'm assuming he's a PI, right? An investigator?'

'Yes. Licensed.' I start to feel my heart race. 'I assumed you knew of him. He used to be police.'

'New York police? He hasn't approached us, Molly. You got his contact details for me?'

I take DeLuca's business card from my pocket and look it over and tell Martinez.

'OK, I just searched all the licensed private investigators in the Tri-state area on the computer and DeLuca does not show up. So either he's from out of town or else he's not legit. Hold on.'

My skin goes cold.

DeLuca lied to my face. What does he want if he's not a PI?

'OK, there's nobody by that name registered in the United States. Molly, listen to me. Do not talk to this guy again, you understand me? Could be he isn't safe. For all I know, he could be the man who killed your sister.'

21

I stare at Bogart DeLuca's business card, my vision blurring a little. My first instinct is to ignore Martinez and call DeLuca directly and ask him what the hell is going on. Who is he?

I Google him.

Zero results.

Zero.

I wipe sweat from my upper lip. Who is this man? I could be in acute danger right this second. Does he really want to help me? Maybe he's Canadian or Swiss and that's why Martinez couldn't trace him. Just because he talks with a broad Brooklyn accent doesn't mean he's ever been to Brooklyn. Or could it be that he really is a private investigator, or freelance detective, and he's working discreetly for Kandee's foundation using a false name?

I look around the diner. It's just past midnight and the crowd of theatregoers is thinning out. They've finished their post-Broadway-show meal and they're heading back to their hotel rooms. Two waitresses huddle around a TV and a fellow patron asks them to turn the volume up. It's a news piece about the incoming storm, about the havoc it's causing to the North Carolina coastline. The head waitress denies the request. The volume stays the same.

I order more coffee. Vigilant of the other patrons. Hyper-aware.

Less than twenty-four hours left in New York. I need to survive a hurricane, as well as the cremation of my beloved twin sister. I need to survive all that while watching the backs of my parents, and then we need to fly safely back to the routines of home.

By two a.m. I'm deep into James Kandee and his affairs and the intensity of my research process is soothing. It always is. The waitress has lent me two Bic biros and a new order pad. I have loose sheets all over this family-size Formica table. Lists of companies owned or majority controlled by James Kandee and his foundations. His web spreads from Switzerland to Liechtenstein to the Cayman Islands to Singapore to Delaware to Jersey to Panama.

The waitress comes over to refill my cup and says, 'You OK, doll?'

I nod and smile.

'Mind if I sit for a minute?'

'Sure.'

She sits down and I see the relief on her face, the relief from taking her weight off her feet for a moment. 'This storm, eh?'

'Is it going to be bad?'

'Nah,' she says, batting the suggestion away with her hand. 'We had Sandy in 2012; this ain't nothin' like Sandy. Grill cook thinks this'll be a breeze, and we're OK in Midtown anyway, it's the folks on Staten Island you gotta worry about. You don't mind me sayin', we noticed, the girls and me: you're the twin of Katie Raven, aren't you?'

I nod.

'We're real sorry. I mean it – we were talking about how tragic it is and all. That kinda thing happened a lot back when I was growing up. I'm from a rough part of Queens. The murders and all, the street crime. Times Square isn't like it used to be, I can tell you, all the chain stores and frozen yogurt shops. Anyhow, I just wanted to say how sorry we all are.'

I look around and there are only two other people in here now besides me. One guy eating an omelette, and one woman reading the paper with a plate of scrambled eggs and bacon.

'Thanks.'

'And we wanted to say – and say no, or whatever, if it makes you uncomfortable – but we wanted to pick up your check for you tonight. Janet overheard you and your folks were flying back to England tomorrow. What I'm saying, doll, is that this is all on the house.'

I sit up straight. This angel is wearing a name badge that says 'Susan'. She is tired, she's been here as long as I have, five hours or more, and yet she takes the time to offer me this kindness.

'Thank you. Before I came here, I always imagined New York to be this massive scary place full of weirdos. But it's not really. It's surprised me.'

'Oh, it's full of weirdos, you bet your life. The stories I could tell you, the subway rides. But yeah, it's the best city in the world even when it's a shithole, excuse my language. Tonight even, all this weather, all the trouble with floods and blackouts that might or might not come, we'll still be here next week. Nothing can hold us down, see. Nothing.'

'I needed to hear that tonight. I appreciate it.'

'You want me to skedaddle, leave you to your novel or whatever you're writing here?'

'No, it's OK. Susan . . .'

'Yeah?'

'Have you ever been to a cremation?'

Her face drops. 'Yeah, sure I have. Too many. You going to a . . . I mean, is it for . . .'

'KT's cremation service is tomorrow near Bushwick. I've never been to one before. I'm pretty scared, truth be told.'

She smiles a sympathetic smile and says, 'It'll be beautiful, you'll see. Your sister will be in a better place.' She points to the ceiling and crosses herself. 'I haven't always had faith but now I believe in something bigger, you know? She'll be in a better place.'

'Was it . . .?' I pause. 'Do you see the fire, at the crematorium?'

'Oh, don't worry. It's a beautiful service, beautiful. Ashes to ashes, dust to dust, just like it says in the Bible. You'll be OK, doll. Just stick close to your ma and pa and you'll get through it, I know you will. Say goodbye to your sister and tell her you'll see her again one day.'

The woman eating scrambled eggs coughs and half-raises her hand so Susan says, 'Excuse me.'

I cannot imagine my sister's body engulfed in flames. I read online that the crematorium heat can get up to nine hundred and eighty degrees Celsius. She and I shared one egg. Most people, in these circumstances, they say, you enter the world on your own and you leave on your own, but that's not true for twins. You enter with your twin. And then you leave on your own. That difference makes it all so much more traumatic.

Susan refills my coffee and then turns the volume up on the TV. The storm's coming closer and the mayor is consulting on whether to shut down the subway system and the New York Stock Exchange. There's a lot of talk about extra firefighters and utilising the National Guard. FEMA are ready. Independent contractors have been put on standby to assist with repairing infrastructure. Outside my window there's nobody walking around. The street is empty.

By three a.m. my heart is racing from all the caffeine but I'm getting closer to the core of Kandee's family operations. There are limited liability partnerships established in the Caribbean that own companies based out of Geneva that fund charitable foundations based in the UK Channel Islands. A web of organisations and law firms. Tax havens and shell companies. James has his fingers in a lot of pies. African desalination projects and joint ventures in oil refineries. Through his Instagram feed I have discovered the hotels he frequents: the Dorchester in London, the Georges V in Paris, the Four Seasons and Carlyle in New York, the Mandarin Oriental in Sydney. I trace three women he's been photographed with repeatedly in the past thirty-six months. They are never named or tagged in the photos. Usually their faces are partially hidden. They all look a lot like KT. A lot like me. A casual observer might even think they're the same person, a long-term girlfriend, but they need to zoom into the photos and pay closer attention to hairlines and mole patterns like I am. James Kandee has girlfriends, or girl-friends, in multiple cities. They make him look good on his social media. They make him look popular.

I focus on his Twitter, Facebook and Instagram on the days leading up to, the day of, and the days following KT's murder. There was nothing posted from New York on that day. The day before KT's murder he was in London. Two days after the murder he was photographed in Dubai. One thing he shares a lot is his transport. Cars and motorbikes and helicopters. But in particular his jet. A Gulfstream G650 with the tail number JK9022P. There are photos of Kandee posing beside his two large dogs and their designer leather-clad travel crates. The jet is white. Nothing distinctive from the outside. There are a couple of Facebook photos from inside the cabin. It has a small kitchen and a main area and a rear bedroom. Three zones. The floors are carpeted and the walls look like they're cream leather. He uses a private airport south of London called Biggin Hill, and for New York he uses a private airport in Teterboro, about twelve miles west of here as the crow flies. I find a plane-spotting online community. I search photos using the tail number of his plane. It's blocked, apparently. I access the plane-spotter blogs and start sifting through Teterboro airstrip photos, jets landing and taking off. Lots of celebrities use the airport so they make up the majority of the posts. What I want to find out is if Bogart DeLuca was in New York that day. If he's some kind of assassin rather than a PI. Maybe not an assassin, but Kandee's security detail, someone with specialist skills who can get rid of inconvenient problems for him.

Susan refills my coffee again and says, 'My shift's over in forty-five minutes; I finish at five.'

I look at my watch and take a deep breath. I need an hour or two of sleep before KT's cremation service. I can't not sleep at all, I'd collapse.

'Could I get some toast, please?'

'Cinnamon raisin French toast?'

'Just regular toast.'

'No problem.'

Cross-referencing the plane-spotter blogs with a website using historical playback facilities of recorded jet flight plans, I locate the flights for October taken by James Kandee's aircraft.

The plane flew on the day my sister was killed.

My vision is blurry, I'm so tired. So wired.

It travelled from London Biggin Hill at 8.50 a.m., landing at Teterboro at 11.35 a.m., and it took off again that night from Teterboro at 6.10 p.m., landing at London Biggin Hill at 5.50 a.m.

There were two pilots on board.

There was no flight attendant on the plane.

There was one passenger listed as flying into New York on the day my sister was killed.

James Kandee himself.

22

I didn't sleep a minute.

By the time I left for the hostel, early-morning commuters were speed-walking down Sixth Avenue with their backpacks strapped tight and their phones in their hands. The sun wasn't up but the city was awake.

I went to bed at five-fifteen a.m. and I lay there next to my baseball bat until nine. Until I heard Mum and Dad talking quietly in the next room. I couldn't make out their words; I think they were speaking in hushed voices so as not to wake me.

The window in my room is rattling in its frame. The storm is set to peak late tonight, at about the time we fly out of JFK. If it's not safe to take off I'll insist we delay. I will demand it.

I put on my robe and slippers and pace to the end of the hall and call Martinez.

'Detective, it's Molly Raven.'

'Hello, Molly. How can I help?'

I pause. Everyone around me can hear my voice; all the strangers in their beds in the rooms behind these thin walls. Better for them to hear than Mum and Dad. They need to be insulated from the facts until after the cremation. I need to protect them, especially Mum.

'I need to talk to you about what I've found.'

'You had any more trouble from the phoney investigator?'

'No.'

'Good. What have you found out?'

'It's about James Kandee, the British heir and entrepreneur. I'm fairly certain his private foundation funded KT's Columbia scholarship.'

'OK.'

'And his private plane landed at Teterboro on the morning of KT's death. It left that same night, a few hours after she was killed.'

'Keep going.'

'I think you need to look into it, detective. From his Instagram I can see he flies young women, all around my age, KT's age, around the world to show off to his rich friends. I think he maintained a kind of harem.'

'Harem?'

'I don't know.' I rub my eyes. This seemed like such concrete evidence at four-thirty this morning and now it seems so flimsy. 'You need to question James Kandee.'

'Is James Kandee here in the USA? Is he in New York?'

'I don't know. Wait . . .' I check my Instagram app. 'He's in Kenya right now.'

'He's in Kenya?'

'He's always flying around. He lives in hotels, out of a suitcase. There are lots of interviews where he talks about it.'

'OK, Molly. Good. We'll look into that. Is there anything else?'

'No. It's just Kandee you need to talk to, detective. I know it.'

He sighs and I hear him sip his morning coffee. 'Can you come to the precinct this morning, Molly? I heard you're flying back to London with your mom and dad tonight. Maybe we can talk about Kandee here?'

'I wish I could,' I say. 'It's KT's cremation today. In Brooklyn.'

'Oh, I'm sorry, Molly. I'm real sorry.'

'I might have time between the cremation and leaving for the airport? I might be able to come then?'

'No, don't worry. I've got your number in London. I'll be in touch when you get back home if that's OK with you.'

'Of course.'

'Look after yourself today.'

I find Mum trying to iron her black dress on the corner of her mattress with a travel iron and a damp towel. I leave the door open so there's more air.

'Did you sleep, sweetie?' she says, looking up through a cloud of steam.

'A bit. You?'

'A little. Your dad's gone out to get us breakfast. You need anything ironed?'

'No, thanks, Mum.'

Behind her are a row of metal hangers with Dad's white shirt and his black suit and a black tie. 'Your father polished his shoes,' says Mum, her smile unsteady.

'I'll look smart,' I say.

'I know you will.'

We eat croissants and takeaway lattes, Mum and Dad on their bed, me standing in the hall in my robe. A woman asks Mum if she can borrow Mum's travel iron after she's done with it and Mum offers to iron for her and the woman laughs out loud.

It's not easy getting ready to say goodbye to the person closest to you in the world. You always imagine important days – interviews, weddings, funerals – to be dignified events where you get to prepare and act at your own pace and in your own way. But money buys that comfort. It buys you options, time and space. It cushions you and gifts you the ability to make choices. Mum and Dad and I have had to prepare for KT's cremation in a communal bathroom at the end of the hall. We have to pack at the same time as we get dressed. We have to console each other surrounded by suitcases and flight documents and backpacking gap-year students.

The storm is blowing strongly outside but everyone we talk to, and everyone writing about it on Twitter, says *it's no Sandy*. The view is dark. Looks like the end of the world out there.

Mum and Dad reignite their old argument about whether we should go directly from the crematorium to the airport, or come back here first to pick up our bags. Dad wins again. We'll come back to pick up our cases.

Mum's wearing her hair in a bun with a black net around it. She's wearing H&M plastic pearls and a handbag we bought together in Camden Market when they came down to visit my new flat for the first time. She looks smaller than usual.

Text from Bogart DeLuca. *Did you know your sister had a life insurance policy?*

Yes, I knew. How do I play this? Do I confront him and ask him who he is? No, not now. Instead I reply, *Have you taken this to Martinez?*

We leave our largest suitcases with the hostel staff but they don't give us a numbered ticket or anything like that, they just pass Dad a Post-it note with the words '3, Raven' written on it in Sharpie.

Three.

Raven.

That is what we are now. Dad goes out to hail a yellow cab and Mum and I wait in the dry. She is trying to be strong.

'It's toughest for you, I think,' she says, opening her eyes wide to prevent tears forming. 'Normally, losing a child, it's toughest for the parents. The worst nightmare come true. But I think it's probably harder for you, sweetie. You two . . .' She fans her eyes with her hands. 'You both hugged in the womb, I ever tell you that? On the scan, you were both hugging each other, clinging on.'

'I know, Mum.'

The wind blows a woman back up the street, her umbrella inside out.

Dad rushes inside, his hair plastered over his face. 'We got one.'

We step on to the street and he holds out Mum's umbrella to shield her but it snaps like a toothpick. We run to the cab and jump inside.

'Where to?'

'Fresh Pond Crematory.'

'Where?'

'Brooklyn.'

He starts driving. 'Where in Brooklyn you want?'

Dad consults his map and then Mum says, 'Mount Olivet Crescent.'

'It's Queens,' says the driver. 'Not Brooklyn.'

We're silent.

Three wet ravens sitting in a cab.

The streets are almost as full as they usually are but people are walking close to the buildings for cover, and the streetlights and headlights are bleeding into the wet cityscape like a montage from a beautiful science fiction movie.

'The flowers will be there when we arrive,' says Mum.

'Lilies and roses,' says Dad.

Mum shakes her head and squeezes my hand. 'It doesn't feel real. It feels like she might call me right now.'

Dad and I stay quiet. We cross the Queensboro bridge, and the East River looks like it's about to burst its banks.

'Storm surge,' says the driver. 'Don't worry, this is an Irene, it ain't no Sandy.'

We keep on driving through old industrial areas and then through quiet streets. We do not speak to each other. They need the silence and I need it too. Hardening ourselves. Steeling for what will surely come.

New text from DeLuca. *Beneficiaries of the life insurance policy are Paul and Elizabeth Raven. 125,000 dollars.*

I don't reply. I just glance at Dad.

A cardboard box gets blown down the street and a police car drives past us with its lights flashing and its sirens wailing.

We reach the crematorium.

'This is it,' says the driver. 'Fifty-one dollars.'

Mum pays the driver and we all step out of the cab and run to the entrance of the crematorium. It looks like a cross between a chapel and a government building.

The manager ushers us inside.

The floor is made of stone and the air inside is chill and it is hushed.

There are small alcoves and nooks in the walls. Urns occupy the spaces. I can hear music in the distance, from another room.

Text from DeLuca. *The insurance policy was taken out last week.*

I turn off my phone. My sister deserves my full attention.

'A service is just ending,' says the manager, a man with thin grey hair. 'You'll be able to go through in about ten minutes.'

Dad shuffles on the spot.

Mum holds my hand tight.

Everything about this feels wrong.

We walk through and there's a long cardboard box, raised on a wheeled platform. On top of the box are two flowers. A red rose and a white lily.

Mum swallows a gentle sob.

We approach the box.

We cannot see her, but we know she is there. At peace.

Beyond the box is a brass door. Mum and Dad opted to see the box enter the oven itself. To say their last farewells.

'You can say goodbye now,' says the manager.

Mum approaches the box and then falls to the ground, her hand up in the air, her palm flat against the cardboard. Her weeping is silent but I can see, from her back, that she is sobbing.

The final words from mother to child.

Dad kneels next to Mum and bows his head and says something to my sister that I cannot hear. Mum rests her head on his shoulder.

A chill runs down my neck.

They look back, both with tears in their eyes, and they beckon me to the cardboard box. They step away and hug each other and Mum sniffs and she cries.

I approach the box. A rose and a lily.

A flame flickers in the background, beyond the doors, some kind of pilot light.

I place my palm on the box.

'Half of me,' I whisper. 'Half. I will never be the same without you. I love you.'

The manager coughs and I step back to Mum and Dad. We hold each other's hands. Dad's is cool and loose. Mum's is hot and tight. Her wedding ring pushes into my knuckle. The doors open and the box moves. Music in the background I didn't notice before. The box is pushed in and the doors lock shut.

And then the fire.

Mum wails.

I feel so desperately sorry for her. And sorry for my twin sister, for living here, for making this tragic life decision, for relocating to New York. And I feel sorry for holding the pillow over her face until she stopped struggling.

23

It takes an hour and ten minutes for the cremation to complete and for the ashes to cool.

The wind is whistling under the door, creating an eerie howl around the crematorium. Mum and Dad have stopped crying.

A man steps through a door carrying a plastic box with a rose and a lily on top. He hands it to my parents and then walks away.

I place my hand on the box.

It's not warm.

We leave the building and the cab's already outside waiting. There's an advert for *The Late Show* on its roof. The wind gusts and Dad shields the box with his body while Mum and I pull the cab door open. The driver doesn't help. We get in and speed away.

There's a team of four guys boarding up the windows to an industrial building, screwing pieces of plywood to the frames. Further on, closer to the East River, there's a woman with a stall, sitting there in a yellow poncho selling sandbags, twenty for a hundred dollars. Her sign says there's a discount for bulk orders. It says the sandbags are military grade.

We don't speak on the way back to the hostel.

Dad's probably thinking about KT, but also about flight logistics, how much time we'll need to check in and clear security, if carrying a box of human remains might hold things up even though they've been assured it won't, whether the storm will delay the flight, and how they'll get from Heathrow back to Nottingham. Mum's likely thinking about KT. About how she lived a full life. They both seem calm. People say relatives need closure and they're right.

I got closure almost a week ago.

Something shifted when her body went limp, when she stopped struggling. I've been calm ever since, but in some ways the cremation was cathartic for me. It marked the start of me coming to terms with the rest of my life as a solo twin.

Statisticians tell us that identical twins tend to die within two years of each other. That gives me less than twenty-four months of life left.

Imagine having an exact copy of yourself, behaving entirely differently in the world, experiencing it differently. There is a well-documented medical condition called twin-to-twin transfusion syndrome. It's where blood from your mother passes through one twin on its way to the other. The donor twin receives the good blood briefly before donating it to the twin, who then receives all the nutrients. This is what I believe happened to us in the womb, only with spirit. I was four when I realised she was the special one and I was the back-up. Same size and shape, but flat. Hollow. I was constantly reminded of my own shortcomings. The mirror-image version was always more important and seeing her, being with her, weighed me down.

Until now.

We pull up outside the hostel in Midtown and the streets are almost empty of people. Dad takes his time with the box of ashes. I hold the hostel door and then together we walk upstairs. He puts the box down gently on their bed. We hug in the hallway outside our rooms and it feels good to be in this hug, just the three of us. They finish packing and then we meet again in the hall.

'Where are your bags, Molly? I'll take them down for you,' says Dad.

I check to make sure Mum is within earshot.

'Mum, Dad. I'm so sorry but I have to tell you something.'

Mum frowns and Dad rubs his forehead.

'What is it, sweetie?' says Mum.

'You're going to be angry,' I say.

'Of course we're not,' says Dad. 'Only tell us quickly, Moll. The cab's outside waiting.'

'I don't know where to . . .'

Dad checks his watch and Mum says, 'Paul, stop stressing. Listen to Molly.'

I swallow.

'I'm not coming with you.'

'I knew it,' says Mum. 'Paul, I told you she wouldn't fly in this storm. Sweetie, I understand, I really do.'

'If it's not safe for planes to take off then they won't let us fly,' says Dad. 'They're the experts. Look, let's talk about this at the airport, shall we? Or in the cab on the way there; we really need to get going. We don't have enough on our credit cards to buy any more tickets; this isn't a game.'

'You two go and I'll come back in a few days, a week maybe.'

'We'll stay here with you,' says Mum.

Dad looks at her. 'Have you both gone mad? We paid almost fifteen hundred pounds for these tickets, on credit. Grab your bags, both of you, and let's get in the cab.'

'It's the way they present the news here,' says Mum. 'They make it sound like the end of the world, like there'll be a tidal wave or something.'

Dad's face is turning red. 'Molly, Liz, please! Let's talk about all this in the cab. This isn't funny.'

'I'll walk down with you,' I say.

I help them with their bags. Dad holds the box.

The cab's waiting outside.

'We can ask about turbulence when we get to JFK, Molly,' says Mum. 'Put your mind at rest. Come with us – it's the safest way to travel, your father looked it up.'

'It's not just the storm,' I say. 'I want to stay for KT. Help the police some more. I think if I fly home tonight they'll prioritise some other case, some missing person or a new homicide. I just need another week here to get my head straight and help Martinez.'

Mum meets my eyes and she realises I've made up my mind. She sees there's no point in debating this.

'Molly, this is not—'

'She's twenty-two, Paul,' interrupts Mum. 'I want her to come but we can't force her.' She puts her palms to my cheeks, cupping my face. 'I love you, Molly Raven.'

'I love you too, Mum.'

She gets into the cab and Dad places the box next to her and helps the driver lift the suitcases into the boot.

Dad looks confused, but doesn't try to argue any more. He says, 'I can't force you to come. But please stay in the hostel until this storm is over, don't go out and about tonight.'

'I won't.'

'We love you, your mum and me.' His voice cracks. 'We think the world of you, Moll.'

'I know.'

He gives me a brief hug and says, 'Call if you need anything,' then gets into the cab.

Mum winds down her window and yells, 'You got money for the hostel for a whole week?'

'Violet Roseberry says I can sleep on her sofa,' I lie.

'Violet's a good girl,' says Mum.

'Fly safe,' I say.

Mum blows me a kiss and Dad winds up the window and their cab disappears into the wet, shiny streets of Midtown Manhattan.

24

I sleep for sixteen hours straight.

When I wake up the storm has gone; it has passed right over me and blown itself out.

I stretch and feel like a brand new person. My eyes are clear and my breathing is slow. I am calm to the core. Renewed.

The first thing I do is check the news notifications on my phone, then the BBC News app, then Twitter, searching for any sign of a lost plane or a crash. Thank goodness there is nothing. And then a text comes through from Mum. *Landed safely. Back home now. Dad sends his love.*

I am in New York all alone and it feels truly wonderful.

After a hot shower I step out on to the street and the air is still. No wind at all. I pace over to Jimmy's food cart.

'Morning, stranger.'

'Hi, Jimmy. You didn't get blown away, huh?'

He shakes his head and smiles, 'I told you it wasn't a big deal, not like Sandy. This was a fart in a paper cup.'

'I need some advice.'

'And you come to me?'

'Do you ever go back to Afghanistan?'

'I thought you wanted advice?'

'You ever go back, Jimmy?'

'I don't go back,' he says, starting to prepare a tropical fruit smoothie. 'It's not like it would be for you, I don't think. I fly back to spend a month with my cousins, catch up with my old neighbour, my best friend he was, and then who knows if I get let back through customs at Newark, you know? I'm a US citizen now, but who can say? Really, for sure? So, I stay right where I am and I work and I live my life. Regular customers. A wife who loves me, and three good boys. I'm lucky to be alive, Molly.'

He hands me the smoothie and I hand him a ten-dollar bill.

'You never ordered it, you don't pay for it.'

'I want to pay.'

He shakes his head. 'Advice, though, now that you might have to pay for. What you wanna know, Molly?'

I eye the smoothie. I didn't see the ingredients, which fruits he blended, but maybe I should take a sip anyhow. Just for the hell of it. Be adventurous.

I sip the drink and it is sublime. I hold it up with a questioning expression.

'Guava, coconut, pineapple and a little ginger root.'

'It's delicious.'

'Of course it is, I made it. You want advice on something or don't you?'

'Best place in Manhattan for lunch under ten bucks. I'm flat broke.'

'Who isn't?'

'Best place?'

He smiles and sucks air through his teeth and looks into the middle distance. 'Ten bucks, really?'

I nod.

He sniffs and says, 'Head down to 37th Street, then walk east to Third. Place called Sarge's Deli. Now, it doesn't look like much from the outside but that's the whole point, right? You walk in there and get yourself a booth, nice and quiet. Hot pastrami on rye with pickles. Dunno if it's exactly ten bucks but it won't be a whole lot worse. Thank me later.'

'I will,' I say, walking away with my free smoothie.

The streets are still wet but the sun is out. I cut around Bryant Park and there are hundreds of construction workers building some kind of structure, some kind of temporary buildings. Maybe for Halloween?

I feel good on my walk. The dark shroud has lifted.

My heart races. I pick up my pace to the New Yorker rhythm, a trot with purpose, a march. I don't wait for the green man at the intersection; I just step over when the locals step over.

I pass the New York Public Library and keep on walking.

It took diligence and careful military-style planning to do what I did. But I managed it. The women and men walking either side of me are oblivious to my past actions. They're the kind of people who grow bored after researching a subject for an hour. They would have failed. Some people can research for twelve hours straight. They're the kind who are confident they will succeed, but they will not succeed because they will overlook a key detail. There are a handful of people in the world like me. A hundred, maximum. People who research for twelve hours, getting deeper and deeper into some esoteric subject, and then, just when they think they have an expert handle on the facts, they brew a pot of strong coffee and strap on an adult diaper, maximum absorbency, and they research for another fifteen hours straight.

And it's not just the researching. If you're playing a part, as I've done these past few days, you need to inhabit that role and commit to the mindset shift. Believe in the task completely. Not just speak and act but actually try to think in a totally different way. Live the role from the inside out, even when on your own. Because it takes that level of focus. Unwavering commitment and dedication. And that is why I can walk down Fifth Avenue the day after a storm and not need to look over my shoulder. My diligence has bought me that freedom. I earned it.

Mum sends me a text with a photo of their dog, a dog I never liked. I reply with a heart. She doesn't normally send me this many messages but I guess she feels the need to step into KT's place in some way. Mum is a good-hearted person.

I walk down to Third and find Sarge's Deli and go inside. I don't research the hygiene report from the New York City Department of Health, and I don't consult Yelp. I don't scroll TripAdvisor to scrutinise badly lit customer photos of sandwiches, and I don't review the menu on my phone. I just walk in like a normal person.

Part of me feels guilty for implicating Dad. Not implicating him exactly, but not standing up for him either. But I knew he'd be fine. He was innocent and I knew he'd be all right. A retired conman, post-prison, once said on his successful podcast that he wished he'd deflected more shade on to those around him. Smoke and mirrors. Decoys, and layers of false data.

I'm seated, and I should normally order a plain cheese sandwich on white bread. But I ask the waiter what he would order. He says the matzo ball soup. I say I'll have it. My temples throb from the exhilaration of this. From living my life in the moment.

The soup is outrageously good. This is what it's like to live your life. To just go with the flow, roll with the punches, see where the day takes you.

Where today will take me is some cheaper accommodation. I may be liberated from my former existence, flying solo for the first time ever, but I am also stone-cold broke. I need to find something cheaper than seventy dollars a night. The thought of discovering a new area, a run-down block in the Bronx or Harlem, scares me.

This all started fourteen months ago.

In a way it started twenty-two years ago when KT received all the confidence and joy destined for us both, and I received none of it. In the womb we were equals, nobody knew our differences back then, nobody judged us. I like to think people looked at our sonograms and saw two equals. But from as early as I can remember, the imbalance between us grew, and after years and years of being slighted, ignored, not invited, and not welcomed, the effects magnified. KT was the person everyone wanted to be friends with. I benefited from that, of course, from the *twin fame*. We were popular at primary school. But KT's default was to smile and laugh and pat her hand on your arm, whereas my default is to look unimpressed and withdraw. Which is no big deal in itself; lots of kids are like me. But they don't have an identical *Sesame Street* version in the same room at all times, *that* is the difference. Compared every second of our lives, by family and teachers and strangers. Scanned, appraised, and analysed. But fourteen months ago things unravelled. They totally fell apart.

I finish my soup and order pastrami on rye like Jimmy recommended. I ask for a small portion and the guy laughs.

We had a kind of pact. It wasn't an overt, spoken pact; more of an understanding. She got to live her fun life and in return I expected complete and unwavering loyalty. I demanded it. If there was ever an issue – a debate, an accusation, a question of taste – I expected her to back me up. Unconditional support. I have to say, in KT's defence, she always did. We were a team, until fourteen months ago. We were a great team.

The sandwich arrives and the amount of pastrami in between the bread slices is astonishing. I take a bite and the salt from the meat makes my mouth water almost before it hits my tongue.

KT and I always lived in the same part of the same place. Not always in the same building, I never expected that level of connection. I always knew she'd marry and have a couple of carefree kids, but at least she'd be close by, two stops on the tube max. I told her that. When I worked my admin assistant job in London she studied at King's College and all was well. I knew she was there. If I needed her, or I needed a kidney due to some horrific road traffic accident, I could rely on her, and equally she could rely on me. And then, fourteen months ago, without telling me, she accepted a place at Columbia over the place she told me about at UCL. She had applied in secret. She had accepted the offer in secret. She had found a scholarship in secret. And then she told me.

I demanded she reconsider. I continued to demand it months after her starting the course. She wouldn't. She distanced herself from me.

I get another text from Mum. A photo of KT's bed in our childhood bedroom, her side of the room covered with One Direction posters and photo-collages of her friends, mine with encyclopaedias and reference books. She's checking up on me just as she has done all my life. Making sure I'm coping. She told me once she worries about me more than she does about Dad and KT combined. Ten times as much. I reply with another heart emoji.

When KT confessed she was leaving me I couldn't talk for a whole minute. It was my worst possible nightmare realised. If she'd said she was studying at Edinburgh I could have found a job up there, or travelled by train every weekend. Even if she'd studied at the Sorbonne in Paris, I could have managed the ferry – never the Eurostar, but I could have used the ferry, we could have made it work. I told her all this. But New York? I pleaded with her. I begged her. And when that didn't work, I told her in no uncertain terms that I would kill myself.

In a way, I did.

The sandwich is incredible but it's way too big so the guy kindly offers to give me a doggy bag. I can have the rest for dinner in my room.

She flew out the following week, early September last year, to start her two-year masters course. A part of me died that day. Withered. And the very next afternoon I began researching how I could fix the problem, and effectively right all the wrongs.

And then I went to work.

25

Accommodation isn't easy in New York City. It isn't easy in London either, but here it's a joke. If you're KT, and you were born charming, then you might get a handsome apartment, fully paid for, on the border of the Upper West Side and Morningside Heights. That might happen. But everyone else has to struggle to make rent or live in an overcrowded dorm room. I've been staying in a seventy-dollar-a-night hostel, and now I have to halve that expenditure. Which is fine if you're the kind of person who's prepared to sleep in a converted shed Airbnb in Staten Island, but I am not that kind of person.

After thorough research I find my new home: the YMCA right next to Central Park on the Upper West Side. I can walk there in fifteen minutes. I've been outside the building so I know the area a little, and I can base myself there, sharing a quadruple room, which isn't ideal, for thirty-five dollars a night. I've already made the reservation.

I check out with my bags. I managed to consume all the bottled water and convenience store food I stored on the tarp under my bed, so now the only unwieldy item is my baseball bat. I stick it in my backpack and it feels like a samurai sword resting behind my head. I pass Jimmy's cart and head up Eighth Avenue towards the Museum of Arts and Design.

My thoughts are clear and positive. A new life for at least one week. A life where I get to live the dorm experience I missed out on. Four young women in a room. Like a pack. I'm a little nervous about the lack of personal space but at thirty-five bucks a night you have to sacrifice something. This way we'll have safety in numbers, me and my new roomies. And no risk of me mistakenly bludgeoning an innocent cleaner with a baseball bat thinking she's trying to break through the door. That kind of thing would result in a mess and it would have ruined my plans. With four of us in a room we can look out for each other. We can defend ourselves.

I wonder who they will be? Maybe students from Arizona or Cape Town. Maybe young medical students visiting from France over Halloween. Or three sisters from Ontario here to see the museums in the daytime and the club scene at night.

I approach the building and it is imposing. I read people here call it the Y. It's a fourteen-storey building right on the park, opposite the ballpark where Violet and I talked that time. Apparently this place has a pool and a fitness centre and a hangout lounge with imitation fireplace. It looks perfect.

'You play ball?' asks the guy who checks me in.

'Sometimes,' I say.

'That's cool.'

He tells me I'm on the eighth floor. Room 812.

I get to the room and I have butterflies. This is how American cheerleaders would live in some Midwest college. I'm about to have my authentic dorm experience. The experience I missed out on.

I unlock the door.

Nobody.

Empty room. Two bunk beds: three messy, and one, mine, made up.

Suitcases by the window, wet towels hanging on hooks, the faint smell of hairspray and cheap perfume.

I unpack some of my things but leave most of the self-defence items either inside my bag or inside my pockets. I make sure my valuables are kept on my person. Until I meet my roommates I must remain ultra-cautious. No wrong moves.

The view is of a brick wall. But it's still perfect. My fantasy come true. I lie on the bed. They left me the top bunk, which I appreciate, it shows they're good people, empathic. I inspect the room. There's an air vent up by the ceiling. Legionnaires' disease. There's a heater. Carbon monoxide poisoning. The window looks loose. No risk of an intruder at this height but there is the risk one of us could fall through if the frame failed. Eight storeys is certain death, statistically speaking. On the wall is a screw head where a picture used to hang. Tetanus. Potential head injury. The wire leading from a standing lamp has duct tape wrapped around it. Electrocution. You wouldn't even have to be the one touching the cable to get the shock; you could be the one touching the person who touches the cable.

But I'm here. No one else chose this place, I chose it myself. No one else is paying the rent, I'm paying. They don't even know I'm here. Nobody does.

My blood surges around my vascular system like it has extra energy, extra vitality, fresh red cells, more plasma than before, stronger platelets. I want to hang out with KT's friends. I also want to watch Scott Sbarra at rowing practice, not just see him walk out of the boathouse; I mean I want to watch him physically pull oars. Later I might walk past KT's apartment again in Morningside Heights. I'm almost in the same part of Manhattan now. Almost the same life.

A bang from a nearby room. I sit up on my bunk. I take my phone and check through the contacts. There aren't many.

I'm so relaxed I almost drift off to sleep. Not sleep, but a deep sense of being at peace with the world. Thoughts of Scott drift into my consciousness. His shoulders. The way he has a dimple in his chin and one on each cheek, a perfect triangle framing his full mouth. I imagine stroking my fingertip over his upper lip, dragging it slightly until my skin makes contact with the moist underside. I imagine placing a pearl in each dimple and them just resting there until he reaches closer to me, and places his hand behind my head and moves my mouth closer to his, and . . .

The door opens.

Three Asian women walk in, each one holding a clutch of shopping bags. Gap, H&M, Macy's, Zara.

They look at me.

'Hi,' I say. 'I'm Molly Raven.'

26

Unfortunately I won't be getting much of a dorm experience from my roomies as none of them speak much English. They're all from Shanghai, schoolfriends, and they speak more of my language than I do of theirs – they're more cosmopolitan than I am – but they don't seem interested in hanging out. Nice of them to let me share their room, though.

The problem with having no fixed return flight is it makes budgeting ten times more difficult. I need money for living, but also for supplies. I need to right certain wrongs. Restore balance. Maybe the need to maintain balance is a twin phenomenon? I need to put the world straight before I leave this city. There are a few people who wronged KT very seriously, and those injustices must be corrected before I fly away.

I step outside into the warm October sunshine and pull on the Yankees cap I bought last week from a souvenir store on Fifth Avenue. I walk a block west to Broadway and locate a Best Buy store. I place one Polaroid camera in my basket. I place extra film in with it. I choose one fully prepaid mobile phone. I pay cash. I leave.

All the packaging deposited into three separate bins.

I walk into the park and towards the zoo.

I set up in a large area of empty grass.

First things first: I text Martinez from my regular phone. He'll have access to immigration systems, and if anyone IDs me in the city he'll wonder why I never told him I stayed in New York. So, I tell him I stayed. That I need another week or so here to help find out what happened to KT. He doesn't reply.

I text Scott Sbarra from my regular phone and tell him I'm staying on for a week and ask if he wants to meet up one last time before I leave for the UK. To chat about KT and say goodbye. He replies immediately with *Sure*.

I don't reply. I'll force myself to wait a few hours.

I text Violet Roseberry from my regular phone and ask her if she wants to catch a movie or something. I say I'm here for another week and I'd like to see her. She doesn't reply.

I scroll YouTube but I do not click on any videos, I just want to see who's uploaded.

Shawn Bagby has uploaded.

Some video about alternate-day fasting, and another about which shirt collar will make you most *alpha* and therefore the most attractive to women. How does he think up all this nonsense?

I check the research notes on my phone. The important points have been coded using a modified version of the secret language KT and I devised as kids. They also have key dates and letter strings interspersed. I find what I'm looking for. The home address of Professor Eugene Groot.

As I scan the rooftops around Central Park I notice the water towers again. These pose more risk than most people care to think about. First of all there's the sheer number of them: some estimate up to twenty thousand in New York City. Then there's the weight. A cubic metre of water weighs a tonne. Some of the water towers I'm looking at, conical things on steel girders, must weigh fifty tonnes. Up there. Just waiting to fall. It'd only take a piece of steel buckling because it wasn't forged correctly, or a gust of wind during a freak storm. But the real risks are contained within. You see, the water in New York City is gravity-fed. It travels via rivers and aqueducts from upstate, and because it isn't pumped it can only reach up around six storeys. Hence the water tanks. But water pumped up into tanks, and left sitting there on rooftops, is a recipe for disaster. Wood rots. Metal corrodes. Pigeons find a way in. Mice breed. Rats build their nests, and even homeless people have been found living inside tanks. Each oversize rooftop barrel is a perfect breeding ground for bacteria. There is sediment at the base of each and every one. The responsibility for cleaning and disinfecting the tanks is left up to each building and some are better than others. There are E. coli thriving on most New York City rooftops. And that's why I only drink bottled water.

Violet replies saying she can meet me tomorrow night.

I hold off replying to Scott even though I want nothing more than to reply to Scott.

And then I turn on my burner phone.

I dial the number from memory.

The phone rings four times.

'Yes?'

'It's me.'

'And?'

'I need to meet.'

'And?'

'When are you here? When next?'

'Now.'

'You're here now?'

'And?'

'We need to talk. Last time.'

'Air,' he says.

He means sea. The twin code. Opposites. By sea, he means the Staten Island Ferry. It's one of our pre-planned meeting places. Top deck, three rows back for him, four rows back for me.

'Not after that storm. Can't do it.'

'Meat,' he says.

He means fruit. He means the Cherry Hill Fountain, less than a mile from where I'm sitting.

'Yes,' I say.

'Twelve,' he says.

That means six. Opposite side of the clock.

'OK.'

He hangs up.

27

I have been evicted from my room. Excluded. Thrown out. Expelled.

The YMCA was pretty reasonable about it, really. They didn't call the police, thank goodness. Once my three Chinese roomies discovered my baseball bat and my hornet spray they asked Reception if they could stay as three and pay extra. Rather than cause a scene, Reception gave me a single room at the same rate I was paying. Said I can keep it until I find something else I can afford.

KT would have had no problems. They'd have all been best friends by now.

But I do get a perk. No private bathroom, nothing that fancy, but now I have a view. No brick wall for me. I can see Central Park from my window. Not a lot of it, the window's too narrow, but I can see the colours. Being able to see nature from my bedroom is a game-changer. I feel relaxed staring at the auburn trees.

And now I have a place to research, and boy, do I need a place to research.

I walk to Best Buy, a different branch this time, a branch in Midtown, and buy a pretty nice Android tablet. Then I go to a store in the Garment District and buy a hundred and eighty dollars' worth of Google Play gift vouchers. Yeah, I'm running down my cash supplies, but I don't see any alternative. And besides, I have plans to remedy the situation.

Jimmy's fine. I check in with him and buy a smoothie and a bottle of water.

'Where you living at, Molly? You someplace safe, yeah?'

'Upper East Side,' I lie.

He whistles through his lips and says, 'You a one percenter now, lady. You walking in Mink Alley now.' And then he whistles again.

'Hardly. Staying on the sofa of a friend's place, that's all.'

'You see him, the Turk over there, fingerless gloves?' He points to the food cart opposite.

'Yes?'

'Cleans his grill with the same dirty rag six days in a row. I'm keeping count. Saw him drop a pretzel one time and look round, wipe it on the rag, put it right back on the stack. He's a dirty little man, that guy, don't eat from his cart, Molly.'

'OK, thanks.'

Another customer approaches so I walk away back up to the park.

My phone rings. 'Hello?'

'It's Scott.'

There's traffic all around, someone's broken down outside Radio City Music Hall, and everyone's beeping their horns.

'How are you?'

'Fine. I got practice.'

'Rowing practice?'

'Racing next week down at Princeton. They're strong.'

'I'm leaving New York soon, Scott.'

'Thought you'd left already. Vi was sad you went back.'

Vi? I loathe the way he shortens her name.

'Few more days. Hope this doesn't sound odd but there aren't many people I can talk to about KT. Memories, you know. My counsellor said it's an important part of the grieving process.' I don't have a counsellor. I've never had a counsellor. 'To keep her spirit alive. Wondered if we could go and get some pizza together some time. Or maybe a diner, whatever. My treat.'

'You like Vietnamese food?' he says casually.

I pause. 'I've never tried it, but I'm sure I'll love it,' I say.

'Pho?'

'Sure.'

'Tonight at eight? You know where Chelsea Market is?'

'Sure.' The lies keep on coming.

'See you outside at eight, then. Will be nice to talk about Katie some more. I miss her.'

'See you there.'

I end the call and my stomach is doing flips. It's not because I'm attracted to Scott, although I am. It's because we're almost repeating history. *Almost.* Some of the joy and anticipation that KT would have experienced before her first dates with Scott Sbarra. Some of the same glances and probably some of the same jokes. Sure, it's not a date exactly, but it kind of is, you know?

I find a cheap café and I stream some movie soundtracks through my phone headphones: *Fargo* and *Pretty in Pink* and *Gladiator.* Setting up the tablet is easy; it's identical to the ones I bought in London this past year. Using the Google Play tokens and a brand new Gmail account under a fake name I manage to buy some video editing software and an app that vocalises, in a computerised voice, anything I type, and I set up a brand new YouTube account. I research and screenshot old hidden Reddit posts deleted by Shawn Bagby. I read about metadata and algorithms and YouTuber strategies. I access the dark web and screenshot posts he made under an alias and then I screenshot the evidence I have that he used that alias. Similarities in cadence, the way he writes sentences. One word he regularly misspells. The way he describes proms as *loser fests* and women as *disposable femoids*. Then I edit some of the screenshots: cutting and pasting. Some of the evidence is true, some fabricated, some exaggerated. The lies are best hidden among the truths. You need more truths than lies, though, that's vital. You construct a pattern, a series, a myth. I have enough raw material now. Which means I can work on it offline, no wifi, untraceable, in the comfort of my thirty-five-dollar YMCA single room with a view.

There are several people milling around Cherry Hill Fountain when I arrive. Joggers stretching and dog-walkers dragging their pooches.

But no sign of *him*.

I walk closer to the fountain, scanning around, my view cut in half by the brim of my baseball cap.

I sit down on a low wall, my hand on my bat.

A minute later I sense someone sit opposite from me. They came out of nowhere. I look around out of the corner of my eye.

'Keep looking the other way,' he says. 'Take out your phone and start talking into it.'

I consider running away.

Because it's not *him*.

But I take out my phone. There are more people around us and right now that's a good thing. If I scream they will take him down – they will come to my assistance and not to his.

I say, 'What the hell is this?' into my phone.

He makes his own phone ring and answers it in a jovial tone. 'My name is Peter. How are you?'

'That's not your name,' I say.

'Peter Hill,' he says.

'No,' I say. 'Your name is Bogart DeLuca.'

28

'How did you know I'd be here?' I ask.

'Does it matter, Molly?'

'He sent you? What do you want?'

'Keep talking into your phone.'

'I am talking into my damn phone.'

'You raise your voice like that again and I will walk away.'

I don't say anything.

'My name is Peter Hill.'

'Whatever.'

His accent is different from before.

'I work with The Man. I work for him.' His accent has shifted from Brooklyn to LA.

'OK.'

'He couldn't make it today in person and he sends his apologies for that.'

More like he never planned to be here in the first place. Sent his henchman.

'OK.'

'What can we do for you, Molly?'

I take a deep breath. 'I need one more favour.'

'The deal,' says Bogart DeLuca, Peter Hill, whoever he is, 'was one favour. One *significant* favour.'

I take another breath. A teenager glides by on roller-skates.

'New deal,' I say.

I can't see him smile because I have my back to him, looking out at the lake, but I sense it.

'Go on.'

'I'm here for another week or so but I have no funds. I need ten thousand dollars in cash – that should be pocket change to your boss – and I need a safe room, a room you guarantee is secure.'

'OK, Molly.'

'Understand?'

'Loud and clear.'

Neither of us says anything for a while. I hold my phone closer to my mouth and start speaking, but then it rings and I almost jump out of my skin.

'You gonna answer that call?' he says.

I silence the call and look at the screen. It's Mum. I let it go to voicemail.

'Real smooth,' he says. 'I'll tell you what we're going to do. You'll get, in full and final settlement of this arrangement, fifty thousand dollars in small used bills, and a hotel room I'll guarantee is clear and secure. I'll select it personally and I'll sweep it for bugs and cameras. I'll inspect it. Is that acceptable to you?'

'Yes,' I say.

'Full and final, Molly. You understand what that means, right?'

'I do.'

'Make sure you do. Because if this goes any further, or any of the project details are ever disclosed, it won't be me dealing with you, you know that, right?'

'Sure.'

'This will go over my head, Molly. Outsourced to someone specifically trained to erase problems. Got it?'

'Yes.'

'I'll meet you outside the Pierre hotel at eleven tomorrow morning. Come alone and ensure you're not followed. I'm going to stand up now and walk. You head in the opposite direction in no less than five minutes. You got that?'

'Yeah.'

'See you tomorrow.'

He walks away and I watch him. No moustache. A different style of clothes and a different gait, but it's him. Bogart or Peter, it's him.

This is a fair deal, all in all. I stay seated on the bench for a full eight minutes trying to square off all the angles in my head, all the risk factors. I haven't written these details down, or typed them into an email, or saved them in a supposedly unhackable app. They're in my head. I can access them whenever I like and I know it's all cast-iron secure.

James Kandee was nothing to me.

And then, for a while, he was everything.

When KT was awarded her sponsorship, which she called a *scholarship* because that sounds so much more worthy and academic and above-board, it took me a good while to figure out who was behind it. Took me six weeks, in fact. She wouldn't tell me. She wouldn't even hint at his identity. Said that the offer and the paperwork all came via a third party. But by cross-referencing Instagram stories with Snapchat posts, diligently photographed by me before they auto-deleted, and making myself aware of his public schedule, meetings with NGOs and UN ambassadors, video footage of him bidding at Patek Philippe auctions in Geneva and Hong Kong, details gleaned from KT's social media and our conversations, I could tell they were in the same place from time to time. By the end of last year I had calculated it was approximately eighty per cent likely that James Kandee, and his foundation, was indeed the sponsor of KT's lavish New York student experience. It's not like me to confront someone, so I had to make sure of my facts. It wasn't until I had reached ninety-five-per-cent probability that I ambushed James Kandee, gently, subtly, professionally, outside his townhouse in Onslow Gardens, South Kensington. I dressed in the exact outfit KT had worn the month before, with him, to Aspen. I worked on my make-up techniques to look more like her, even plucking a line of eyebrow hairs with tweezers to mimic her scar. And it worked. He thought I was KT. By the time I was inside his house and he'd worked out I was not actually KT, it was too late. I had access. I had his ear. I told him everything I had worked out and I told him I'd communicate my evidence to the *Guardian*, the *New York Times* and the *South China Morning Post*. Details of the young women he'd sponsored over the years, and the trips he expected them to accompany him on. He pleaded his innocence, maintaining the trips were optional, and that he'd never crossed the line, he'd never slept with any of the students he sponsored. He was actually very open about the arrangement. He also claimed he was asexual. A virgin by choice. He flew beautiful young students with him, all for his public image. For his Instagram profile and to ensure he never lacked company when dining at the Hotel du Cap-Eden-Roc in Antibes or at the French Laundry outside Napa. He wanted their faces next to his and he wanted their conversation. I didn't believe a word of it at first, but later, after finding some of his boarding school friends from Rolle, Switzerland, and talking to them through a proxy, I worked out he was most likely telling the truth. Or *part* of the truth. I still suspected dark forces were at play somehow but even my research couldn't uncover exactly what they were. He asked me what I needed to guarantee my silence. He knew the public would never believe the sponsorship deals were a hundred per cent platonic. He said he realised the 'optics were dreadful'. He asked what I wanted.

So I told him.

The YMCA is busy when I return, international students trying to use some kind of translation app to communicate with the receptionist.

I pick out my best clothes, an H&M top and a pair of jeans that fit tight to my hips. I clean my ballet pumps with wet wipes. And then I hit the showers.

On this floor I don't get a public shower room with three showers, each with a clingy curtain. I get an individual shower room down the hall. As soon as I open the door and find clean tiles, a toilet, a sink, a shower, a lockable door, the relief washes over me. *Lockable*. I take my time under the jet of water, and my mind wanders. To Scott in his training gear. To how his arms and shoulders would look heaving back the oar of his boat. To how he and I walking around Chelsea later on tonight will look exactly like the way he and KT might have walked around Chelsea a month ago. There isn't a person alive on the planet, save for Mum and Dad, who could spot the difference.

I let my hair dry wavy, more like KT's, and then I blow-dry it and apply my make-up. I spray perfume on to the insides of my wrists and rub them and dab behind my ears, just as she did. I never normally wear perfume. It irritates my eyes.

The walk down Ninth Avenue is a dream. I understand this city now. The noise and the way the sunbeams cut between the tall buildings. The fire trucks and the steam rising from pipes in the middle of intersections. People hustling and people kissing. The metropolis is starting to grow on me.

Pumpkins outside stores: large, medium and small. I guess Halloween is a big deal here.

The occasional waft of my perfume puts a spring in my step. An extra level of confidence. It's Armani Mania. The scent KT used. I straighten my back and start smiling. I never usually smile when walking around like this, never.

Scott will be waiting for me outside Chelsea Market. Maybe he's bought me a going-away gift. Maybe a book or a trinket, something he thinks I'll take back with me.

The Avenue is longer than I'd expected and my pumps are getting more grimy with each block. But I arrive in time. Eight o'clock.

There's nobody here.

No Scott.

I wait, and I circle round the block in case there's another exit I missed. A row of four yellow school buses sit parked opposite under a metal fire escape.

The waiting fuels my anxiety but it also makes me excited. What are his expectations for tonight? A fifty-minute bowl of noodles then he runs off to drink tequila shots with his rowing buddies? Or has he carved out a few hours for me?'

And then I see him.

Walking towards me from the East Side, from Eighth Avenue.

He's backlit by headlights and his silhouette is perfect. The breadth of his shoulders and his chest. The easy way he walks. The glow from his hair and the length of his legs. Suddenly I'm awkward, shy, grinning like a fool. He crosses the street and I can't look him in the eyes. He comes closer and I look up and he is smiling.

'Shall we?'

29

It's just like a real date.

Scott seems relaxed. He tells me he trained for two hours today. We are walking next to each other. Like a normal couple.

He holds the door open for me. The restaurant is called Co Ba. Vietnamese food.

We're seated and people look at us as we pass their tables. The tall chiselled athlete and his date. A natural pairing. I smile and sit down. We're not at a good table, not in the corner, not at the back of the room, no good lines of sight, and you know what, I don't even mind. Who's going to hurt me with Scott Sbarra right here? Nobody, that's who.

He orders a gluten-free beer and I order water.

'You don't drink?' he says.

'I tried a glass of wine one time,' I say.

'You're not much like Katie, are you?' he says.

'Same and different,' I say. 'She was the wild one.'

'There's a GoFundMe at school. We're not sure what to do with the money yet. Maybe a plaque or an assistance fund for international students? We're already up above fourteen thousand dollars.'

'That's great,' I say. 'You organised that?'

'Me and some of the others,' he says. 'It wasn't just me.'

I should really order plain white steamed rice. I should ask for a spoon. I should check out the toilets before I touch the food, just as I do in every restaurant I eat in for the first time. But I don't. There is what I should do, and there is my own free will. That tension is there. Tonight, with Scott, I choose to be carefree, relatively speaking.

'You like your pho spicy, Katie?' His eyes widen. 'Oh, shit, oh, no. I'm really sorry, Molly, shit, I am so sorry, Molly.'

'Don't worry about it.'

He shakes his head and I think he's blushing. 'My bad,' he says.

'Happens all the time,' I say. 'Really. Don't worry about it.'

He looks down at the floor. 'So weird at school with her not there, you know? Like, she was always there, studying in Butler Library, in John Jay, at swim practice. She was so public, so out there. And now there's this vacuum.'

'That's exactly how I feel,' I say. 'A vacuum.'

He nods.

'More than a vacuum,' I say. 'She was an extension of myself, if that makes sense. She wasn't like a sister, nor was she part of me – more like an extension. Since the day we were born. And now it's like walking around with no shadow.'

'Must be hardest for you,' he says.

'I don't know.'

'I'm real sorry.'

'It's hard to explain,' I say. 'She was always there for me to text or to share news with, even the tiniest thing. Like my conscience.'

The waiter comes back with our pho. Hot steaming bowls of broth with flat noodles and spice and handfuls of fresh green herbs topped with thin slices of beef brisket. Scott asks if he can have more brisket.

'I need the protein,' he says. 'Training.'

I dip my spoon in the broth and sip, waiting for the heat burn. But it's not as spicy as I'd expected. It's delicious. Warming. I slurp noodles and the noise is outrageous.

Scott smiles. 'My mom eats like that.'

'Your mum?'

'She likes her soup,' he says.

Spring rolls arrive at the table. Crispy deep-fried spring rolls, and according to the menu they contain grilled tiger shrimp and honey plum grilled pork, along with rice vermicelli, salad, herbs, and a chilli-lime dressing.

'You have any brothers or sisters?' I ask.

'Two brothers,' he says.

'Older or younger?'

'One of each.'

'You get on well?'

'On and off,' he says. 'Much better now than a few years ago. Katie met both of them. They really liked her. Mom and Dad liked her, too.'

'Everyone liked KT,' I say.

He pulls off his V-neck sweater and now he's sitting here wearing a white T-shirt. I start to feel warm. Women at the other tables glance at him. Those at the back of the room are looking at his back, and the V-shape of his torso. Women to my left and right are looking at his chest through his cotton T-shirt, at the profile of it. Men are looking too. They are looking at their wives and girlfriends, and then they are looking at Scott Sbarra.

Scott wipes sweat from his brow. 'Chilli, eh?'

'I like it.'

'How long are you staying in the city for, Molly?'

'About a week. I want to help the police some more before I leave for London.'

I need to right wrongs.

Restore balance.

'I might be flying to London next year. There's a boat race on the Thames we might qualify for, don't know yet.'

'*The* boat race?'

'It's in a city called Henley-on-Thames. You know it?'

'Not really,' I say. 'I've heard of it. Not sure it's a city.'

'People wear hats and stuff, old-fashioned preppy boat race, some real nineteenth-century shit. But the trip's fully funded if we qualify, so it would be kinda cool.'

'Maybe I could see you in London,' I say. 'Just for coffee or something.'

'Could be cool,' he says. 'Excuse me.'

He stands up and walks off to the gents'. The way he walks, the stride, the posture, the movement of white cotton over his shoulders, it makes me want to chase him down. The room watches him walk and he is unaware. At least half the room. Three-quarters.

But it's wrong. All of it. Who is worse here, me or him? Me for being here, with KT's man, or him for being here, with his dead girlfriend's identical twin? It's disgraceful whichever way you look at it. Evil, almost. Twisted. He should be grieving more than he is. KT was worth more pain than I can see in his face. But I'm the one to say stop. I'm the one who must do the right thing.

He comes back and finishes his pho.

'You're probably not in the mood for anything,' he says. 'But it's Halloween in a couple of days. You ever experience a true American Halloween, Molly?'

'Not really my thing,' I say.

'That's what Vi says. She hates Halloween with a passion.'

Vi again.

'Violet hates Halloween? Why?' I finish a spring roll.

'She hates anything commercialised. Anything wrapped up in shopping and materialism and plastic garbage. Vi's practically a communist. Always stays home on the 31st.'

'I'll probably do the same, to be honest. Stay in the hostel and work on KT's case.'

'Any leads yet you know of?'

'A few,' I say. 'Nothing concrete. Nothing to justify an arrest.'

'I just wish they'd lock me in the cell with the guy. Just for five minutes.'

'You never know, you might get your chance.'

He grits his teeth and says, 'Cops talked to her neighbour, you think? Kid living down in the basement?'

'I don't know.'

'They should.'

I don't say anything.

'Something wrong with that kid. Like he has a dark side.'

'I'm looking into him.'

'Be careful around that guy, Molly. You need to talk to him, you let me know and I'll go in with you. We can talk to him together.'

I smile at him and he blushes again. Six-four with a square jaw and yet he blushes. Red around each cheek dimple.

He orders another beer and the restaurant lights dim.

'Katie told me you guys were inseparable as kids. Told me about your secret language and the way you hardly spoke to your parents for a few years, just each other.'

I take a sip of water. 'We used to make fun of them behind their backs. It was cruel, really.' I start to laugh. 'One time we swapped salt for sugar and Dad spat out his tea. We planned the whole thing. Well, I planned it and KT actually *did* it. We were a good team.'

'Don't take this the wrong way,' he says, leaning back, his shirt stretching over his midriff. 'And I know I said it before. But you're *so* different, the two of you. You look almost the same, obviously, but your faces, your expressions. It's like I'm here with Katie but I'm not, you know?'

'We've always been pretty different,' I say. 'Same, but different.'

'I liked her a lot. She was a special person.'

'She liked you, too, Scott.'

He doesn't place his hand on my hand but he moves it closer. On top of the table, in full view of the room, his little finger is almost touching my little finger. I can feel it. The heat and the energy. I can feel the potential of him through my body. Like I'm getting drowsy from a hot bath, every muscle in my body easing. I want to push my hand so our fingers touch. I want to feel his skin against my skin. But I pull back.

'Check?' he says.

They bring it to us and we split it.

'I'm heading back up to school. You still in Midtown?'

I nod.

'Walk you there?'

We set off.

The evening is warm for the end of October, and there is a stillness in the air. Couples walk entangled. The woman in front of us has her hand in her lover's back pocket, and his arm is loose around her waist. I start to think about how my hand would feel in Scott's pocket. Just casually placed there. The movement of him as we walked.

'I said, do you think you'll ever come back to New York?'

'Sorry, I was miles away. I don't know. Maybe? Probably not. Probably won't be able to.'

We cross the street heading north.

'It can be expensive, but try to live your life to the full,' he says. 'Sorry, that sounds like greeting card bullshit. I mean, that's what Katie would have wanted, you know?'

'You think?'

'Well, she never talked to me about her dying or anything,' he says. 'But in an indirect way, watching movies – can't remember which ones; she usually chose them – she said she thought couples who are in love and then one of them dies from cancer or whatnot, she said the other should move on and marry someone else. That life is for living and you only get one shot.'

'That sounds like KT.'

Our arms touch as we walk. Not much, mere grazing. I walk close to him and he does not back away.

I catch a sense of his aftershave in the breeze and I just want to stop and sniff him, breathe him in, open up my nostrils and smell him.

'Hey, Stevie!' he yells, then jogs off up the street.

Who the hell is Stevie?

They hug and pat each other's backs and I realise how tactile Scott is and how I've not been close to him tonight, not really.

He runs back to me and says, 'The guys are going to play pool, get some beers. I'm gonna join them. You want me to get you a cab or something?'

'No,' I say, and my voice fails me. I squeak, 'I'll be OK.'

He's leaving me by 34th Street to join his friends? Leaving me here alone?

'It was nice seeing you, Molly,' he says, leaning in for a kiss. I feel his smooth, hard cheek next to mine. I reach round for a hug and we hold together for perhaps half a second. The smell of his hair. His chest pushing into mine.

'It was good to see you,' I say, my breath close to his ear.

He looks down at me and he's blushing again and he pulls away and runs off to his friends.

I head north up Ninth Avenue. After the initial shock of his leaving I reassure myself, safe in the knowledge that I can see him again if I choose to. I can spend quality time with him again.

I'm not walking, I am gliding. Floating just above the pavement. My skin feels softer than it has ever felt and I am oblivious to all the water towers, cranes and scaffolding around me. I cross ten more blocks, daydreaming. About how his chest would feel against the heels of my hands. How his fingers might push through my hair.

And then I catch sight of someone.

In a shop window.

He's staring right back at me.

Suddenly, I'm cold.

There he is again, in a car wing mirror.

I cut down a side street and into a Starbucks.

He's gone.

I step outside.

No sign of him.

I walk to the corner to hail a cab.

And he steps out from a 7-Eleven and walks right up to me.

30

I increase my pace and walk with a group of three middle-aged couples, all of them wearing jeans and white sneakers. We cross over to Port Authority and go in.

He is nowhere.

I leave the group to collect their tickets and I walk further inside and buy a grey beanie hat from a chain store.

He's not here.

I'm sweating.

People drag their bags around, looking for buses, and I scan from left to right, my pulse racing inside my temples. Is this it? Is this the moment when Bogart DeLuca takes me away, silencing me, neutralising a problem on behalf of his boss? Here to end me with a stab to the heart or a suppressed 9mm round to the back of the head? Maybe the plan to meet at the Pierre Hotel tomorrow was merely a ruse? The generous pay-off was a lie? A misdirection? Maybe this had been the true plan all along?

I take cover behind an escalator.

No sign of him.

I see people walking around with wet hair. One of them

shakes an umbrella. I buy a disposable plastic poncho and slide it on.

I walk to Seventh Avenue.

Up to Times Square.

Everyone tells me how this was once a dangerous part of Manhattan, full of pimps and crack dealers. But that was then. Now it's all Disney and Gap stores. I fit in perfectly wearing my poncho. I'm one of a herd.

I cross towards Sixth and he's right there on the other side of the road.

Mets cap pulled down low, ill-fitting suit, black shoes.

Or is this when Martinez and a crew of his non-uniform colleagues swoop in and arrest me because my research wasn't quite thorough enough and I missed a crucial detail: a fibre or a fingerprint?

No.

I was obsessively careful in the apartment. Scrupulous in the extreme. There were no fingerprints.

Did I miss something, though? No. I didn't miss anything. I can't have.

I walk close to a woman who looks like she can handle herself.

He's still there. I see him in the reflection of a truck window.

Or maybe he's another detective? Someone Martinez sent. A colleague on the homicide team. FBI, even. They got to me. They somehow figured it all out with some piece of new technology we don't know about yet. Is this me getting arrested? Is that what this is?

I dip into an AT&T store and out the other door and then I sprint up to Jimmy's smoothie cart.

'Someone's following me,' I say, out of breath.

'Get in,' he says, clicking a button and letting me into the cart. 'Stay down, don't say a word.'

It's spotlessly clean in here. No discarded fruit peel or old paper napkins on the floor. Just gleaming stainless steel and Jimmy's Crocs and Jimmy's white socks.

Up at his hip level I can see a small photograph of his family back in the '80s or '90s. A group of four or five children, all smiling, and a woman of thirty or so. On a shelf under the till is a baseball bat. And the emergency go-bag I asked him to store for me.

I stay down for twenty minutes. Jimmy serves seven customers in that time. Then he says, without looking down or gesturing to me, 'Don't think nobody's following you now, Molly. Nobody out here.'

'You sure?'

'Yeah. Can you call an Uber or something? Get you home?'

'I don't know how to call an Uber.'

'You wanna cab, then?'

'Yes, please.'

'Hold on.' He steps out on to the street and hails a cab.

I jump inside and thank Jimmy. He waves that away.

We set off.

'Where you going?' asks the cab driver.

'The YMCA on the park, West 63rd Street.'

The driver stops the car and says, 'No, no way, Jesus,

you can walk there, it's five minutes at the most, just walk there.'

'I have a bad leg,' I lie. 'I'm injured.'

'You're not bleeding back there, are you?' he says. 'I don't need blood on my seats. You need a hospital or something?'

'No. Just take me to the YMCA.'

I unlock the door to my room and take stock of my arsenal. I run to the bathroom, do what I need to do, run back, and use my belt to, in effect, lock the auto-closing hinge that connects my door to the wall. Another trick gleaned from a retired Green Beret on YouTube just before I left for New York.

Now I'm in.

My last night here.

I fall asleep thinking of Scott. How I'm starting to want him more.

The next morning I wake early to pack my belongings. I work on my Shawn Bagby video in two different cafés using my burner tablet. Then I retrieve my bags and walk through the park between the pond and the zoo to reach the Pierre. I arrive at the ornate hotel gates at two minutes to eleven.

My new base.

He walks out to greet me, a zip-up attaché case under his arm.

Were you following me yesterday? I think.

'Good morning,' he says, in his LA accent.

'Morning, Bogart.'

'It's Peter,' he says, gesturing for me to follow him away from the Pierre, back into the park.

'Wait a minute,' I say, looking back to the doorman at the hotel. 'The room. You said . . .'

'*You* said,' he whispers sternly, 'somewhere safe. You coming or not?'

I follow him across Fifth into the park.

'Where are we going?' I ask.

'Give me your phones.'

'What?'

'Phones. All of them.'

I shake my head.

'OK, then I'm leaving.'

I hand him my burner.

'The other one too.'

I hand him my iPhone.

He places them inside a black case.

'What is that?' I ask.

'Faraday bag. Now we can talk.'

I know what a Faraday bag is. People place their devices into metal-lined containers to prevent them from being hacked, screened, traced, or damaged in a solar event.

'Where are we going? I need to know.'

'There,' he says, pointing across the park.

'Where?'

'The Ritz-Carlton. Your new home for the next ten days, maximum. Junior suite on the eleventh floor. It's as secure as we can make it. Booked in the name of someone who isn't alive any more, paid for in cash. You can order as much room service as you like and it'll be covered.'

'Really?'

We pass by horse-driven buggies and cross the road. I can't think of him as Peter Hill. DeLuca is the name stuck in my head. He's Bogart DeLuca to me.

The doors to the Ritz-Carlton open and the doorman says, 'Welcome home, ma'am,' to me.

We travel up in the lift and DeLuca hands me two key cards. 'I don't have copies,' he says. 'Hotel management will have master keys, but I don't have any copies. Keep your internal lock on, your chain attached, and always display your *Do Not Disturb* sign.'

I use the keycard to open the door.

The room is larger than my London apartment. The view is of Central Park and there's a telescope positioned in the window.

DeLuca sits the attaché case down on the end of the king-size bed.

'Fifty, as agreed,' he says.

I open it and the bundles of used notes are stuffed tight into the bag.

'What now?' I say.

'It's over,' he says. 'It's all over. Is that clear?'

I nod.

And then he leaves.

I lock the door, attach the chain, cover the peephole with gum, and tie my belt around the door lever just like back in the good old YMCA. I take my time unpacking, sipping chilled orange juice from the minibar and playing Sinatra through the in-room music system. This is, by a magnitude of ten, the nicest room I have ever set foot inside. I hang up each of my shirts. I shower in the incredible marble-clad rain shower. I douse myself with luxurious lotions and creams. I relax on the bed in a fluffy robe with white hotel slippers.

I switch on the TV.

The message says, *Welcome to the Ritz-Carlton, Violet Roseberry.*

31

Dinner last night was room service. A trolley wheeled in by a very polite young man. He set up the tablecloth and unveiled the roasted half-chicken with Béarnaise sauce and crispy courgette strips. The view was perfect, as you'd imagine. The darkness of Central Park laid out in front of me, not an oblique sliver as from the YMCA, or a poster in Reception as in the Bedfordshire Midtown, but an expansive, private panoramic view through a perfectly clean windowpane.

This city is unimaginably beautiful seen from this perspective. The skyline, the oranges and reds of the trees, the horses making their way out on to West 59th Street. And from this height even the Manhattan traffic is mesmerising. Lights and colours moving round the park, entertaining me up here.

The fact that I'm checked in as Violet unnerves me somewhat. Even the stationery on the desk is personalised with her name. I think it must be some kind of sick joke.

I slept the sleep of the dead after my room service dinner, and then I ordered breakfast. I ate in bed, a stack of divine pillows supporting me. American pancakes with maple syrup and blueberries, fresh black coffee and orange juice with ice. I'd never ordinarily order ice. I only eat ice if I make it myself, especially with the water towers in this city, but the woman on the phone assured me they make their ice with Evian so I took the plunge.

The luxury of this place. But it still feels dirty coming from Kandee. In KT's emails sent in May she said that she was worried about delivering some kind of package, part of 'Project H', whatever that meant. And then someone with an email address made up of only numbers and consonants advised her to take out life insurance shortly afterwards. Whatever James Kandee and his foundation are involved with, it's not purely charitable. There are sinister forces at play.

I have a mid-morning bath and pick out my 'grey man' outfit for the day. 'Grey man' in Midtown Manhattan is different from 'grey man' where I'm headed, so I've adapted accordingly.

The phones stay in their Faraday bag. I didn't have a signal-jamming bag in London because I wanted my phone to establish a regular uninterrupted pattern in case the records were ever analysed. I didn't want that drop in signal.

I walk over to Fifth, over to Madison, over to Park, and down to Grand Central Station. Its creamy stone glows warm in the autumnal sunshine. I order a Starbucks to go, and buy my Metro North ticket, standard class, to Stamford, Connecticut. I'm not going to Stamford, I'm not even going as far as Rye, but that's exactly the point. On a train you can get off before your destination; you can't do that on a plane or a ship. It's more private.

I locate the correct train and choose a relatively empty carriage. The journey will take around forty-five minutes. By the time I've found his house, scanned the neighbourhood and made my preparations, the window of opportunity remaining will be sufficient. I have some wriggle-room.

Through Harlem and further north.

The view from the train changes from brick to dilapidated industrial to green weeds to trees and major arterial roads.

I enjoy the motion of trains. I like the rattle of them, the pace of them. Air travel is unnatural in my opinion. It is discombobulating and uncomfortable, even on a private Gulfstream G650.

The view passes me by and my mind wanders.

DeLuca's predecessor picked me up in her Volvo SUV at a quiet North London petrol station. She parked, filled up with petrol. I walked over from the shop and I stepped into the back seat as per our plan. Nobody noticed anything out of place. Why would they?

Private air travel, if you stay within your domestic airspace, is a piece of cake. If you travel domestically by air it's not that much more complex than driving or taking a bus. You drive right on to the runway, you load up your bags, you fly away. The pilots need to do their job and communicate professionally to air traffic control, of course, but there are no real security or customs controls.

When flying internationally it's a whole different story. Even celebrities and billionaires get checked when they fly across a sovereign border. But there's the rules and then there's the reality.

James Kandee had been flying internationally for years on his customised Gulfstream jet. He'd fly from Biggin Hill, the location of his private hangar, to Teterboro, New York, roughly once every two or three weeks. He used Teterboro as his entry point into North America, even if his eventual destination was LA or Austin. And that's partly because it's so convenient, just a short drive from the apartment he's having built on the sixtieth floor of a skinny new tower on West 57th Street, or, as Violet Roseberry calls it, Billionaire's Row. Sometimes he'd fly on to the Caribbean from there, or to Buenos Aires for the weekend. He might take a girl from Harvard or a girl from Rutgers or he might take KT. And James Kandee, like most of his ilk, values convenience and speed. He does not want to answer questions from a customs official and he sure as hell doesn't want any of his bags opened. That one per cent of the one per cent demand frictionless travel, as far as that is possible. Sometimes, when he has to fly direct from London to Las Vegas or Chicago, airports that aren't so familiar with him, he'll meet more friction. But not at Teterboro.

We pass through small towns with quiet railway stations, and the world looks more like Nottingham outside the train than New York.

In the Volvo that night, on the way to Biggin Hill, I kept low in the back seat covered with a blanket.

At the airstrip we drove straight to the hangar. The hangar doors were closed. I was taken out of the car and carefully placed inside a large reinforced suitcase on wheels. I was then loaded into the Gulfstream along with other matching pieces of luggage. The customs official in

London, by now almost a friend of Kandee's, checked the passport of him and the two pilots, and wished them a pleasant flight.

It was dark and strange inside the suitcase but it was not unpleasant. I had rarely experienced that much adrenaline; neither before nor since. The feeling of getting away with it. A free jet ticket to the United States. Completely off the grid.

Two more stops on this train until I get off.

We're close to the ocean here. I can see gulls flying against the breeze.

Once we were airborne, James unzipped my case and let me out to stretch. He never allows the pilots to walk around or open the door to the main part of the plane, and I expect that's because he wants them to assume he's busy having sex with the attractive girls he sponsors, rather than sitting on his chair with his phone while they sit on their chair opposite, staring out of the window. When we were due to land I got zipped back inside my case and stowed in the rear bedroom of the aircraft along with his other matching bags.

One stop left. My ticket gets checked.

When the plane came to a halt at Teterboro I could hear the pilots open the cockpit door and talk to James. I could hear them walk down the steps, and I could hear a customs official board the aircraft for a five-second glance around. Passports were checked. Bags, including me, were offloaded into a Suburban. And then we drove straight out of the airport on to Route 17.

This is my stop.

Two before Stanford.

One before Rye.

I'm on my way to Greenhaven. One of the most expensive and prestigious suburbs north of the city. A district known for its waterfront properties and its coastal beauty. An area with excellent schools. This place is home to eminent bankers and industrialists, gallery owners and patrons of the arts.

It is also home to Professor Eugene Groot and his family.

32

It takes me forty minutes to walk from Harrison railway station to Groot's house in Greenhaven. The houses get larger and grander, the maintenance standards higher, the lawns greener and the cars more discreet. There are no Ferraris or Lamborghinis here, not that I can see, anyway. But there are brand new Audi SUVs and Jaguars. One man – I'm not sure if he's the householder or a member of staff – buffs and waxes a vintage Porsche with all the skill and care you might expect of a specialist historian restoring an oil painting in a museum.

I don't walk to Groot's family house, but I manage to position myself one street away. I'm almost three minutes behind schedule. I have no phone and I have no notes. All the facts are engraved in my hippocampus, neocortex and prefrontal cortex. The location of the ideal park bench, as identified on Google Maps, specifically the satellite photo mode. The house and garden, again gleaned from Google, this time in 3-D mode. I know where Groot's trees are, where he parks his car, where his wife parks her car, where the front door is situated, where the back door is situated. They bought the house two years ago and the main listings on Sotheby's Realty are now gone. They're also missing from three compiler sites

– sites that exist to aggregate the listings from individual estate agencies. But I found them eventually, via a blog based out of New Jersey. A blog linking to interesting or luxurious houses. They had the link, but they also had screenshots and photos and some extra information about the area. So now I know this house inside out.

I walk round the block to ascertain exactly where Groot's cameras are and where his neighbour's cameras are. I also want to see who is home.

The houses are immaculate. The leaf-blowers have been out at work and the paintwork is flawless. Imagine the house in *Home Alone*, except more historical. Each building on its own acre plot. Mature trees and fine landscaping.

Seeing this life, this way of living, is eye-opening to me. My first instinct this morning, before I reprimanded myself, scolded myself, was to hire a driver to take me to Greenhaven. I have almost all of my fifty thousand dollars left, after all. I have forty thousand hidden in four separate locations in my room, one thousand as decoy in the safe, and eight thousand seven hundred on my person. Left shoe, right shoe, bra, inside zip pocket of my coat, wallet for muggers. The at-risk money is in the safe. You walk into a fancy hotel room and you think the safe is safe. Let me tell you: the safe is never safe.

I briefly had notions of flying back to my London life first class. One of those flatbeds with hot meals served on bone china. Crystal glasses. Privacy and personal space. I witnessed that other class of flying when I walked through to economy just a few days ago on my way here. But a first-class ticket would be foolish. Business class would be stupid, too. Even premium economy might raise suspicions, if anyone were to ever probe into my affairs and finances. No, it'll be economy class for me. The grey woman of Camden.

On the walk back round I double-check camera orientations and infra-red garden security systems. This would be more difficult at night. You might think it would be smarter, but not only would it not work with my narrow window of opportunity, as calculated from Eugene Groot's public class schedule and from Jane Groot Esq.'s 'work from home' Friday afternoon routine – but also it wouldn't work with neighbourhood watch vehicles or security lights.

I settle back down on the public bench adjacent to the property. My observation base. I'm wearing a grey wig I bought for ten dollars in the Garment District. I made sure to combine it with a few other items so the cashier wouldn't notice. On its own the wig would barely work, but under my beret it looks just fine. I look seventy years old. Eighty, even. Disguise works best by layering, that's what the CIA's finest minds taught me through several well-produced YouTube videos. Let's talk posture: I'm walking more slowly and more hunched than normal. Clothes: I'm wearing an unfashionable dress than ends just below the knee thanks to some rough alterations this morning with my complimentary Ritz-Carlton sewing kit. Socks and plain black sneakers. A fifteen-dollar handbag I bought from a street vendor with cash. A freebie magazine I took from the hotel.

I look like I'm reading the magazine, but really I'm watching his house.

If there is one thing I know, it's that retribution is essential for moving forward with your life. There is a primal need to cleanse. You are responsible for your own survival and your own happiness. You cannot rely on anyone else – any government organisation or family member. Take responsibility. Act, don't just think. Form a plan and execute it perfectly.

Groot leaves in his dark green Mercedes and I stay seated. I have between nineteen and twenty-five minutes.

After five minutes I check for neighbours then walk part-way past his house. The good thing about an expensive neighbourhood like this, one with historically important houses and strict landscaping codes, is that there are no new walls or chain-link fences. Residents *want* you to see their beautiful rose beds and their well-clipped box bushes.

I step on to the lawn in an area not covered by any CCTV cameras. I sidestep around a compost area to a small lawn shielded by a dense privet hedge. The clock is ticking. I remove my wig and fix my hair, and then I take out my Polaroid camera and make sure the house façade will be in the frame of my selfie shot. I hold the camera at arm's length and take the photo. It develops. I put it down on the ground and take another, this time pulling down my bra, which is stuffed with fifty-dollar bills. I move the cash and expose my nipple. The picture develops. Groot's front door canopy and my breast in one shot. I take more, some with half my smile and the roof of the house, others with my tongue sticking out. One photo with my hand over my breast: the background a beautiful Georgian style window with old glass. I use my Ritz-Carlton pen to write a heart on the back of the photo together with a date: *Sept 19th*. And then one final photo. I may be wearing an old lady dress hemmed at the shin but I am not wearing any underwear. I take an upskirt photo and it develops but I can't bring myself to look at it. I collect wet sticks from the compost area and take lighter fluid from my bag and stack the sticks and photos to form a pyramid and set the whole thing alight. The one photo of my face, breast and the Georgian window, I leave to one side. When the other photos are mostly burned, I put out the fire, leaving just charred glimpses of what they showed.

And then I put the wig back on and walk away.

Towards the beach and then back to the bench, my pace slow and stiff, the sea air blowing my thighs through the material of my skirt.

I sit down and watch Mrs Groot arrive home right on schedule. An immaculately dressed black woman in an ankle-length cashmere coat. She notices the smoking embers and runs into the garden. And that's my cue to depart the neighbourhood. Part of me wants to stay to watch her reaction, but that is the undisciplined part, the part that could get me into trouble. I have no wish to get into trouble. Besides, I have no real issue with Jane Groot Esq., attorney-at-law. None whatsoever. It's her lowlife husband who seduced my twin sister and then dumped her, claiming he couldn't hurt his family – that's who I have an issue with. More like he couldn't afford to live this kind of life without the earnings of his successful wife or the validation of their social contacts. If I hadn't taken this action today, then she'd have suffered on. I'm righting a wrong. He slimed his way into the beds of his students, impressing them with his Harvard Club membership. Let Jane Groot free herself from this swine. Better still, let her take the Polaroid to the police. A photo has more impact than an email or a witness statement. Let them reach their own conclusions about respectable Professor Groot and his rule-breaking relationship with a now-deceased student.

33

I take a different route back to the Harrison train station. I maintain my old lady posture and appearance. But it is difficult to suppress my joy. Revenge, retribution, punishment, karma, whatever you label it: rebalancing a wrongful act is a powerful sensation. Groot wronged KT. An eye for an eye. He wronged her. And now he is to be punished for it.

The train will arrive in fifteen minutes. I spend that time in the ladies' toilet, or *restroom* as they call it here. I am resting, I suppose. Resting well away from security cameras. I need to be completely invisible. KT used to walk around with her head held high, making eye-contact, smiling. People noticed her. I don't smile or make eye contact. I don't want to be noticed.

The train arrives.

My ticket is stamped.

There's a woman sitting opposite and she must be thirty. She keeps staring at me. She's trying not to seem too obvious, staring while her eyes are swivelled round in their sockets, her face pointing out of the window, but she is focused on my appearance. Perhaps on my wig and the way it doesn't give me a natural hairline. Or how my facial collagen is too young-looking for my skirt length or shoe choice. This woman is trying to work out my back story. But she'll never get close.

The Suburban dropped me off in Manhattan that day, five or six blocks from KT's apartment, in the northernmost part of the Upper West Side. It was my first time in New York City. My first time outside of the UK.

A family boards the train and sits opposite, the eldest child trying, and failing, to master her yo-yo.

KT's building was a sculpted brownstone with heavy, ornate steps. There were shrubs growing outside her windows, and her blinds were finished at the hem with a line of small fabric spheres on pieces of string, like a line of soft ping pong balls.

I checked that nobody was watching. And then I buzzed her.

A message pings on the phone of the woman opposite and she stops staring at me. She's not a cop, there's no way, I've been too careful. She's just inquisitive. Some people are not good at hiding their stares, that's all. It'll be OK. I believe wholeheartedly in this role, in this disguise, and so will she. Maybe it's weird to see someone, anyone, on a train these days who isn't looking at their smartphone. Perhaps that's why she's staring.

KT opened her door. I expected a look of horror on her face for some reason, an expression of mortal fear, but she burst into tears and smiled and led me inside.

'What the fuck, Moll? How are you even here? Oh, my God, this is amazing. Did Mum and Dad organise it?' She looked behind me. 'Are they here? Did you come by cruise ship? Is this a surprise?'

'They don't know I'm here,' I said. 'It is a surprise. I've been saving up.'

We didn't hug. We didn't even shake hands. We never really touched each other. No affectionate punching of shoulders or brushing each other's hair. None of that. Never. We're too similar. It'd seem weird.

'I cannot believe you are here – you're such a bitch not letting me know, God, I would've tidied up or something. Fuck. You're staying here with me, right? How long are you in New York? Oh, my God, you're really here, Molly!'

And then we made a pot of tea and sat down and got to talking. No phones or distractions. We talked and we covered so much. How she was coping in New York. Her new boyfriend and the awkward affair with her tutor that he ended despite all the promises that he loved KT and that he was going to separate from his wife and buy his own duplex apartment by Morningside Park. I told her about my job, how my mid-year assessment went, the movies I'd seen on Netflix, the new fire safe I'd invested in. She told me about Violet Roseberry. How they had drifted apart a little after Violet started acting strange, but they still hung out after class or in the library. I asked about how Mum and Dad were enjoying New York. She told me Dad loved it and Mum was worried about the family business, how they were probably going bankrupt and this was Dad's last splurge; one of many, and how she didn't know how they would manage after the court had dealt with them.

The train slows for a stop and the kid with the family does a half-decent yo-yo and her mum gives her a big cheerful hug to congratulate her.

KT started talking about the dinner we'd have with Mum and Dad that night at her favourite Italian place close to her apartment, and it was then that I told her exactly how I'd got here, how I had found out about the foundation that was sponsoring her and that I met James Kandee and persuaded him to fly me here secretly in his Gulfstream. I told her that I was going back in a few hours, I didn't even have a passport with me so I couldn't be here officially, but I'd just wanted so badly to see her, to make things right between us. And then we opened up about how we both felt. Finally. How we *really* felt. We worked our way through two full pots of tea and a packet of digestive biscuits. I tried to explain the betrayal I felt, her leaving me alone in London. She opened up about how suffocated she was and how she needed two years just to be herself. How Mum and Dad were so focused on me they pretty much ignored her. We didn't cry but we talked and talked. We were exhausted. So I suggested we do what we did as children, as young teens even. I suggested we take a power nap before dinner with our parents.

The woman opposite gets off at Harlem 125th Street and the train trundles on towards Grand Central.

As kids we'd sleep in single beds in the same room. But at five or six years old we started to take naps at the same time. They'd often be just twenty minutes long, that's all. We got tired at the same time every day, so the synchronised naps worked well. We both fell asleep quickly if we were in the same room and we both woke up together. So, at age twenty-two, we took another power nap. The talking, the honesty, it had all been so tiring. KT told me to take the bed and she'd take the sofa. I insisted she take the bed and I take the sofa. She made it up for me with a tartan blanket and a pillow. She closed the window shutters and got into bed. We both fell asleep in minutes.

Only I didn't fall asleep.

Because sleep wasn't part of my plan.

I waited another ten minutes so she'd be in deep sleep. I know her patterns off by heart because they are also my patterns. Her breathing slows the way mine does. She sleeps on her back the same way I do. Her face is turned to the left side to start with, just as mine is. She sleeps with her arms down by her sides under the covers the way I do. So when I crept over to the bed and straddled her holding the pillow she'd lent me, she was pinned down by her own sheet. Her arms were underneath my weight. She tried to move them as she woke and saw me, felt me. But my knees dug into her armpits just as Martinez described. She fought me and I didn't want that, I wanted a peaceful sleep for her. She's strong and she tried to wrestle me off but by the time the pillow had been tight against her mouth and nose for a minute or so the fight was leaving her exactly as I had researched. The carbon dioxide poisoning starts to kick in. Consciousness weakens. She went limp. And then she fought back one last time, thrashing with her feet and hands but she couldn't move. We're equal weight and almost equal strength and I was on top of her and she was under the sheet. Weakened. I couldn't hear her words through the pillow, just a dull, distant scream. And then she went quiet.

I disembark the train at Grand Central and walk west towards my hotel.

That afternoon I'd breathed a sigh of relief, the pillow still covering her face, me standing three feet or so away, coming to terms with it all. I steadied myself and then removed the pillow. There are times as a twin when seeing your sibling is a shock. Most times it's not, it's perfectly normal, but once a year maybe there is something inexplicably unsettling about seeing yourself away from your own body. One time I saw my twin wearing a dress I'd also bought, unbeknownst to her, and the shock of seeing what it would *actually* look like on me shook me to my core. You see yourself in a dress through the mirror in a store and that's one thing. You never get to see a full three-sixty of how it fits your hips or how your legs really look. That night I saw her face. I closed her eyelids, my fingertips covered the whole time because, although our DNA is practically identical, our prints are not. I straightened her sheets. I placed the blanket on her bed and the pillow back with hers. The room was quiet and dark, slivers of streetlight meeting her cheek from the slats of the window shutters. I knelt at her bedside and I told her I loved her.

34

I walk from Grand Central to the park. I find a quiet place away from all the tourist hot-spots – the lake, the fountain, the zoo, the rink – and, using my bag as a shield, I slip off my wig and hat. Then I unpick the hem of my skirt until it's down to my ankles.

Nobody ever tells you how fast you'll become accustomed to luxury.

I walk into the Ritz-Carlton.

Serious luxury, I mean. I'd have been ecstatic with a superior double in a four-star business hotel. But this. That incredible double-window panorama of the park. My bathroom is the size of an average living room, with a tub that fills in about a minute and a shower that makes me want to stay in there all day long. I open the door and climb in. All the complimentary toiletries are Asprey, a brand I've never heard of, but now I'm not sure I can live without them. Maybe, with almost fifty thousand in cash, I won't need to.

I let the water heat the back of my neck. My mind wanders. To Scott Sbarra. What he's doing right now. Who he's with. What he smells like and if he feels guilty about our 'date'.

After an hour I slip out of the hotel and head down Sixth Avenue clutching the Faraday bag with my two phones within. Luckily my room is available again in the Bedfordshire Midtown Hostel, so I pay up front in cash for six nights. I leave, and take out both phones. I'll appear on cell tower maps now. I'm traceable. I have a register.

Two messages from Mum. One is a photo of her, taken by Dad, sitting on the floor of our living room outside Nottingham surrounded by photo albums. Her eyes are red and wet but she's smiling. In her hand is a photo taken at school the week we turned six. Matching outfits, matching pigtails, matching poses. The other message is her asking if I'm OK and if I'm eating. If I have enough warm clothes.

At 46th Street I head west a couple of blocks.

Three missed calls.

One from Martinez.

I call him back and he picks up on the second ring.

'You OK, Molly?'

'I'm fine, thanks.'

'OK, that's good. Listen, we may have a significant breakthrough on the case. We've had a witness come forward, a reliable one from what I've seen.'

I stop walking and two people bump into me and one of them turns and says, 'Watch it.'

My temples throb. 'What's the lead?'

Don't say it's me. Do not say you want me to come down to the precinct.

'I can't say just yet but I'm working on getting a slot on *Crimestoppers* tonight, on network TV. High dollar reward for information, the works. I wanted to let you know that we're working round the clock here, Molly. I give you my word.'

'Thank you.'

'Your parents OK?'

'Yes, they're back home now.'

'When are you flying back to England? Soon?'

'Next week.'

'Right. I'll text you with the details of the *Crimestoppers* show if it comes off. No promises, but I pulled a few strings, called in a favour, you know.'

'I'll watch it in the hostel,' I say.

'You still in the Bedfordshire Midtown?'

'Yeah.'

'You take care, Molly. Any concerns or questions you call me, OK?'

I find a Starbucks but I choose not to go inside. Another block over there's a Dunkin' Donuts. I step inside.

Two hours later I've drunk three cups of coffee and one glass of bottled mineral water, and I've eaten two donuts. Four out of five things have been crossed off my mental to-do list. I've edited and pieced together all the stock footage, screenshots, Reddit posts and photographs I've collected relating to Shawn Bagby's incel past. It's not the violent misogyny that will ruin his reputation. It's not even the direct threats to women or the death threats made to so-called Chads. It's the snarky comments about his own followers. A loyal subscriber will forgive many things: a lack of uploads, poor audio quality, lapses of judgement, ethical mistakes, proven cruelty. But ridicule your own subscribers, the people who watch your vlogs day in, day out, who see the embedded adverts that pollute each clip, who put food on your table through ad revenue, and you are done for.

A man walks into Dunkin' Donuts. He looks more Californian than New Yorker. Baseball cap, board shorts, work boots, light grey V-neck shirt. I hear him order. He's Australian, not American. He has beach-tousled hair and the back of his neck is tanned deep brown. When he stretches to one side I see the V-cut of his lower abdominal muscles and I am entranced. That line. It reminds me of Scott. The area where his hip meets the side of his torso. The indentation.

I pick up my phone.

'Scott, it's me, Molly.'

He talks, but I can hardly understand because he's chewing something. He apologises for eating and talking.

'I want to see you again before I leave New York.'

'Sure, great idea.'

My breathing quickens.

'I don't think I'll ever be coming back, so I want to say goodbye. Have a night out, one to remember. Are you up for something like that?'

'I'm a student in New York City. I'm up for anything.'

'Tonight?'

I don't want to want him this way.

'No can do, sorry. I have this thing, see, with my study group.'

'Tomorrow night, then?'

'Tomorrow is Halloween, Molly.'

'I want to say goodbye to you *properly*,' I say. 'Fully.'

There's a pause on the line.

'Oh, I don't know,' he says. 'Just, with your sister and all. With Katie. I mean . . .'

'It's because of her that I want to see you, Scott.'

'Oh . . . I don't understand?'

'You're grieving, I know you are. I'm grieving as well. Being together . . .' I hush my voice and turn my face away from a teenage guy who's obviously eavesdropping. 'We should be together. One time before I fly away. I want to be with you.'

Another pause.

'Tomorrow night, then,' he says. 'I got a party on campus from midnight, but we could do dinner or something?'

I hush my voice even more. 'I have a hotel room,' I say.

He doesn't say anything.

'It'll be healing for both of us. Closure.'

'You still in the hostel?'

'No,' I say, thinking fast, back to the Harvard Club, that area. I can't take him back to the Ritz-Carlton. He can't see my suite, he'll ask too many questions. 'The Sofitel on 44th Street.'

Another pause. 'Time?'

'Eight-thirty sharp. Listen to me, though . . .'

'I'm listening.'

'You must not tell a soul, not even your best friend or rowing buddy. This is strictly between us. A one-off private thing. If I hear from Violet or anyone else in KT's circle that you've talked about this then I will not even show up. OK?'

'Yeah, of course.'

'OK. Pick up a key at Reception and make yourself comfortable in the room. You can get there any time from three p.m. I'll be there at eight sharp. You bring . . .'

'Who?'

'No,' I say. 'Bring, you know . . .'

'What?'

'Protec—'

'Oh, OK. Sure, yeah. Molly?'

'Yes.'

'Are we doing the right thing here? I mean, I really like you and all, but . . .'

'Healing,' I say. 'Healing is always the right thing.'

35

Tomorrow is for Scott.

But today is for Violet.

I need to experience one true night out in this city as a solo twin. If I'm to live a full life in the next twenty-four months, then I need to break out of my comfort zone. I'm not sure my sister made me anxious, but she definitely contributed. Even when we were kids she would play mind games. She treated it almost like a sport at times.

I need Violet for this. We need each other right now.

New clothes. Nothing crazy expensive or outlandish, but some classic KT style items. Bold designs. A top that reveals more of my back than I'd usually show. I buy them all from Bloomingdale's. I spend four hundred dollars in cash. James Kandee's cash. It feels good.

Violet's waiting outside the Ethel Barrymore Theatre wearing a red dress cut above the knee. She looks amazing.

'You know we're gonna run into all sorts of skeleton-pumpkin-ghost-bullshit tonight, right? Mainstream freaks out in force the day before the day. You know that, right?'

'I don't care,' I say. 'I just want to have a night to let loose in New York with a genuine local. Talk about KT some more, remember her the way she'd want to be remembered. Celebrate her before I fly back to my boring old life in London.'

We start walking downtown.

'She'd have loved your outfit,' says Violet.

'Oh, I know. It's more her than me, really.'

'You can pull it off,' she says. 'New York attitude is rubbing off on you, Molly Raven. Subway?'

That's a step too far. 'Not just yet. Sorry. Yellow cab?'

'Uber.'

I don't normally travel by Uber because I suspect they're not regulated to the same extent as traditional New York yellow cabs, but I agree to this compromise. A minute later a Toyota Prius pulls up and we climb inside the back. Could be anyone driving us. I check my seatbelt four times.

'Rooftop bar?' she asks.

'Erm . . . OK.'

The car stops and we travel up in the elevator to the fortieth floor. If there were a catastrophic fire, this kind of building would not fare well. It's too old to have a top-grade inbuilt sprinkler system; this place will have a retro-fitted version. And forty floors is a lot for a firefighter laden down with gear and oxygen tanks to climb up and rescue us. If there were a serious fire, I could imagine people jumping.

'What are you drinking, girl?' asks Violet.

Water.

Coke.

Or should I risk it?

'What are you having?' I ask.

'Espresso martini. I need the caffeine.'

'Make it two.'

'Yeah, you do!'

She orders the drinks and there's lots of shaking and mixer-theatrics. It's like being in a movie. Like the movie *Cocktail*, in fact. Tom Cruise and Bryan Brown. Our bartender is no Tom Cruise, but I can't deny I'm getting thrills from this place. The cool breeze. The bass thump of the music. The anticipation of tasting strong liquor. I had mouthwash yesterday. I've inadvertently licked some anti-bacterial gel. But this is the real deal.

'To Katie,' says Violet, lifting her triangular glass.

'To KT,' I say, raising mine, taking my first sip and making a face. 'People do this out of choice?'

Violet just laughs and leads me to a rattan sofa near the perimeter wall of the rooftop bar. Brazilian R&B plays from the speakers. People laugh and flirt all around us. 'Just drink it real slow,' she says. 'We're not racing here.'

Two guys approach us and Violet shakes her head. They leave.

'I don't mind,' I say. 'It's my first time in a rooftop bar. My first martini. Tonight is my last big night out before I'm normal quiet Molly Raven again in Camden Town. Let the boys in.'

'One of them had short trousers – like, not ironically short, just clueless short. When the *men* arrive I'll let them through, but those two? No, Molly. No way.'

She finishes her drink in half an hour. Takes me forty-five minutes.

'Club or bar?' she says, getting up.

'Expensive club,' I say. 'The kind you see in music videos. With table service.'

'Well out of our budget I'm afraid, Molly. I only have fifty bucks left.'

'I'm paying,' I say.

She frowns.

'A loan came through from my bank in London,' I lie. 'We can afford it, tonight. Whatever we want.'

'That's what you think,' she says. 'But this is New York.'

'Expensive club,' I say firmly. 'I'm in your hands.'

We get an Uber to the Black Flamingo in Williamsburg and she tells me all about the counselling and treatment she received in the Catskills. How she's learning to trust people again now. Then we hit the Blond, GoldBar and Marquee all before two a.m. I try to drink lots of water to stay conscious. Then we enter the Flying Hippo and that's the last thing I remember.

I wake up in my hotel room.

My eyes are crusted together.

I feel dreadful. I reach over for a glass of water and find Violet there. We're both fully dressed. She wakes up and we stare at each other for a while and then she laughs.

'Great night,' she says. 'Those three guys, fuck.'

I have no recollection of three guys.

'This place, Molly. What is this, the Plaza? What kind of loan did you get?'

She sits up in bed and rubs her eyes.

'Place is bigger than my mom's house.' She swings her legs off the side of the bed and focuses on something by the bedside table. 'The Ritz-Carlton, Molly? Fuck me.'

I look at the view through the gap in the curtains and then I check the time. Just past ten a.m.

'I need to get on,' I say, my heart racing from all the alcohol and caffeine. 'I have plans today.'

'You got time for breakfast? How the hell do you afford this place?'

I scold myself for being so reckless. So stupid.

'It's just for one night. Last night, I mean. This place. Just for our big adventure. I'm back in the good old Bedfordshire Midtown tonight. I know it's stupid, a waste of money, but I had to say goodbye to KT's city this way. With her best friend, fancy hotel, the works.'

'Good for you. I need the bathroom.'

She stands up and I point to the door for the bathroom.

And then I remember what she told me last night in the Uber back to the hotel. Did she really share that, or am I imagining it? My head pounds, the pulse throbbing behind my eyes. No, she did say it. She actually apologised for it.

I hear a flush.

She told me, earlier this morning, how she and Scott slept together. How they had sex a few times before KT died. And how . . . I must be remembering it wrong. No, she did say it. She told me how they had sex *after* KT died, just last week. How it was like medicine or something. What's the phrase she used? *Like a Band-Aid.*

'Mind if I take a quick shower?' she says, emerging from the bathroom. 'You want to go get breakfast? I need a cigarette and then I could murder some pancakes.'

'I can't,' I say, and I can hear the coldness of my tone as the words leave my mouth. 'I'm too busy.'

And then I notice the stationery on the desk. Beautiful personalised stationery complete with the heading *Ms Violet Roseberry*.

'All right,' she says, frowning. 'Just a shower, then?'

I sprint across the room so I'm standing in front of the desk.

Keep calm.

'I think you should leave now.'

'Molly, I need a fucking shower,' she says, frowning. 'The state of me. I'll be five minutes, tops.'

'Please, Violet,' I say, spreading my arms, trying to conceal the letter paper and envelopes. 'I don't feel well.'

She collects her coat and her bag. 'What happened?' she says. 'You OK, Molly?'

'I have a lot to do.'

'Fine,' she says. And then she leaves the room and I watch, through my peephole, as she trudges angrily down the corridor.

I breathe out. I order room service breakfast. I shower. I leave.

Reception gives me two Tylenol for my head and then I head out into the city. I have my phones in their protective bag and I have my unregistered tablet.

In a minimalist café in the Meat Packing District I upload my video to YouTube. I use fake Twitter and Instagram accounts to amplify the reach using the same hashtags Shawn Bagby uses. I'm careful to implement all I've learned in the past week to leverage the algorithm and get the video seen by his followers. Tags, the description, the title. You have to make the metadata do the hard work for you.

It's out there.

And now I walk away with a spring in my step. I'm going shopping again.

This time it's for tonight. I have six items I need to buy, six items on my mental checklist for my date.

Twenty minutes later I find the Victoria's Secret boutique on Fifth Avenue.

I walk inside.

36

By six I've thoroughly prepared for my date with Scott, every last detail. I'm hungover and tired. But I feel ready.

I take a long, hot, well-deserved bath. The bubbles overflow the tub and I soak and wash myself with lemon blossom shower gel. I shave and pluck and preen and thoroughly scrub myself, and then I slather my body with lotion.

Room service dinner. Something light because I don't want to feel bloated later. A chicken Caesar salad with a lime and ginger sorbet.

I go over everything in my head once again. I have never done this before, not even close. We went to discos together, my twin and me, but nothing like this.

The Sofitel superior room is booked and paid for in cash. The room's reserved under the name Scott Smith. The concierge at the Ritz-Carlton handled the reservation expertly, and I had to spend an extra two hundred dollars as a deposit to avoid any credit card details being handed over. I guess, if anyone ever checked, the breadcrumbs would connect the Sofitel room to Violet Roseberry, not me. It's important that nobody ever finds out about me and Scott. He might have checked in already. What's he thinking about?

How he'll seduce me? What he'll do to me? How he'll kiss me?

I pull on some of the items I bought today from three separate downtown stores. I have normal clothes, attractive but normal, covered with an ankle-length *Scream* costume and *Scream* mask. It's Halloween. It's vital that I fit in.

In the lift down to the ground floor I'm the only adult in costume. You might think that would be awkward but it's not awkward at all. You gain power when you wear a mask.

I take Sixth Avenue and walk south. I buy a single ticket at the Broadway Luxe movie theatre. I pay cash. I also get a box of popcorn and a large Coca-Cola with ice and a straw.

The Shining.

Two hours and twenty-six minutes.

My ticket's stamped and I say *thanks* in my best approximation of a New Jersey accent.

Inside there are only a dozen or so people seated. They're all in the middle of the middle of the auditorium or else they're down at the front. According to my Google research the larger crowds will come later at the nine o'clock showing of *The Exorcist*, and the midnight showing of *The Texas Chainsaw Massacre*, and the three a.m. showing of *The Blair Witch Project*. I sit at the back near the aisle. A few couples walk in and sit near the front. The lights go down. I eat a handful of popcorn and the kernels stick to my fingertips. Adverts play. I feel my heartbeat race. The thought of Scott Sbarra in a king-size bed. The shape of his body. The scent.

Trailers play and then the movie begins. When the sweeping shot of landscape appears – the Torrance family driving towards the Overlook Hotel – I carefully set down my Coke and popcorn, and then I walk quietly to the exit. Nobody sees me leave. I walk for twenty seconds and enter the ladies' restroom. Third stall, the one with the window, the one I've visited twice in the past week, always in a wig and hat. I take out my multi-tool and select the Phillips screwdriver. It's not easy loosening the screw but eventually I work it free. I open the window.

Someone comes into the ladies' and I stop dead.

After four minutes I hear a flush, and then running water in the basin, and then the blower, and then the door. I climb out of the window, scanning around for pedestrians. None. I drop five feet into an open dumpster, falling into the cardboard boxes I bought, constructed and placed in said dumpster earlier this afternoon.

I sit low, surrounded by dented cardboard and packing materials. My pulse is fast. I remove the eighteen-dollar *Scream* outfit and mask, and leave them inside one of the cardboard boxes along with my phone. Then, slowly, I raise my head above the metallic wall of the dumpster. Sirens, but no people, not in this alleyway. I climb out.

If you saw me walk to the Sofitel hotel you'd see someone in a white hazmat suit costume. You'd see a woman with red hair, another cheap souvenir-store wig just like the grey one I wore to Groot's house, this time covered with a plastic Nixon mask secured at the back with elastic. I pass Jimmy's cart, and the Bedfordshire Midtown Hostel. I pass the Algonquin and the Iroquois, and then I reach the Sofitel. I am getting turned on. The anticipation of Scott, his stubble, his sweat – but also the buzz in the evening air. Halloween. My skin is tingling and everyone is dressing up, ready to party. The city coming alive.

The entrance to the Sofitel is long and lined with sofas. Mood lighting, fireplaces and stacks of antique Louis Vuitton luggage. I wait for the lift. Elegant French tourists, not in costume, wait with me. They look at my mask but they do not comment. The doors open. I make a gesture of letting them all in, like I'm a grey-haired gentleman, as the mask might suggest, and they laugh and touch their keycard to the console and select floor seven. More people arrive and I hold the door open. They select floor seven and floor twenty-one. Then another guy says, 'Hold the elevator,' and steps in and says, 'Nine, please.'

I hit number nine.

We exit together, the man and me. He says, 'Have a nice evening, Mr President,' and I reply, 'Very good, thank you so much,' in the best New Jersey accent I can manage.

He leaves to find his room. Maybe he has the same plans for tonight as I do?

Probably not.

I hold back and then I follow the signs to Room 919, the room I booked earlier.

My heart is beating so hard I can feel it.

New lacy underwear, moisturised skin, shaved legs.

Beat, beat, beat, beat.

Deep breath.

I ring the buzzer and the door opens almost immediately. Has he been waiting by the peephole? I think so.

He's standing right in front of me wearing a Sofitel robe. I can see his chest muscles and I can see his stomach muscles. He has damp hair. He's holding a glass of whisky and he looks nervous and excited. When he sees the mask he smiles and gestures with his head for me to come in.

'Nice place you have here,' I say.

'Why, thank you,' he says, and then he drops his voice and whispers, 'You sure this is OK?'

I nod and take off the mask and then he pushes himself to me and tries to kiss me but I pull back. 'Easy, mister boatman. I'm not like those other girls.'

He snorts a laugh.

'Go and get all the towels from the bathroom and lay them on the bed.'

'What?' he says.

'Oils,' I say. 'I don't want to lose my deposit.'

He lays the towels on the bed and then he sits down on them, drink in hand.

I take my time removing my hazmat suit costume, and then I slip off my shoes and socks.

He watches my every move, sipping his whisky.

I walk over to him and stand between his open legs. I drag the cord slowly from his robe and hold it loose in my hands.

'We have the whole night,' I say. 'Check out at eleven a.m.'

'I was going to a party after this,' he says. 'I think I might have to cancel.'

He tries to place his hand at my waist and I shake my head. 'You wait your turn, boatman.'

He smiles and his teeth gleam at me.

I lean down so my lips are almost touching his earlobe and I breathe on to his skin. I don't say anything for a full thirty seconds; I just breathe him in and watch him breathe me in.

'Molly,' he says, his voice low.

'Shhh,' I say, and then I move my face so I'm directly in front of him and I look him straight in the eye and I push my mouth close to his. He lunges forward to kiss me but I lunge back, maintaining the smallest of gaps between us. His breathing is heavy now. The room is hot.

'Lie on the bed,' I say softly. 'Your head on the pillows.'

He complies. He doesn't ask any questions.

'You want Show A or you want Show B?'

His smile broadens. 'Fuck – Show A. You English girls.'

I approach him with the robe cord and tie it loosely around his head as an ineffective blindfold. He wolf-whistles.

I say, 'Safe word is Violet.'

'Safe word?' he says.

'You always need a safe word, boatman. Safety is paramount.'

He smiles and says, 'Be gentle with me, Molly.'

I take the paracord from my pocket and loop it around the bed posts and tie knots around his wrists in the formation I've practised thirty times before. They're loose and comfortable, the kind of thing you find in a Bondage for Beginners kit. Until, that is, you pull on them.

'We can't tell anyone about this,' I say, pushing my index finger to my lips and then dragging it across my lip, sliding my finger inside my mouth for a moment.

'Not a soul,' says Scott, trying to see me through the robe cord blindfold.

He is aroused.

I am aroused.

I take an ice cube from his whisky glass and run it down his chest and his navel, and then up to his neck and over his Adam's apple. I drag it across his lips and then I place it gently inside his mouth.

I remove a new pair of lace panties – paid for with cash – from the Ziploc bag inside my pocket, and I drag them lightly over his face and over his thighs, and then over his groin. He moans and starts to squirm. The paracord hand-ties tighten around his wrists. It's standard 550 paracord. It can hold five hundred and fifty pounds of weight. I'd say Scott weighs two hundred and twenty.

I push the panties across his lips and then I ball them up and push them inside his mouth.

He groans with anticipation.

I zip up my hazmat costume and pull the Nixon mask over my face and then I take my four-inch fixed-blade NYC-legal knife from my pocket.

And I drag the blade firmly across his throat.

37

Scott tenses up on the bed.

It's a horrible scene.

He is writhing, his eyes still covered, the panties still bunched in his mouth. The bed is red. Gurgling noises. The towels are red. I pick up a pillow and hold it to his neck and face. To stifle the noises, but also to give him some privacy in his final moments, some dignity. It takes minutes, just as it did with KT. It would be better if these things took seconds the way they do in movies, but in truth it's an ordeal for all concerned.

The amount of blood is considerable but I make an effort not to get too much on my costume or hands. After five minutes he is still, no pulse, but there's so much blood soaking into the towels, pooling on the sheets, that I have to arch my body to avoid it.

When it's over I step back and check the peephole. Nobody coming. In a hotel like this the rooms are extremely well soundproofed. This isn't a converted late-nineteenth-century building, it's purpose-built. Not a soul heard his muffled noises, his screams of *help* and *please* and *Violet* and *mommy*.

I check the time on the alarm clock and I'm two minutes ahead of schedule. I check the hall is clear and then I leave, careful to place the *Do Not Disturb* sign on the door. The room is fully paid for three days. With any luck, he'll be discovered when I'm already safely back in my flat in Camden living my same old predictable life.

You don't need a keycard to take a hotel lift down, only up. I press the button and the relief is overwhelming when the lift arrives and is empty. Some blood-splatter on my hazmat suit but it looks like red paint. It looks like I applied it. I ride down to the third floor and then it stops. My breathing quickens. A woman in a tiger-print mini-skirt steps in, her face painted to look like it's been ripped open, a zip revealing the fake flesh below.

'Oh, I love your outfit,' she says, staring forwards as the doors close. '*Point Break*? So practical as well, with the cold and all.'

We arrive at the ground floor.

'Happy Halloween,' I say in my best New Jersey accent.

And then I'm out on the street. I walk away from the hotel, west, back towards the Broadway Luxe cinema, and the exhilaration is grotesque. I am leaving that scene. Him. There. His wrists tied to the bed so firmly that his circulation would be cut off if he still had any.

I cross Sixth and walk on.

A mob of five zombies lift their arms in front of them and stagger towards me.

I go two blocks the wrong way then double back to the side street and the dumpster. Three minutes to make sure nobody followed me. Then I climb up inside and crouch down on the nest of boxes. I carefully remove my hazmat outfit and load it into a black garbage bag, and then place that into another bag full of food waste. I nestle the bag inside a bag under a dozen other identical bags. I collect my *Scream* outfit and put it back on. Then I use the boxes to help me climb back up to the window ledge, constantly vigilant for lovers sneaking down here to make out or men needing to relieve themselves. I check through the dirty, frosted glass to make sure the third stall is unoccupied. And then I push the window up gently and heave myself, my boot getting purchase on the lip of a line of bricks, and I step down on to the toilet seat. Quietly. I screw the window tight again with my multi-tool and then I remove my blue gloves and stow them inside my pocket. I considered cutting them into small pieces with the scissors on my multi-tool and flushing them down the toilet, but there's a risk it'd block. So I stow them and flush and open the door.

Nobody here.

I wash my hands and walk back to Screen Two.

Quietly I take my seat and pick up my popcorn and my soda.

Jack Nicholson is out in the snow, carrying his axe, hunting his family. I can't watch, it's too awful.

I count heads. Two more than when I left. Latecomers. But both sitting in the middle section. Nobody knows I left during the opening credits and nobody knows I returned. There are cameras near the tills, near the popcorn stands, near the main atrium. But not near the Screen Two restrooms. Not there.

It takes the entire last part of the movie for my heart to return to its usual rhythm. There are some things you must do for yourself, for survival, and dealing with my sister was one of those things. Then there are other things you do because they are the right thing, to restore balance, to right wrongs. Tonight wasn't so much about punishing Scott, even though he cheated on my twin. No, it's Violet who will be most cut up by this action.

Either because she loses the man she cared for.

Or because she gets arrested for his murder.

38

I don't walk back to my suite at the Ritz-Carlton.

First thing I do once the movie is over is make sure people see my *Scream* mask and costume, the one I stored in the dumpster. I made sure they noticed me when I came in before the movie and now I make sure they notice me when I leave. I was with them the whole time, sure, I was right here, *The Shining*, All Work and No Play, RedRum, all two hours and twenty-six minutes of it.

I know where all the cameras are and I make sure I get picked up on each one. I don't look up at them, nothing so obvious, but I walk slowly, with nobody immediately in front of me. When I exit out on to the street I head to Times Square, to the world-famous ticket booth.

The area is heaving with skeletons and ghosts and men in hockey masks. There's a dog dressed up like a demon and two babies in a walker, each one with a clown mask.

Dinner is Shake Shack and it is delicious. The queue is long and the restaurant is packed. When I'm done with my cheeseburger and fries and frozen custard I discreetly deposit my rubber gloves with my food carton in the garbage bins. This place, tonight, this many people – they'll fill a hundred black bags or more. There won't be any DNA in the dumpster bag because I used gloves at all times to handle the costume. Gloves to remove it from its packet, and gloves to put it on. There won't be any of my sweat on the costume because, although I didn't wear any underarm anti-perspirant – a measure to mitigate sweat from elsewhere – I did have extra-absorbent night-time sanitary towels taped under each armpit. That minimised any sweating from my forehead or neck, and made sure it was collected in the towels. I'm not a sweaty person anyway, far from it, but you need to take extra precautions. Before conducting a covert mission it's always prudent to scrub down. So that's what I did. I scrubbed down, scraping my skin, cleaning my nails thoroughly, clipping them short, violently brushing my hair, scouring my eyebrows and lashes. Those measures, combined with the sanitary towels, hazmat suit, mask, hat, wig, gloves and back-up liquid Band-Aid fingertips, should ensure there isn't any trace of my DNA in that hotel room. And if there is, well, then I have the argument that maybe KT slept with him there on a previous occasion. Can you imagine how many DNA samples are present in one Manhattan hotel room? I feel almost sick just thinking about it.

I want to walk home because I'm exhausted. The adrenaline's burnt away, leaving me tired and chilled.

I want to lock myself in my room and run a deep bath.

Instead I find a late-night electrical store near Madame Tussaud's. There are a few dozen people checking out tablets and phones and TVs. Text message from Martinez apologising for no *Crimestoppers* coverage of KT's case. Says a kid's missing and that took priority. I reply *OK, thanks*, and then I use my back to shield one of the wifi-connected display iPads, so the camera can't pick up the screen image. My *Scream* mask is still in place.

I load YouTube.

I search for my first ever video to see how it's doing.

39

I accidentally have 3.2 thousand subscribers.

The video has been viewed almost seven hundred thousand times in fifteen hours.

It has already been quoted, reviewed, critiqued, ripped apart and lauded by seven well-known YouTubers, each with over a hundred thousand subscribers. The #BagbyTroll hashtag has gone viral. The anonymous Gmail linked to my anonymous YouTube account has over three hundred messages in the inbox.

No response yet from Shawn Bagby. How will he recover from this? Will he ever recover? That's the thing about stars created by social media. The fans giveth, and the fans surely do taketh away. And there's not a single thing he can do about it.

I walk home, tired, treading over the obliterated remains of a jack-o'-lantern left out on 57th Street. The crowds have thinned and the morning light is starting to reveal itself.

Bath.

Bed.

I wake at eleven and order room service. Canadian bacon, free-range eggs, La Colombe coffee, orange juice with ice. It's nice that I can trust the ice. It's one less thing to worry about.

The wrongs, I realise, in the most part have now been righted.

I take a bite of crispy bacon and dip it into an egg until the yolk bursts. It's top quality. All the food here is top quality. It's not going to be easy adapting back to powdered soups and microwave meals. But I'll manage. There will be a period of post-Ritz adjustment and then I'll be fine. The forty-seven thousand, five hundred dollars I'm still in possession of should cushion the blow.

Nothing relevant on the news channels.

Maybe the story will break after I've left, just as it did last time. There is no better alibi than being halfway across the world. Of course, my alibi is weaker this time as I'm known to have been in Manhattan recently. It's not *as* perfect. But I have enough layers of subterfuge to hide what I did. I have layers *within* the layers. I was careful.

It was easier before because I wasn't in the system. When the police checked where I was on KT's death day, they would most probably, using their contacts and data, have seen that I'd never applied for, nor been issued, an ESTA visa waiver. They had no record of my fingerprints as I'd never travelled through US customs or immigration channels. They might, using their contacts in Europe, have ascertained that my passport had never once been used to cross an international border. I was one of many people who never leave their home country. I was in the UK on the day KT died. I didn't fly to New York privately then fly back to London then fly on a commercial airline back to New York. Nobody would do a thing like that.

The world outside is preparing itself for the New York marathon. There are signs up all around New York explaining which roads will be closed and at what times. There are colour-coded routes for élite runners and standard runners. I've decided to fly back the day after the marathon. Part of me wanted to leave earlier, today, to simplify things, to mitigate risk, but the view from my suite window is too scintillating to resist. I'll do what KT would have done. I'll live life. The telescope on my window ledge, combined with minibar and room service, means I have the best view of the twenty-six-mile-mark finishing line in all of New York. That's just too good a chance to give up.

Approximately one quarter of my cash is stashed behind a plug socket by my bed. I used my multi-tool to ease out the plug and then I inserted the roll of notes in the cavity before tightening it back up. One quarter is hidden beneath a piece of carpet, itself hidden and weighed down by my luxurious king-size bed. I sliced the carpet with a razor blade. It took considerable time and patience. The bump is almost imperceptible. You'd never notice it. One quarter is located inside a large torch I bought from Macy's. The torch has no batteries, just a roll of twelve thousand dollars in used bills. And the other quarter is on my person right now as I wander down Park Avenue. Some in each sock. More in my bra. Some concealed in a zip pocket inside my coat. I have sixty bucks in my main pocket in case I get attacked. You must always have mugger money.

I find the corner store I'm looking for, but there are too many people and I get a bad vibe from the place. I walk on past Madison and head west.

Past St Patrick's Cathedral, past Barnes & Noble, past Washington Square Park. This city has a grip on me. The next two years – my final two years, statistically speaking – living them out quietly but fruitfully, I'll think of this place often.

My phone rings.

'Molly Raven?'

'Molly, it's Detective Martinez. Listen, where are you right now?'

'What? I'm in the Village, I think. Greenwich, maybe, I'm not sure of the areas just yet.'

'I'm coming to pick you up.'

'What?' I start sweating, looking around for an exit. 'Why?'

'For your own protection, Molly, that's all. There's been an incident. I'll explain when I see you. Can you get to the corner of Seventh and 33rd, Penn Station? Can you get there?'

'Yeah, I can find it.'

I hear some banging. A door closing.

'Be there in thirty minutes.'

40

The unmarked car pulls up and the window winds down.

'Get in, Molly. I'll explain as we drive.'

I climb into the back seat of the car next to Martinez. His partner is in the driving seat.

'How are you holding up?'

'I'm OK. What's going on?'

'We're working hard on your sister's case, even though the *Crimestoppers* thing didn't happen. I'm sorry about that. There are a lot of moving parts to this.'

'Why did you pick me up?'

The partner takes a call as he drives and Martinez says, 'It's for your own protection. You can leave any time you want to. There've been developments.'

'What developments?'

He rubs his hand over the stubble on his jaw and says, 'Scott Sbarra, your late sister's boyfriend – he's been found dead in a hotel room.'

I cover my mouth with my hands. 'No!'

'I'm afraid so.' Already? Something's gone wrong. He shouldn't have been found yet.

The partner watches me in the rear-view mirror.

'What happened? Did he kill himself? Oh, God. He did, didn't he? Scott killed himself.'

'We don't know all the details just yet, Molly,' says Martinez. 'The crime scene is still being investigated. I can't tell you much, but I can tell you we're working on the basis that this was a homicide. And, as he and your sister were in a relationship, we're also assuming that these crimes are likely connected.'

'You mean . . .'

'There's a risk someone is here in the city with some kind of vendetta against Katie and Scott, and we don't know if that's the end of it or if they have anyone else in mind. We need to make sure you're safe. That's why we're here, especially as you look the same, you and Katie.'

'Do I need to get out of the city? Am I not safe in New York?'

'We'll make sure you're safe,' says Martinez. 'That's our job.'

'Scott's really dead?' I say.

'I'm afraid so.'

'Was he a suspect? You think he might have . . . to KT?'

Martinez clears his throat. 'Scott Sbarra was with someone else at the approximate time of your sister's death. His alibi wasn't rock-solid, but it was something.'

'OK.'

Violet Roseberry. He was with Violet. *Vi.*

We don't drive to the precinct, we drive to some other government building.

'Where are you taking me?'

'A safe place, Molly. Police property.'

Suddenly I'm afraid. What is going on here? Am I being naïve? The building has no police shield and it has no uniformed officer standing guard outside. There are no marked cars parked on the street. No sign that this is an official police building.

The car stops and shakes on its axle.

'Let's go,' says the partner.

We walk in through a door with a key-code lock, and through a corridor, up a flight of stairs and into an open-floor room. People are making calls, having meetings, drinking coffee, reading files.

'In here,' says Martinez.

We go into a small room with a table and a bin in the corner. There's a mirror on the wall and a camera mounted up near the ceiling.

'You want a water? Something hot?'

'Water, please.'

His partner leaves the room.

'Molly, where were you last night between eight and nine p.m.?'

'Where was *I*?'

He nods.

'I was at the cinema. Why?'

'Who were you with?'

'I was on my own.'

'On your own? You saw a movie all on your own?'

'Yeah, I always do.'

The partner walks back in and places a plastic cup of water down in front of me.

'Molly was at the movies last night. All on her own.'

'Really?' says the partner. 'All on your own, eh?'

'I saw *The Shining* at the Broadway Luxe in Midtown. It's close to my hostel. I didn't know what else to do, I don't really know anyone here.'

Martinez sniffs. 'That's OK, you're not under arrest or anything, relax, Molly. We're not interrogating you here. We just want to make sure you're safe is all.'

'Do you think I'm not safe here?'

The partner shrugs and looks at Martinez. Martinez says, 'I think you're safe but we want to make sure. You notice anyone following you, anyone photographing you, anything of that nature?'

I think about the man following me after the dinner with Scott. But I'm pretty sure that was DeLuca. 'I don't think so.' I sip the water.

'You had any contact with a Eugene Groot, professor of humanities at Columbia, your sister's teacher – you seen him or talked to him since you been here in the city?'

I swallow. 'We had dinner together one time.'

They both look at me but they don't say anything.

'At his club, the Harvard Club. He suggested it. But I didn't enjoy the dinner much. He was drinking a lot. I felt uncomfortable so I left early. You don't think he's responsible for Scott, do you?'

'We're keeping an open mind,' says the partner.

'Groot mention Scott Sbarra at the dinner, Molly?'

'I don't think so. Maybe, I'm not sure.'

Martinez scratches his chin and says, 'No hurry, have a good hard think. Try to remember if Groot mentioned him in any way, even indirectly.'

The room falls silent. I glance up at the camera and then down at my hands. 'I don't know, detective – I'm telling you the truth. I'm just not sure. He didn't talk about him much, at least.'

'But he did a little?' says Martinez. 'What did he say, you remember?'

I shake my head. 'It was such a weird dinner.'

'How so, Molly?'

'I'm not used to those places – private clubs. Just felt out of my depth. And then he started drinking too much, expensive wine, you know. He . . . I don't know, it was like he was flirting with me at the end. Not even flirting, just coming on strong. He told me they had rooms upstairs for members. How I looked like KT. So I left. I didn't feel at ease. But I did get the impression he disliked Scott. He did seem to snarl a little when his name came up.'

'Snarl?'

'A little. Some hostility.'

'You know anyone else connected to both your sister and Scott Sbarra, Molly? Can you think of anyone, besides Groot, who knew them both?'

I shake my head doubtfully.

'Nobody?' says the detective, moving a biro around between his fingers.

'Well, there's Violet, I guess. You think she might be in danger as well? Oh, God, we need to call her.'

'I'll take care of it,' says Martinez, calmly. 'Anything else you can think of? Something Katie told you on the phone earlier in the summertime? Anything she wrote you? About someone threatening her and Scott, about someone jealous, someone angry at them?'

'I think I told you everything already,' I say.

'Think on it some more – you'd be amazed what people remember when they really try,' says the partner.

So, I try.

'No,' I say.

'Nothing?' says Martinez.

'Well, there's the guy living in her building, I guess. Shawn. He always seemed a little off to KT, like he was angry at the world. She was concerned about him the first few months she lived there but nothing ever happened. Not that I know about.'

'Shawn Bagby,' says Martinez.

'Lives in the basement. I've told you about him already. Looks like an athlete.'

'He have anything against Scott Sbarra you know about?' says the partner. 'Any grudges, fights, anything of that nature that Katie might have told you about?'

'No.'

'You think of any reason he could be angry with Scott?'

'Jealousy, maybe. He was infatuated with KT for a while. Used to slip notes under her door, leave flowers outside her apartment – freaked her out in the early days. But that all stopped. He might have been jealous of Scott.'

'Thanks, Molly,' says Martinez. 'You've been real helpful. Just so we know how long to keep a protective watch over you, make sure you're OK, when are you planning on travelling back to England? You booked your flight yet?'

'Day after tomorrow,' I say. 'But I can change my ticket if I need to. It's a flexible ticket. You need the details?'

'Sure, that would be useful,' says Martinez. 'I'm confident it'll be fine. We want you back to your normal life as soon as possible. We'll be in touch in the meantime if there's anything we're worried about. You call me if you notice anyone acting strange. You still in the Bedfordshire Midtown, right?'

'Yeah.'

'Good. Let me walk you out.'

We head out, and the partner doesn't say goodbye.

'What happened to Scott?' I ask. 'You say you think he was murdered?'

'Can't tell you much, Molly,' says Martinez. 'Seemed like a nice kid, real future ahead of him. Varsity athlete, excellent grade average. Hell of a shame.'

'I always heard stories about New York as a kid,' I say, stepping out into the sunlight of the street with Martinez. 'How dangerous it could be, gangs and drug dealers and organised crime. But I always thought they were exaggerations, you know? It really is dangerous here. It really is.'

'It's dangerous everywhere, Molly,' he says. 'It's not New York, it's *people.* Never underestimate the capabilities of a person, no matter how reasonable or normal they seem. It's not any particular city that's evil. It's the people who live there.'

41

Returning to my hotel room takes time because I have to check I'm not being followed. Every three or four blocks I take a walk into a fast food restaurant or a sunglasses shop, and leave via a different exit. I use ladies' bathrooms so men aren't able to follow me. If there are women following me then I'll lose them in the labyrinthine clothes sections of mid-price department stores, walking behind racks and into changing rooms, joining lines to pay, then taking the back street exits.

The Ritz-Carlton is my sanctuary, real or perceived. It's real in a way because nobody apart from James Kandee and his team, whose interests are almost completely aligned with my own, knows I'm staying here. I still pay for my single room at the Bedfordshire Midtown Hostel, and I still keep some of my belongings there. Each day I visit on my way to wherever I'm going and I make sure to move the sheets around. Sometimes I even dampen a towel and hang it on the rail next to my tourist poncho and my spare sweater.

When I get to my suite I feel hot. Not feverish, although this is similar. I'm hot because I've reached that mental tipping point where I've taken so many micro-steps to cover my tracks and throw people off the scent that it's exhausting to remember all the details. The human brain wants to forget these things. Grey matter excels at retaining useful facts, skills, memories attached to feelings and pleasant recollections; but logistical details are there to be deleted after they've been utilised. I work to go back methodically over my tracks – all the steps I have taken, times and dates, lies, contingencies – to reassure myself that I haven't made any errors, that I'm safe. Scott being found so quickly was not part of the plan. This will have consequences. So now I need to refocus. Redouble my attention. It's a coping mechanism I use to cool back down. Work through exactly how all the risks were countered. And then, after some time has passed, after I have reassured myself with facts and mental timelines, I start to feel almost normal again.

The TV news stations periodically mention the body of a twenty-two-year-old Columbia student found unresponsive in the Sofitel hotel on West 44th Street. I want to watch each and every bulletin but I ration myself. I slog through other shows, one on gardening, another on cooking, then a documentary on the Appalachian trail, and then a news show. I want to know what the newsreaders know, or at least what they think they know. The details they are sharing. But I can't simply listen to the news on a loop. Hotel rooms are well soundproofed, I know that now, but I'm still cautious of a maid or a neighbour listening in. *Why does that woman watch back-to-back news shows about the man who died in the Sofitel? Is that level of interest normal?* So I ration myself. It's a risk factor, albeit a slight one, so I manage it best I can.

After a long, hot bath, and an hour of in-room stretching and exercises facing the kaleidoscopic tones of Central Park, I set out into the world.

My instinct is to only walk the streets I have walked before. To visit a Starbucks because I've already been there, and because it's a chain that serves millions of customers each month so maybe it's more likely to be safe. But today I choose to walk the other way. I head towards Roosevelt Island, that needle-thin strip of land separating Manhattan Island from Queens. I find an independent coffee shop adjacent to a synagogue and I order a toasted panini and a hot chocolate.

My seat choice is optimal. At the rear, by an emergency exit; solid planter close by that I could use for concealment in the event of a gunfight.

I lied to Martinez.

I told him my British Airways single ticket to London Heathrow was flexible but it is not. It's the cheapest ticket available. Economy. I'm not sure why I lied. There was no upside to the lie, no plan. It isn't like me. It was irrational.

My last few experiences in New York City.

Maybe my last journey outside of the UK ever, although I do have fresh ambitions of visiting, in a low-key fashion, France and maybe Rome one day. Seeing the Mediterranean. And the buildings of Florence. The canals of Venice. There's a ticking clock inside my heart. Two years, more or less, until I join KT in the grave. Or in the urn. It might not be two years, of course, it might be two months. It might be two weeks. Statistics are statistics, nothing more. I'm sure the data is more relevant to twins who die from natural causes but I still can't shake the idea from my head. Twenty-four months. You can't plan your life according to a mean average, but you can let that probability guide you when making key decisions.

He's uploaded.

I take a long swig of hot chocolate and plug my earphones into my tablet. The café's wifi is excellent. Anonymous IP address, anonymous YouTube identity linked to an anonymous Gmail account created in another anonymous café on an anonymous no-contract tablet.

It's an apology video. Eight minutes long. Nine hundred thousand views and counting. Forty thousand likes and seven hundred dislikes. Over five hundred comments.

There he is, glassy-eyed, looking into the screen. The backdrop is a plain wall and the lighting is perfect, angled to highlight the line of his jaw and the sadness in his expression.

He's sorry for what he's done. He takes full responsibility. He says he owns it.

I roll my eyes and bite hard into my panini.

Shawn Bagby says he's not the boy as portrayed in the other video – my video; he's a man now, and he'll accept full responsibility. He's said that word twice already in the first ninety seconds. He says he's grown as a person. Grown? He says he was under the influence of prescription painkillers, an addiction he's beaten, a rehab process he's shared or possibly overshared in earlier videos. He says the medication was responsible for souring his world view for a time and making him depressed and negative. He says he's genuinely sorry for any hurt he has caused.

Well, Shawn Bagby, you're rather good at this, aren't you? You know exactly how to wrap your subscribers around your little finger.

He says life was tough when his father died ten years ago. What's this got to do with making fun of your fans and creating misogynistic content?

He says life can be cruel sometimes but you need to man up and face it head on, you need to alpha it out, you need to lead your pack even in the most trying of situations. *Alpha it out?* What does that even mean?

He finishes the video by suggesting that the anonymous person who made the attacks, who collated all the old deleted posts and sub-Reddits, is bitter and dangerous, and he would like to hold out a virtual olive branch and offer to pay for therapy, no strings attached.

My mouth falls open and a piece of tomato drops on to my plate.

How did he manage to do that? I mean, Professor Groot will get his comeuppance, Mrs Groot Esq. will surely see to that one way or the other. Scott paid dearly for his betrayal. And his demise means that Violet, though I haven't spoken to her yet, will most likely be distraught. The wrongs I unearthed here in New York have been righted. Order has been restored. Yet somehow, through some mastery, some slippery sleight of hand, Shawn Bagby has survived his ordeal. Not only survived, he has gained an extra thirteen thousand subscribers in the past twenty-four hours.

I'm not angry, I'm just surprised.

He did a bad thing and yet he thrives.

This will take some more work.

42

I walk south and my phone rings.

My screen tells me it's Violet.

'Hello,' I say, 'Molly Raven.'

She's crying.

'Hello,' I say. 'Who is this, please?'

'It's me,' she says. 'Haven't you heard?'

I turn to get a better view of the intersection. There's an armoured truck collecting money from a jeweller's.

'Yes, it's so awful,' I say. 'I can't believe it. I don't feel safe here any more. Who's doing this?'

'Some sick bastard,' she says, sniffing. 'Some sick fuck. God, I can't believe he's dead. I can't take it in, Molly.'

'Martinez told me they might not be related incidents,' I lie. 'Because the attacks were so different. One quiet and one ultra-violent. I don't know what to believe. This kind of thing doesn't happen in London.'

'Ultra-violent?' she says. 'He wouldn't tell me how Scott died but there are rumours at school. What did they say?'

'Nothing,' I say, startled. 'I just gleaned it from his demeanour. That it was violent. I don't think Scott died a good death, Violet. But I don't have any details.'

'Where are you right now?' she says.

I look at the street sign.

'Corner of 55th and Lexington. Where are you?'

'I'm in school. I don't want to go home, Molly. I don't want to go to work and I don't want to go home. Nowhere is safe.'

'You think you're in danger, Violet?'

She sighs and I hear her blow her nose. 'Maybe, I don't know. Maybe not. Who knows what to believe? They killed Scott, that's all I know. I heard it was some kind of BDSM thing gone wrong – guy at Columbia said he was found with his wrists tied to a bed. Some sicko.'

'What's BDSM?'

'You know, sadomasochism. He was into erotic asphyxiation, you remember I told you? Never tried it with me, but . . .'

'What did you say?'

'Nothing. Can we meet?'

'Sure. Somewhere near the library?'

'The Butler Library?'

'The Public Library,' I say.

'Oh, OK. Bryant Park? At four?'

'OK. Take care, Violet.'

'Yeah, you too.'

I haven't had lunch yet. I walk into Zuma with a strut in my step, and get guided to a table in the corner. A handsome guy in black brings me a menu and then he brings me a bottle of sparkling water that costs more than my average London lunch budget. Twice as much.

KT would have loved this place. I know I still need to be careful – but I also feel a strong urge to experience this life one last time. KT's life. It's balancing risks, it's always about balancing the risks. For these final hours in this city, surely I can risk being more like KT.

I let the server choose the dishes for me. All I say is I'm medium hungry, because that's true, and that I don't want puffer fish, because I read it's potentially fatal if it isn't handled properly. Especially the liver. I read that only the most experienced chefs in the world are qualified to prepare the delicacy. He says they don't offer it in the restaurant.

The food is sublime, each dish better than the last. My first taste is salmon sashimi, just tipping my toe in the water. This is the real deal: salmon so velvety and soft it melts on my tongue. It's not fishy. It's not cold and hard. It's divine.

My favourites are the eel, the yellowtail sashimi with jalapeño peppers and ponzu, and the black cod. I savour the flavours and the textures. Maybe KT ate good sushi a hundred times in her twenty-two years, in Aruba with James Kandee, in Paris with James Kandee, in Hong Kong with James Kandee, but she never experienced this. The undiluted joy of mono-dining at a quiet table during an off-peak lull; each mouthful a surprise and a delight. I am determined to fully enjoy this moment.

Dessert is green tea ice-cream. I pay, and tip the waiter thirty per cent, because he's outrageously attractive and he did a good job. Credit where credit is due.

I feel like KT when I walk to the New York Public Library and then wait in the centre of Bryant Park for Violet to appear. I feel cosmopolitan and cultured. Less afraid. Less of a perennial outsider.

There's construction work going on in the park. I find two green chairs, each one with a small table attached, and try to figure out what they're building. Someone talks about the marathon and someone else nearby talks about a Christmas market. Then the woman's husband corrects her, saying they're building an ice rink, same as they always do, it's a tradition like the big tree outside the Rockefeller Center.

Violet arrives and bursts into tears when she reaches me. I didn't expect this from her. Not because she didn't like Scott – I know all too well that she liked Scott very much – but because she's a hardened New Yorker, and because I never saw her cry like this for KT. There are people staring at us out of the corners of their eyes. She says, 'I'm sorry, it's just . . . shit, can we go somewhere?'

'Sure.'

We walk north and we do not speak. She loops her arm around mine and I like that. It's as if we're in a play or something.

'You want to talk in my room?' I ask.

'In the Ritz-Carlton?'

'Hardly! That was just for one night. No, I'm back in the hostel. Come up?'

She nods, and when we get there I unlock the door with my key and go inside. I glance at the door next to mine, wondering who's sleeping in Mum and Dad's bed. My room smells fusty.

Violet sits on the bed. There's a six-pack of bottled water under there, a back-up I bought in case my suite is compromised in some way. She says, 'Like . . . only a block away from here, in his hotel bed, murdered.'

'I know. It's utterly horrific.'

'I told the police there's a madman on the loose. A psychopath. Some guy killing Columbia students.'

'What did they say?'

'They said what you said. That there's a chance they may not be connected. Not connected? You believe that? A girl, and then her boyfriend? Same school? Of course they're fucking connected.'

'It's a nightmare.'

I'm still surprised his body was found so quickly. I'd expected him to be discovered after forty-eight hours, some manager or cleaning supervisor knocking on the door and yelling a warning, then opening the door. But within twelve hours? Did I forget something? No, I did not. The door sign was on, I know that. Maybe he bled out so much it dripped through the floor to the ceiling below? Scarlet raindrops. No, that's impossible. Not with all the towels and bedding. The smell? Even though I turned the air-con down to sixty Fahrenheit? There wouldn't have been any smell.

'What are you thinking about?' she says, opening her water bottle.

'My sister,' I lie.

'Oh, Molly, fuck, this is even worse for you, I know it is. I liked Scottie so much but this is much harder for you. Goddamn, I wasn't thinking, I'm sorry.'

'Grief isn't a competition,' I say. 'Mum told me that before she left for London. Saw it on *Dr Phil* or something.'

Violet smiles. 'I've talked to some friends, some people who knew Scott, and people who knew Katie, but those two mixed in such different circles, you know. Not many people were friends with them both. Talking to you, it helps make sense of it all.'

'There's no sense in any of this,' I say.

'Amen to that. I hope whoever did this rots in hell.'

'Oh, I think they probably will.'

'Scottie's parents are on their way down from Connecticut. His dad's not well as it is – heart arrhythmia and a pacemaker – so I'm not sure how they'll cope with all this.'

'Thank God they have each other,' I say. 'Mum and Dad have been supporting each other these past weeks. People talk about marriage being outdated, but my parents lean on each other for support. If they'd divorced years ago, as they almost did – money worries, you know – I don't think either one of them would have survived this.'

Violet looks away, over at the wall.

'What?' I ask.

'Not important,' she says.

'Tell me.'

'You talking about divorce reminded me. Professor Groot's wife served him with the paperwork this morning. Right there in front of his fucking class. Served him as cool as ice and then walked right out of the lecture. Groot could not believe his eyes.'

43

The hostel room is too narrow to sit and talk for long. Too tight. Airless. We step out on to the street and there's some kind of news crew: a woman with an umbrella held over her head, a guy holding a camera, another guy making sure pedestrians don't get too close.

Violet looks at me and I look at her.

'The Sofitel is right over there,' she says.

'I know.'

We walk a block to the diner and there are even more film crews. The police have taped off an area outside the hotel reception and there are two squad cars parked on the pavement.

We go inside the diner and it is warm and familiar. Zuma was nice and all, but I prefer this place.

'I'm not sure I can eat anything,' says Violet. 'I feel sick to my stomach.'

A waiter I don't recognise approaches and I say, 'Two coffees, please.'

'Coffee?' she says, shaking her head. 'Scottie's dead in a morgue and I'm drinking coffee. What the fuck, you know?'

'Are you going to talk to his parents when they get here?'

She takes a paper sachet of Sweet'n Low from the pot and flips it between her fingers. 'I don't know, I'm not sure. Maybe. I wasn't his girlfriend or anything so I don't know what to say to them, you know? Like, where the hell do I even start? I don't know what to think any more. Those poor people.'

'I wish I could go to the funeral,' I say. 'I know it sounds morbid or whatever, but attending KT's cremation, the service, the peacefulness of it all, coming to terms with the truth – it helped me. I think I'd have broken down if it wasn't for that goodbye. I think I'd have lived in denial of what really happened.'

'It helped? Really?'

'I mean, I'm still lost without her.' I shake my head. 'Honestly, it feels so alien not having her around, not knowing where she is. I know that doesn't make any sense but you understand what I mean.'

'Yeah.'

The coffees arrive.

'He seemed like a good guy, Scott,' I say.

Violet covers her eyes with her hands and takes a deep breath. 'He truly was,' she says. 'Everything ahead of him.'

'Life is short,' I say. 'I have learned that this month. Life is very short. You have to live it.'

She sips her coffee.

'How did Groot react?' I ask.

'What?'

'Your professor. How did he seem when his wife stormed in all furious and screaming angry.'

'Oh, no, she wasn't angry at all,' says Violet. 'She was calm and collected. A real pro. She served him divorce papers is all. At least that's what we assumed they were. It was a file of papers. She told him to find an attorney and she said if he returned to the family residence he'd be met by security. Then she walked away with her head held high.'

'He must have been devastated.'

'At least he still has his life,' she says. 'He can still live on, fix the mess, maybe. Reconcile, get couples counselling or whatever. It's not like Scottie. I keep expecting to get a WhatsApp from him, you know? A message about seeing a movie or getting a bagel in Wu + Nussbaum together after class.'

'What if the perpetrator is still in Manhattan?' I say.

'Who knows,' she says. 'Could be anywhere. Could be halfway across the world by now. Say, when are you flying back?'

'Day after tomorrow from JFK,' I say. 'I'm not looking forward to that flight one bit.'

She looks at me quizzically.

'The turbulence. Bird strike. Both pilots getting sick. Or maybe a hijack by some lunatic with an improvised weapon. A bomb in someone's luggage. A bolt failure in the wing. Engine fire. Multiple engine fires. Freak crosswinds. Some new strain of avian flu. Or Ebola, even. Mid-air collision. Crashing on take-off, crashing on landing. I don't like to think about it.'

She frowns and says, 'So swallow a Valium and don't fucking think about it.'

'I can't do that.'

'That's what your sister always did,' says Violet, smiling. 'I used to give her sleeping pills every time she flew to some fancy vintage car rally or art auction someplace. She'd doze all the way there on the jet, and all the way back. Used to wash them down with fine champagne. She knew how to live, your sister.'

'She really did.'

'I'm gonna miss you, Molly.'

'Same. I'm glad KT had you as a friend.'

'You mind if I get in touch if I ever get my bank account healthy enough to visit London?'

'I'd probably kill you if you didn't.'

'You'll take me to Buckingham Palace, eh?'

'Where else?'

We're too sore to laugh, too sad to smile much. We drink our coffees and get refills. I get a call from Mum but I don't take it. She calls back three times, so I apologise to Violet and accept it. 'Mum, I can't talk. I'm with Violet.'

'Did you hear about Katie's friend Scott? They murdered him.'

'I know, Mum. That's why we're talking right now. Violet's really upset.'

'You have to come home, sweetie. I mean it. Call the airline up, they'll put you on an earlier flight, just explain all this. You need to get back to England now, where it's safe.'

'I'm coming home, Mum. The day after tomorrow. I need to tie up some loose ends but I'll be really cautious, I promise.'

She starts getting flustered on the phone, talking about asking for police protection. 'Violet's with me,' I say. 'I'm safe. I'm not alone.'

We end the call. Violet pays and then we step out into the street.

Jimmy waves from his food cart and I try to ignore him.

'That guy wants to talk to you, the guy in the smoothie cart.'

I wave at him and then start walking the other way with Violet. He shouts, 'Molly, come over here.'

'We should go over, no?' says Violet.

I nod, reluctantly. 'He's a nice guy. I buy smoothies from him.' We turn and walk to his cart.

'You heard, eh? In the French hotel.' He makes a gesture dragging his index finger from ear to ear and Violet bends over double at that image.

'Jimmy . . .' I say.

'I'm sorry,' he says. 'Poor kid.'

'This is someone who knew him. I mean, I knew him a little, but she knew him pretty well.'

'I'm really sorry, lady. I apologise. I didn't know.'

'It's all right,' says Violet, straightening up. 'Not your fault, man.'

'I didn't know,' he says again. 'It's getting like the old days round here. Bad for business, y'know, the marathon and all, busy times, I'm sorry, none of that's important right now, I'm sorry. Say, Molly, there's a guy been asking after you, asking if I'd seen you around.'

'A guy? What guy?' Bogart DeLuca? Martinez?

'Man around fifty, maybe fifty-five. Real fit-looking, you know, the athlete type, real lean. Wire-rim glasses. He was asking if I'd seen you go into the hostel.'

'And what did you tell him, Jimmy?'

'I told him I didn't know what he was talking about. I said if he didn't want to buy a smoothie maybe he could move aside for a real customer. Don't worry, I didn't tell him a thing.'

44

I'm sitting on my bed in my junior suite reading the Ritz-Carlton *Things You Must Do In New York* book. I have a Ritz-Carlton pen and a hotel pad. I'm drinking Ritz-Carlton mineral water and I'm wearing a Ritz-Carlton robe.

Apparently I must see twenty different things before I leave this place to return to my normal existence. Nine of the twenty I've actually done. That leaves eleven.

I must visit the Met, or the Museum of Modern Arts. Next is Top of the Rock, the viewing gallery of the Rockefeller Center, or the Observatory at One World Trade Center. The views look spectacular.

Brooklyn Bridge, Staten Island Ferry, Statue of Liberty. All tourist hot spots with all the risks that entails: pickpockets, terrorists, muggers. But on the plus side they're all free.

The Highline. Also free. Coney Island. Again, free. A Broadway show. Very much *not* free, but they're close by and if it wasn't marathon week I'd probably try to get a ticket. The concierge here could help me get great seats but I'd rather not talk to him again because I read in a book they sometimes give tip-offs to law enforcement. Ballet at the Lincoln Center. Same problem.

There are some less obvious options: a speakeasy bar in some Lower East Side basement. Performing Arts in Bushwick, Brooklyn.

The thing is: money.

Money is often, in my experience, the thing.

I have it now for the first time in my life. Even after making a few extravagant purchases there's still over forty-seven thousand American dollars left. And if it was just me in this world, operating in a vacuum, I'd hit Bloomingdale's and see a Broadway show and I'd maybe take a helicopter tour up and down the Hudson. No, I wouldn't go that far. You climb in a helicopter and you may as well be riding a motorbike. Both are statistical death traps.

But Mum and Dad are as good as bankrupt. KT's insurance policy won't pay out quickly enough to save them, and even then it wouldn't cover their debts. They have no business any more, and, even though they managed to pay off some of their creditors through voluntary agreements these past years, they don't have much goodwill in the community. No outside family to speak of apart from Mum's sister, and they haven't had an easy relationship since Grandma died.

So it falls to me. I can't afford to keep them in our childhood home, but I can afford to help them rent a flat above a fish and chip shop or something. I can help them buy cereal and pasta. Beans and loaves of bread. My dollars, converted through multiple innocuous currency exchange centres in the Midlands – by them, not me – will see them through. I'm all they've got now, and they're all I've got. I don't begrudge them a penny.

Outside my window, down in the park, officials in fluorescent tunics are swarming, making sure the finish line is prepared. Who was the man asking Jimmy about me? Another cop? Or a journalist, maybe? Through the telescope I watch them stack multi-packs of water on, and underneath, fold-up tables. There are hundreds of boxes of space blankets: silver foil wrappers to keep exhausted runners from catching hypothermia. It's a real risk this time of year after so much exertion. It can kill a fit person stone dead.

What would KT do if this were her last day in New York? Her last *ever* day in New York? She'd probably spend all the cash, blow through it all. She was always more carefree with her expenses. Maybe she'd buy a pair of calfskin boots from a Fifth Avenue boutique, or dine out with a bunch of friends in the Tavern on the Green. That's what she'd do; she'd get together with four or five friends and they'd have a long boozy lunch. But I choose sobriety, thank you. I need to be on my guard until I'm safely back at Heathrow. For the next two years I need to live my life, travelling and experiencing things, while also staying on my guard. I need to balance those two things.

I choose a walk in the Upper East Side.

It's picturesque. The cool people might hang out in Williamsburg or East Harlem, they may favour some hip new place in Corona, Queens, but the streets above 59th, east of the park and west of Second Avenue, are a haven for the risk-averse. Quiet, clean blocks with not a single dangerous-looking tenement or street corner. Women in long coats and doormen with hats. It's not cutting-edge here, it's sterile and sanitised.

My phone rings.

'Molly, I don't know who to call. It's the police, the cops.'

'Slow down, Violet, I can't hear you. What's wrong?'

'They want to talk to me. Oh, God, about Scottie; they want to interview me or something. Do I need a lawyer or will that look bad? Would you hire a lawyer? How do I do this?'

'You don't need to be afraid,' I say. 'They've already talked to me. They're just trying to figure out who was where, who was doing what. They're looking for clues is all.'

'I have no alibi, Molly. I have nothing.'

'You probably do, you just don't know it. You go to a corner shop – sorry, a *bodega*? Did you leave to buy milk or something? You see a neighbour? A takeaway delivery driver?'

'No.' Her voice is strained. 'That's what I'm trying to tell you. Shit, I was home all night like I always am on Halloween. That shit freaks me out. I was home on my own. I ate frozen pizza and re-watched *Gattaca*. Read for an hour or so. They're not going to believe me, are they? They'll arrest me, right? Charge me?'

'Calm down,' I say. 'Take a deep breath, I'm serious.'

'*I'm* serious,' she says. 'The police sounded very fucking serious.'

'If they thought you'd killed Scott they would have turned up in a car and arrested you. You're a witness, someone with information, that's all.'

'You're right!' she says, her voice lifting. 'Of course you're right, Molly. I know you're right. Jesus, they'd have cuffed me by now if they thought I'd murdered him. Yes? Of course, you're right. What would I do without you? I'm such a dummy.'

'You feel better now?'

I head north past 66th Street. The houses are grand up here.

'A little,' she says, sighing. 'A little better. When's your flight tomorrow, Molly? I want to come to the airport and say goodbye.'

'Come out to JFK? You don't have to do that. You're sweet.'

'I want to, really. If you don't think I'll ever see you again, well, I'd like to wave you goodbye is all.'

'I'll get there around six.'

'What terminal?'

'I don't know. I'll text you it . . . but you really don't need to come.'

'I know I don't need to, I want to.'

'That's really nice. Oh, and Violet . . .'

'Yeah?'

'If you feel uncomfortable when they're questioning you, just ask for a lawyer. They'll stop and appoint one for you. They have to, it's the rules. You can do this.'

We say goodbye.

They might question her about Scott's murder but they won't charge her. There's no risk she'll be convicted. Beads of sweat run down my back. Maybe I did too much, too fast? I should have slowed down and been more methodical. I look up to the sky and take a deep breath. If I'd wanted her charged I'd have plucked a hair from her head when she was asleep in my Ritz-Carlton bed, root and all, and I'd have planted it in the Sofitel room. Or maybe I'd have offered her a bottle of water – she was hungover so she'd have taken it – and then placed that in the Sofitel. To be honest I considered both options. But then I decided it would be grossly disproportionate. The right must fit the wrong. Balance is necessary – nature abhors imbalances. Violet lost Scott, and that was sufficient. More than that would have been unconscionable.

I cross Park Avenue and on towards the children's zoo in Central Park. I need to be careful. There are road barricades and volunteers everywhere, preparing for the first runners to come through.

A van drives ahead of me, then indicates and slowly pulls over.

The doors at the rear of the van push open.

It's a man in a dark suit.

Inside his jacket I see his hand resting on a gun.

45

I turn to run the other way and he says, 'DeLuca sent me.'

I face him.

'Bogart DeLuca sent me, Molly.'

I look at his gun and he closes his jacket.

'Listen. Walk two blocks south, that way. Guy on the ground.' He reaches out to pull the van doors shut and then he says, 'You should go now.'

What is this? I'm at the intersection. I can run east to the river, west to the park, north towards Yorkville. But I head south. My senses are on high alert. Why didn't he just call me if he wanted me? Leave a message at the hotel?

Guy on the ground? What does that even mean? James Kandee and I have ways to communicate, codes rooted in the language KT and I used as kids, but *guy on the ground* doesn't make any sense to me.

I pass by a building covered in scaffolding and past a homeless guy with a paper cup.

'It's me,' says the guy.

I turn back.

'Come closer,' he says.

'Bogart?' I say. 'Or is it Peter Hill?'

'Bogart.'

'What happened to you?'

'Come closer and squat down,' he says through gritted teeth. His skin is dirty and his clothes are torn. 'Come close.'

I squat down.

'Put money in the cup, Molly.'

I put a dollar bill in the cup.

'You need to get out. It's not safe here for you no more.' His Brooklyn accent is back.

'What do you mean?'

'What I said. You need to leave.'

'I'm flying home tomorrow,' I say. 'Is it the guy who murdered Scott? You think I'm in danger?'

He looks at me with an impatient, disappointed expression and says, 'The picture, Molly. My contacts found out earlier today. The damn picture.'

I shrug.

A couple walk close and Bogart says, 'Just a coupla dollars for a shelter, lady. God bless you.' They pass on by.

'Picture?'

DeLuca looks left and right. 'Picture of Katie outside the professor's house out near Rye. That ring any bells?'

I try not to change my expression.

'Lawyers are involved. Smart, expensive lawyers. That picture was scrutinised, and, even though it was just Polaroid, they noticed it.'

Shit.

'I don't know what you're talking about, Bogart.'

'Yeah, you do.'

'I need to leave.'

'The pumpkin, Molly. You took your sexy photo in his garden and you burnt the rest but in the background of the shot there's a very noticeable pumpkin. A jack-o'-lantern. It isn't real clear with the naked eye but once the image is cleaned up, zoomed in, expensive software . . . bam, there it is.'

'I don't know what you mean?'

'What I mean is that Mrs Professor Groot was pretty confused when her legal team told her this piece of information, owing to the fact that the Groots only carved and placed out their organic Wholefoods pumpkin two days earlier. Meaning Katie was already dead. Meaning it was actually *you* who went into their garden, Molly, up in Greenhaven, real nice area, and you took the photos pretending to be Katie, and dated them, and burnt most of them. It means, Molly, that the professor and his wife took the matter straight to the cops. Their divorce isn't happening no more but you can be damn sure Martinez is on your case. It doesn't look good. What the hell were you thinking?'

'I . . . I don't know, I was – I'm in shock still. You know? PTSD or whatever. I wasn't thinking straight.'

How could I have been so reckless? I thought I could pull this off. I'm useless. My God. And Kandee seems more powerful than I thought. He finds out everything.

'I thought he hurt my sister,' I say, blurting out the words. 'Maybe he killed her. The police weren't making any progress and I wanted to see him hurt.'

'Martinez is gonna grill you real good,' he says.

'Why did you book my suite in Violet's name?'

'What?'

'Why did you do that?'

'We don't have time.'

'Why?'

'One of a hundred tactics to delay, stall, throw shade, mask the scent. Same as why I switched to the name Peter Hill in the park that time. Lip-readers, bugs, covert surveillance. You have to assume someone's always on your tail. It's part of a larger strategy which you have now wrecked. Now listen carefully. You have to leave today, Molly.'

'OK,' I say. 'OK, I get it. I'll leave.'

'Give me your phone.'

'What? Why?'

'You know why.'

'I'll keep it in the Faraday bag. I promise.'

'I'm not asking, I'm telling.'

'I need to get back to my room. I need all my stuff. I'll go back to the hotel and pack and stay somewhere else tonight.'

'We don't know if your room's compromised. Assume it is.'

'A pumpkin?' I say.

'Yeah, a pumpkin.'

He holds out his hand and I give him my phone.

'And the other one.'

I look around and then I give him my burner.

'You got two choices, and you're lucky you got two. In some ways your interests are lined up with The Man's interests, otherwise . . .'

'What are they?'

'One. Listen close. You leave at two o'clock, that's what Katie would have said, you understanding me clear?'

'Two o'clock,' I repeat.

'That's what your sister would have said, you get me? Might have lip-readers watching us right now. We just don't know. Two a.m., as Katie would have said.'

He means eight o'clock. The opposite side of the clock. Eight p.m.

'I understand completely.'

'OK, two o'clock. Leaving by sea. 31st Street usual. You got that?'

'Yeah.'

'You understand what I'm saying: like your sister would have told you.'

'I'll remember it.'

'What street?'

'31st Street usual.'

'OK, Molly. The Man will take care of the rest, you understand?'

My legs are aching from crouching down for so long. 'What's the second option?'

'You don't turn up, and then The Man sends a clean-up team to go pay a visit to your parents in Nottinghamshire. You don't want that, do you, Molly?'

'I'll be at 31st. Two o'clock.'

'You mind you are.'

'Let my parents know I may be out of touch for a while? That I'm OK? Not to worry?'

'Sure.'

'OK, I need to go and pack. Get my stuff. Thank you, Bogart.'

'Don't thank me yet. And there's no packing your stuff, Molly. The room might be compromised. Watched. You leave with the clothes on your back. That's all you got.'

'No,' I say. 'No, I need to go back, I'll make sure it's safe first. I have . . .' I lower my voice. '. . . nearly forty thousand in the room.'

'In the safe?'

'No, not in the safe.'

'Tell me where it is and I'll send a guy I know. Give me your key.'

'Is this some kind of trap?'

'Yeah, it's the kind of trap where we save your ass. The key.'

I hand him the key. 'Some of it's behind an electrical socket so he'll need a screwdriver. Some is under the bed – I sliced a piece of carpet and hid it underneath. The rest is in a torch.'

'Like a flashlight?'

I nod. He looks at me like I'm crazy.

'What?' I ask.

'Nothing. Listen to me: watch your back, don't go to any of your usual places, don't even think about visiting the professor over at Columbia or any such shit. Do not seek out Violet and do not visit your sister's apartment, is that clear?'

'It is.'

'I mean it, Molly. You got one shot at out and you're lucky you even got that.'

'I'll lie low. It's not long.'

'Don't get followed, stay away from cameras, stay away from the TV crews and people filming near the marathon route. Stay low-key and meet us in the agreed place. You got it?'

'I got it.'

46

The van drives away slowly.

I need to blend in, to hide, to keep my head down until two o'clock. Which is eight p.m. in the real world. The police might be expecting me at the hostel. No. It's too obvious. They know I won't go back there. If DeLuca's right and they know about my junior suite then I should probably stay well away from the Ritz-Carlton. I have to assume the authorities have connected some of the dots already, and I have to trust DeLuca will collect my cash. My gut says if they can't gain access to retrieve my money they'll reimburse me. I have to believe that's true.

A man passes by me. He's wearing an aluminium foil poncho and he's drinking Gatorade. He's an early finisher, I guess.

The park is full of spectators filming on their phones. I walk over towards the West Drive and the finishing line area is cordoned off, staffed with hundreds of volunteers and dozens of police. My first instinct is to flee but my second instinct is to wait a while. Sometimes your gut needs some time to work things through.

After thirty minutes the slower élite runners are finishing.

After an hour the first people in fancy dress start to come through. The park is full of families celebrating with their loved ones. A man walks past me with blood-stains running down from his nipples, his shirt attracting shocked glances from children and adults alike.

Close to the lake, near the Bethesda Fountain, I pick up a discarded foil space blanket and wrap it around myself. Nobody seems to notice. I sit down on a bench and pull my trousers up so they end above my knees. Do I look like a marathon runner? Not yet I don't.

Close to the finishing line I find a discarded drawstring bag. It's sponsored by the same banks and insurance companies who sponsor the space blanket and spectator stands. Inside I find a bottle of water, a protein shake, an oat and honey granola bar, a bottle of Gatorade, and a bag of pretzels encased in a packet modified to read *You Did It*.

I certainly did.

What I need now is a discarded baseball cap to hide my face. I see one but it's in the secure area of the park, the area for registered runners only, people with wrist-bands, so I walk on. Eventually I spot a cap sponsored by the same bank that sponsors everything else. It's been left up on a rock near the Plaza hotel. I walk over and pick it up and check it's clean, and then I rinse it from the water bottle and pour the remaining water over my head as make-believe sweat. I put the cap on. You see me up on this rock and you see a triumphant runner, a sub-four-hours athlete, someone who trained for months and months and who finished her race.

I have *almost* finished my race.

The Ritz-Carlton is right in front of me, I can see my floor through the orange foliage of the trees. My window and my telescope. My belongings. My clothes. And my cash.

I look at my watch. I have several hours to stay lost and unidentified before my exit out of here. I'm tempted to board the Staten Island ferry and wait there until nightfall. Somewhere away from Manhattan, but still accessible. The subway is too dangerous; there are too many cameras. The main thoroughfares are littered with aboveground CCTV systems, and who knows how good the facial recognition technology is these days?

So, I stay in the park.

I'm looking south from my rock.

To my left is the Upper East Side, where DeLuca warned me, and further east is Brooklyn and my sister's crematorium in Queens, and Violet's home and JFK. South of me is the Bedfordshire Midtown Hostel and all the memories I have with my parents, those two tiny next-door rooms, the kindness the diner waitress gifted me the night I stayed there researching before the storm, conscious that my search history might get investigated, keen to have a headstart, eager to be the one who found James Kandee's jet details to direct shade away from myself. Of course he had a cast-iron alibi. He gave speeches and hosted lunches that afternoon. He walked to the board meeting of a private equity fund based downtown with two of its founding partners, and he had a meeting at the UN regarding one of his charity projects. He wasn't alone for a single minute, and he wasn't anywhere near my sister's apartment in Morningside Heights.

To my right is the YMCA, and further up is Columbia University: one of the finest colleges anywhere in the world.

A passer-by gives me a thumbs-up for finishing the race and I tip my cap to him.

I eat the pretzels. I need to keep my strength up and I need to stay away from shops and cafés until my eight o'clock pick-up.

I'm licking the salt from my lips when I spot them.

Four uniformed cops in the distance walking towards me, one of them pointing. Are they pointing at me?

They can't be.

They are.

47

I clamber down the rock and start walking towards Fifth Avenue. I don't look back, but from the reactions of the people walking towards me I can tell the cops are running. So I run.

How did they find me? Undercover police? CCTV? I sprint and I feel my trouser legs fall down to my ankles and I sprint harder than I ever have before.

At the Plaza hotel intersection I run through traffic and clip the wing mirror of a yellow cab. Drivers honk their horns and one guy in a chromed delivery truck yells, 'You crazy, lady?' from his open window.

The cops get slowed down by the traffic. I head into the Plaza and straight through to the other side.

In the mirrors I see them in the distance: two cops. One fast, one slow.

As I burst out of the hotel doors and run down Fifth I see Martinez on the street talking into a radio. I cut into a store. Bergdorf Goodman.

The staff look aghast as I run through in my space blanket. I sprint through two departments, then slow and ditch the blanket. I crouch behind a rack of coats and remove my jacket and pull it inside out. It was red and now it's grey. I ditch the bag of food and I ditch the cap, scraping my hair into a ponytail.

A uniform cop walks in and I buy a beret at the counter for a hundred and forty dollars cash.

I walk out of a side door carrying the empty store paper bag and wearing the beret. I walk, slowly, with purpose, across the street. Six more blocks. I cut across to Lexington and walk a block and then cut back to Fifth and down 46th Street.

It feels like home.

Past the Sofitel and on towards the hostel.

I can't see any cops there but I know there's probably one in the room waiting for me to show up. I pass back to Fifth and circle through Bryant Park and up to the west end of 46th, away from the hostel, just to cover all the angles, before heading back there. Five minutes later a man in a long raincoat walks into the hostel. I see the bulge on his hip. He's a detective.

I stay close to the hostel but I do not go inside.

My beret is tight on my head, almost covering my eyes.

'Jimmy,' I say, walking fast to his smoothie cart. 'It's me, Jimmy. The bag.'

He reaches under the counter and pulls out my go-bag. 'You safe?' he asks.

I nod and grab the bag and walk down to the Sofitel.

You can't enter the lift in an establishment like the Sofitel and get access to the floors with rooms, you just can't. But if you press down then you'll go down. It's because hotels need to sell gym memberships to non-guests in order to maximise their profits and please their shareholders. So I go down in my beret and I check myself into a spotlessly clean and air-conditioned restroom.

My chest's pounding.

I unzip the go-bag.

I remove the beret and my jacket and fold them and place them on the toilet seat lid. I remove the high quality latex mask I bought in a costume store on my second full day here in New York, and I remove a cheap crumpled old man suit that I bought for cash in a thrift store in Gramercy. I stuff my clothes into the bag and then I listen to the room. There's nobody out there washing their hands or fixing their make-up.

I step out and it feels terrifying to be in a public place wearing this thing. I look in the mirror and an old man with grey hair and grey stubble stares back. You cannot see that I'm not an old man.

I stuff my bag down into the waste paper basket and cover it with tissues.

As I turn to leave, a woman walks in and gasps. I mumble something apologetic in a deep voice and then I walk out towards the gents' restroom. She watches me leave: a short man in his seventies wearing an old suit and new black sneakers.

Inside the gents' there are two men washing their hands and neither one of them notices me.

I wash my own hands and walk out and take a tiny pebble from an ornamental plant. I place it in my right shoe and I call the lift and ride it up to the ground floor. A hotel employee opens the door for me and says, 'Have a nice day, sir.'

I nod my thanks and limp out of the hotel on to 44th Street.

The third person I see outside is Detective Martinez.

He's thirty yards ahead of me.

We're walking towards each other.

He puts his hand inside his jacket.

48

I keep on walking.

Martinez pulls out his phone.

I keep going. Hobbling. A retired CIA operative on YouTube explained this method of disguise as *onion-like*. You layer up and you layer down. I look like any other old man with this cutting-edge mask because my skin appears wrinkled. I have liver spots, thin grey hair, jowls. But I also have a wrinkly neck: the mask extends under my shirt line. You have to inhabit the role. *Believe* in it. No half-measures. Maybe I would get noticed without this limp. It's hard to fake a limp – if you try you'll look like you're faking it. I'm not faking it, my limp is real and the pebble digging into my foot is causing me genuine pain.

Ten feet from me.

He walks closer.

I limp on.

As we pass I look straight into Martinez's eyes. I can almost smell his cologne.

He stares straight past me.

I go on.

Fifth Avenue.

This is a significant operation. FBI, possibly. Could be

they're after James Kandee and I'm just a small part. A pawn.

Back up to Central Park. Slowly. The police wouldn't expect anyone to return to the central location where they were first spotted and that's exactly why I'm headed back there.

The post-race clean-up operation is in full swing. I have an hour to wait before my extraction.

The park's getting dark in places but it's still open. Doesn't close until one a.m. I checked once why a place like Central Park isn't well-lit and covered by cameras. The best answer I could find was that if they lit the place then it'd need policing. You light an area and you make it safe and then you need to police it to make sure it continues to stay safe. All 843 acres of it. With an already stretched police department. So they leave it wild. The only *truly* dark place in Manhattan outside of the waterways.

I pass the lake and head north.

I read somewhere that the Ramble used to be a late-night cruising spot. Back in the time before the internet. I doubt they'd have been keen to see me without my disguise and, looking the way I do in this mask, I doubt they'd have been pleased to see me now that I resemble a septuagenarian man.

The air is cool and I'm alert to every siren, every distant yell.

Past Cleopatra's Needle and on to the dark water of the Jacqueline Kennedy Onassis Reservoir. This park is about two and a half miles long. It's a miracle it still exists here, in one of the densest, most expensive cities in the Western world.

I pass a park policeman and he ignores me completely. Why wouldn't he?

The only food I have is the marathon granola bar I took out of the bag and hid in my pocket earlier. I'm hungry but I'll wait a while. I'm not sure how long this night is going to last.

Past the tennis courts and into the thick undergrowth.

I check my surroundings because the last thing I need is some do-gooder mistaking me for a dementia patient and calling me in. When the coast is clear I shuffle down into the bushes and I crouch low and I eat my granola bar.

It is sweet.

DeLuca told me two o'clock and now it's seven fifty-five so I'm right on time. DeLuca told me we'd be travelling by sea so I know what's coming next. DeLuca told me to meet him at '31st Street usual' so that's why I'm squatting in a dead bush beside the 97th Street Transverse, close to the bridge, near the place I was picked up on the day I killed my sister. If you look at a clock face 3 is opposite 9, and 1 is opposite 7.

With thirty seconds to go I scramble to the other side of the bushes. I'm ready, crouching, waiting, on top of a steep-sided concrete bank. It's forty-five degrees and when the time is right, when there are no vehicles on the road, I scoot down to the pavement below.

Two cars pass me by and then a Volvo appears.

It slows.

The door opens.

I climb inside.

'Get down in the footwell and cover yourself with the blanket.'

I do as he says. I don't utter a word.

We drive and drive. I try to judge the direction and the distance by focusing on the buildings and light I can see through the material of the blanket. I already know where we're headed, I just don't know the route he'll take.

'They got close,' he says.

'I know they did.'

He drives on. The car smells brand new. I'm guessing we're travelling at five per cent below the speed limit. I'm guessing he's careful to use his mirrors and his indicators. Just another Volvo driving to New Jersey.

The lights are few and far between.

We drive off the expressway and into what feels like a suburb.

Five minutes later we slow to a crawl and pull into what looks like a residential, two-car garage.

Everything goes dark.

'End of the line,' he says.

'What?'

'Get out.'

49

The garage is lit by three fluorescent strip-lights and the floor is squeaky clean. It looks rubberised, like a hospital floor.

There are clear plastic sheets on the walls and on the floor.

The man from the car is wearing latex gloves.

There's a barrel of liquid covered in hazard warning labels.

At the far end of the room is a wall of tools and machines, each one attached to a pin board and circled in white.

DeLuca walks through a door and hands me a bottle of water. The seal is secure. It's a fresh bottle.

'Drink. You need to go to the bathroom, there's a bucket in the corner.'

I scowl at him and take a sip from the water. 'What is this place?'

'You've never been here. You'll never be here again.'

'Where am I?'

'Nowhere,' he says, opening the rear hatch of a Mercedes SUV. 'Get in.'

'In the back?'

'No,' says DeLuca. 'In the box.'

There's a black leather box with name tags and tassels. It has air holes and vents.

'In the box?'

'The other one's already at the hangar. Twin boxes. You'll need this.' He hands me a Dictaphone. 'And this.' He hands me a sheet of folded fur.

'What?'

'The Man has two dogs.'

'I read about them. St Bernard's?'

'Bernese mountain dogs. Two sisters from the same litter. Krista's already close to the hangar and this crate belongs to Milla.'

He explains that the suitcase method of entry, the way I got back to London from New York a week ago, with me folded inside reinforced wheeled luggage, may not work this time. Too risky. The airports have heightened security. He doesn't know if it's connected to the recent spate of murders in Manhattan, or if it's just the TSA tightening up. So we have a new method. There's no way this would work with a commercial airline, but private is different. This box solution, combined with the fact that James Kandee has two officials at the airport on his payroll, will suffice. Though he says 'payroll', no cash has ever changed hands, of course. Just two sponsorships so one guy's daughter can study at Brown and the other guy's son gets put through Penn State. A favour for a favour: an easy passage through customs for a free college education.

The bespoke leather container is roomier than the customised suitcase I travelled in last time. I ached for two days after that journey and I had a cramp for the second half of the flight. I wore an adult diaper, supplied, but I didn't need to use it. I'm used to wearing them for research marathons. They don't bother me. That suitcase was reinforced; this is even more luxurious: French leather from the house of Hermès. I'm the same weight as the dog, apparently. And this long leather box allows me to stretch a little. DeLuca explains how the matching boxes were built to exacting specifications, with mesh vents and air holes and full coverage, unlike traditional crates, to ensure the anxious dogs are calm in transit. I have a water bottle with a straw and a kibble feeder full of organic granola.

Before we leave in the Mercedes another guy walks through and drives off in the Volvo we arrived in. Two minutes later we drive out of the door.

It's a strange feeling being encased in a box of your own volition. The human instinct – my instinct – is still to scream. To fight. I was zipped into this thing voluntarily, clutching my Dictaphone device and my folded piece of fur. But still I want to yell and force my back up through the zipped leather lid. I want to break this open, but I just stay as calm and as quiet as I can.

'Test the devices,' says DeLuca from the driving seat.

I press button one and the Dictaphone emits a growling noise. I press button two: a different growl, more aggressive. Three and four are both barks, one short, one more of a howl. He opens the Velcro hatch and I hold the patch of fur as instructed and he scans it.

'Good,' says DeLuca. 'Any questions.'

'Did you get my money from my room?'

'The Man will fill you in.'

That doesn't sound positive.

'All good?'

'All good.'

We drive about thirty minutes and then pull into Teterboro airport. I can't see anything from inside here unless I open a leather hatch on the roof section of the crate.

When we arrive in the hangar I close the hatch and spread out inside the box, my senses on high alert, my finger on the Dictaphone button.

I wait, listening.

My breath moistens the inside of the leather box.

The sound of men talking.

DeLuca opens the rear of the Mercedes and he, along with, I'm guessing, one other guy, maybe James Kandee, unload my box. What I didn't realise is that the crate has integrated wheels. They pull me outside the hangar on to the taxi area. I'm deposited next to an identical dog crate. I can smell Krista through the material. Dog odour and expensive leather.

She growls.

The men outside my crate are joined by others and I hear laughing.

Then the sound of jet engines starting up.

More talking. Are they checking James Kandee's passport? Do they even check in a place like this?

I get a kick to my side so I unfold the piece again and it feels like pony skin complete with black and brown and white fur. I hold it up to the leather hatch and then I press button one. A low growl. Krista responds with a similar growl from her own crate. The men laugh again. Someone rips off the hatch and holds a microchip scanning device to the fur and it beeps. The hatch closes.

'Beautiful dogs,' I hear the customs official say.

'Yes, they are,' says a boyish voice. Nasal. The voice of James Kandee.

I press button two for a longer growl.

More laughing and then the men leave DeLuca to manhandle both dog crates into the jet. I get bumped around through the plane door and back into the rear of the aircraft, where I know the private bedroom is located.

Silence.

I'm on board a Gulfstream G650 jet and the dog in the next crate over is sniffing and scratching at her box.

The engines scream and Krista barks.

As the plane taxis I dig my nails into the soft pads of my fingers, focusing, trying not to pass out with terror.

The plane picks up speed.

Krista barks and howls.

The plane is in the air, and I am leaving New York City once and for all.

50

It's not as bad as you think, taking off while you're trapped inside a leather dog crate.

I'd rather have a comfortable seat and a seatbelt, but there is an illogical reassurance that comes from being confined in a small space. I'm surrounded by Hermès calf leather and the crate is jammed between the on-board bed and the fuselage wall.

Once we're in the air I take a sip from the water bottle tube.

I wait for a long time. What feels like hours.

A noise.

I hear the door to the jet's bedroom open.

The hatch lifts and I see his narrow, clean-shaven face. He smiles down at me and then he opens the lid of the crate and offers me his delicate hand. I take it, contorting my limbs to climb out, stretching, bent double for a moment before straightening up.

'You look like you need a drink, Molly.'

'Is it safe?'

'On here?' he says. 'Completely. The captain and co-pilot have been with me for eleven years and seven years respectively. They know the score, I told you last time. They're not to come out of the cockpit unless they need the restroom, which is directly next to the cockpit. They will not enter the rear two-thirds of the aircraft. You're safe. Please, come through.'

He leads me into the centre portion of the jet. A sofa with a film projector, twelve large cream leather armchairs, each headrest monogrammed JK. Just as I remember it.

'Was the dog crate better than the suitcase, or worse?'

'Better,' I say. 'The pilot has the flight plan?'

He nods. 'Good choice, Molly. You did your research. I mean, all three options I gave you had effectively zero extradition risk, but your choice, for my money, was the right one. Palm trees and easy living.'

I made my choice after news of KT's death came out. I contacted James Kandee and told him he had to help me, otherwise he would be accessory to a murder. I needed a back-up plan in case things went wrong.

'How long before we're there?'

'Not long now.'

'Did DeLuca's people get my money out from the suite?'

He smiles and points to the chair opposite. We both sit down facing each other. 'No, he did not.'

I stand back up.

'Relax, Molly. Please, sit down. The day you've had. Please, take a seat and let me explain.'

I sit down.

'Drink?'

'My money?'

'Well, in reality it's *my* money, but I understand your concern. They couldn't get into your suite; the NYPD were all over it. I'm sorry, I know you had some sentimental items stowed away.'

'I had thirty-eight thousand dollars stowed away.'

He reaches down under his seat and lifts up a black leather portfolio folder. It matches the dog crate. 'I rounded it back up to fifty.'

He pushes the leather folder across the table to me and I unzip it. 'Fifty?'

'Count it if you like, Molly.'

I flick through a wad of notes. 'I trust you.'

'After what I've done for you, I would say you should trust me. Now, that drink. Gin, whisky, champagne? I don't have an attendant so I'll serve you myself.'

I hesitate and then I say, 'Gin and tonic. A weak one.'

He steps over to a small kitchenette and prepares two gin and tonics. 'Lemon, lime or cucumber, Molly?'

'Lime and ice.'

He finishes the drinks and sits back down, pushing one of the glasses over to me. The tonic water bubbles explode under my nose and I relax for the first time in a long time. It tastes strong.

'What happens when we get there?' I ask.

'Simple. They think Milla is booked in for a residential obedience course at a beachside resort. So, when we land, I step off the plane with you in the crate, and you're carried to the outsize-baggage area inside the building, to be picked up and driven an hour from the airport, to the boarding house you requested. I take a meeting with an art dealer at the Grand Hotel, buy a Matisse sketch, and then I'll board the plane and head to St Kitts for a three-day trip.'

'And then that's the end of it.'

'That, Molly, is the end of it.'

I drink.

The plane turns to the right and I grip the seat with my hand.

'It's OK,' says James. 'They're the best in the business.'

I put my seatbelt on anyway.

'I need to ask you, Molly. How has it been these past days? I mean, I expect you've had nobody to talk to about any of this. How has that affected you? Psychologically, I mean.'

'I've worked through it.'

'DeLuca told me you've been punishing some of Katie's friends and associates for their wrongdoings.'

'I don't know what he means.'

'You can talk freely here, Molly. It's probably the only place in the world where you can talk freely. I have the aircraft scanned for bugs and surveillance devices before each and every flight. Now, one thing I'd like to know. Why did you lie to me?'

'I didn't lie to you.'

'You demanded I fly you to New York so you could reconcile with your twin sister while your parents were visiting. You told me you didn't have a passport and you didn't have any money.'

My neck starts to itch.

'But you did have a passport, Molly. And you didn't reconcile with Katie – quite the opposite.'

'Things went wrong,' I say. 'You can't predict how someone will react.'

'I'd bloody say so.'

I don't like his tone. I unfasten my seatbelt.

'You put me and my organisation at unnecessary risk, Molly. DeLuca and his team have been working 24/7 to clean up your trail, to avoid anyone linking us.'

'I know.'

'Why did you do it to your sister?'

'I don't know.'

'You do know. What had Katie ever done to you?'

I shrug.

He shakes his head. 'Let me tell you, from experience, that if you don't talk about it, if you don't let it out, it'll eat away at you until you grow tumours. What happened in Katie's apartment that afternoon, Molly?'

I take a deep breath and then sip from my drink.

'That's a beautiful watch you're wearing,' I say.

He looks confused for a moment, glancing down at his left wrist. 'It's a vintage Rolex. Used to belong to a racing driver. I won it in Geneva.'

'I know,' I say. 'I was there when you bid for it.'

'No, Katie was there.'

I dip the cuff of my sleeve into my gin tumbler and wipe at my eyebrow. The look on his face as my make-up smudges and the scar reappears.

'What are you . . .?' he says.

'Yes,' I say.

'Katie?'

I pull the snub-nosed .38 revolver lighter I bought from a souvenir store out from my sock and hold it casually at table level, the barrel pointed at his chest.

He swallows. 'Don't do anything stupid, Molly.'

'Katie. My name is Katie.'

He frowns. 'What did I whisper in your ear when I won this watch at the Phillips auction?'

I smile. 'You whispered, *One day, Katie, this watch will be yours.*'

His mouth falls open.

51

'You?'

'Me.'

He shakes his head and then he focuses on my gun. 'Don't kill me. I can get you more cash, just don't kill me, please.'

'You do exactly as I say, your perfect life won't change one bit. And I've had enough of your money, your sponsorship, your secret packages, your conditions, your precise stipulations about how I should dress when attending the opera with you or how I should look at you when dining out with your friends in Italy. I've had enough of your foundation.' I can feel my face reddening. 'Enough of deliveries, and enough of men in dark suits from half a dozen countries tracking me because of my connection with you and Project H. Enough of Bogart DeLuca or Peter Hill or whatever his name will be next month. This is the end.'

'Whatever you want.' His hands are up by his cheeks. 'Just put the gun down.'

I ignore him. 'You flew Molly out to New York to fucking kill me. What did I do to deserve that, James?'

'I didn't know she came to kill you! She said she was coming to make up with you, start afresh, heal the wounds with you.'

I narrow my eyes.

'She said she couldn't afford the flight. I offered to buy her a commercial ticket but she said she didn't have a passport and she demanded to see you urgently. She knew about what we were doing, Katie. I don't know how, but she knew. I was forced to help her.'

'You're lying.'

'I'm telling you the truth.'

'You flew her from her pathetic little London flat to my apartment.'

'I'm sorry.'

'She did start out by making efforts to repair our relationship that day. She apologised for overreacting when I told her I was moving to New York. I listened. She said she always felt like the boring underachieving twin. Like she didn't get as many of the good genes as I did in the womb or some bullshit. She was tired of people comparing us both, looking down on her. And then I moved to the USA.'

'She was vulnerable.'

'No,' I say, draining my gin. 'Molly wasn't vulnerable. She was fucking dangerous. Unhinged and detached from reality. It was always me that was at risk. From her extreme nature. If anyone was vulnerable that day it was me. Having her inside my apartment.'

'What happened?'

I keep the gun lighter pointed at his torso.

'She talked. I listened. I was pretty stunned when she turned up unannounced like that. We drank a pot of tea and we chatted. Real, genuine talk like we'd done as kids. She told me how she'd got there, all about the journey over to New York, how it was done, how *helpful* you'd been, and that she was flying back later that same evening with you, meeting your car in the park. It was the most exciting thing that had happened to her for years. She told me how you used our childhood code in emails. We even spoke in our code together for a few sentences until we started laughing about the craziness of it. And then we both cried. From laughter to sadness. I don't know what she felt, but I felt loss that afternoon. The impossible closeness turning into distance. Not just physical distance, but emotional distance. After the tea and the crying we were both exhausted. I suggested we sleep before dinner. She took the sofa and I took the bed. But I knew something was off. I don't know how I knew – some kind of intuition. So I rested, but I didn't sleep.'

'She tried to attack you?' he says, shuffling in his seat.

'You move and I'll shoot you in the abdomen,' I say. 'A slow and painful death. Molly did try to attack me, James, yes. She waited until she thought I was in deep sleep. We both sleep the exact same way: on our backs, with our faces pointing up to the ceiling; it's an unusual sleep pose. I was under the sheets. She started to creep towards me and my pulse started racing. I thought maybe she was going to stab me or inject me with something. But then she took the pillow and she raised it up towards my face. Her expression was cold marble. Not evil, more blank. She started to push the pillow closer to me and I flipped her in one swift move. I'm a swimmer; she wasn't.'

It's possible she just wanted to lie down next to me. I've thought about that. But her expression suggested differently.

I've come to terms with what I did. I know in my heart that she was in my apartment to kill me. She couldn't take it any longer and she wanted me gone.

'I can't believe it's you,' he says. 'Where did we stay in Monaco for the Grand Prix?'

'First night in the Hôtel de Paris, second night on your schoolfriend's yacht, the *Lunar*.'

He shakes his head again. 'Your eyebrow scar?'

'It took longer than I expected for her to go quiet. Even with my weight bearing down on her she fought, and I hardly had any advantage. I kept the pillow in place long after she'd settled. And then I told her goodnight.'

I've been suffocated my whole life. She only experienced it for a few minutes.

'But the scar . . .?'

'I plucked a line in her eyebrow so she'd look like me. I swallowed the plucked hairs.'

'And your parents didn't notice?'

I stroke the barrel of the gun lighter with my middle finger. 'She didn't look like either one of us by that point. Her eyes were red from burst capillaries and her skin was pallid. Her face looked awful. But she was at peace. She came to finish me and I turned the tables. It was self-defence. Completely justifiable.'

She'd smothered me ever since I was a young girl. Weighing me down. Making me feel guilty for living my life to the full. A professional energy thief even way back then, demanding Mum and Dad's attention, forcing them to worry about her every day: emotional blackmail to ensure they kept her going, kept her on the level. She would make demands from across the Atlantic and I would distance myself, ignoring her, protecting my life, knowing that my actions would fuel her anxiety. An identical twin is in a uniquely powerful position to do something like that. The levels of trust are unfathomable to most people.

'I'll give you more money – just let me go.' He's sweating and I can see his hands shaking. 'You can have the plane, you can take the pilots.'

'I don't want your plane or your pilots. I want to truly disappear.'

He frowns, not understanding this concept. James Kandee's identity is so wrapped up in his foundations and his charities and the hospital wings named after his ancestors. He *is* his Instagram account.

We never did find out what we were delivering. Some of the girls suspected they were collectibles: stolen gemstones or lost artefacts that are impossible to trade on the open market. One girl from Yale had a theory about a new experimental drug: a non-traceable, safe-to-use psychotropic substance used only by the super-rich.

I don't care what it was. I just care that it's over now.

'I want a normal life,' I say, 'for however long I can have it. Statistically speaking, identical twins die within two years of each other. I want at least two normal years.'

'You think that's possible? After what you've done?'

'What have I done? I defended myself against a maniac. And then I righted some wrongs is all. Wrongs inflicted upon me. Betrayals and lies. If people do wrong they must be punished. The punishment must fit the crime, I appreciate that, and I made every effort to make them fit. In my eyes, I'm leaving New York City a better place than I found it.'

Molly was born three minutes after I was, and I often think about those precious moments. What we must have looked like together, Mum, Dad and me. The three of us. Complete.

The jet starts its descent and the pilot announces *fifteen minutes to landing* and I grip the arms of the seat. Because I worry too, you see – about safety, about threats in the world. I follow YouTube accounts and I know how to make improvised weapons. Molly made a drama out of her anxiety levels – always the most scared, the most timid, the most in need. She took all the attention, and all our parents' time and care. So I was forced to go the other way, to be confident, outgoing. Self-reliant. I had no choice.

And it wasn't enough for her: she wanted all of my attention too. She forced me to move to New York. I needed space to breathe. And, in a way, I found that space. And a new family of sorts, people who focused on me and never even met my demanding little sister. They only knew me. My side. My ways. Scottie was sweet – until he started to stray. He was focused on me for a while. Unwavering attention. I never wanted to hurt him like that. But the way he flirted at the restaurant, mere days after what he thought was my death. How he acted around Vi. How he was so keen to meet me at the Sofitel. There was no other option in the end. The cut to his throat was necessary, to differentiate his death from my sister's murder. It was important to me that the police would suspect two different people. Scott broke my heart over and over. So I broke him.

James squirms in his seat.

Groot should not teach after this. He should go work in consulting or maybe a museum. Well away from young students. He's just one more man who can't tell the truth. I have to turn to elaborate disguises and subterfuge but men seem to have a natural aptitude for deception. It's like they don't even need to try. I considered ending him. But he has a wife and children and ultimately I was too fond of the man. I hated him and I loved him. On balance I'd say he got off too lightly. Further action may be required.

'Molly lived a miserable life,' I say, calmly. 'All I did was put her out of her misery. It would have been different if she'd been enjoying herself, but she wasn't. If anything this was an act of mercy.'

James starts to say something and I show him the gun again.

'Don't kill me,' he says.

'Take off your clothes.'

'What?'

'I said take off your fucking clothes, James.'

He stands up.

'One wrong move and I will shoot you – you know I'll do it.'

He takes off his jacket and then he pulls down his jeans.

The plane shakes as the landing gear emerges from the undercarriage.

'Shoes,' I say.

He slips off his sneakers and then starts to take off his socks.

'Keep your socks and underwear,' I say. 'Get in the bedroom.'

He doesn't resist as I duct-tape his mouth and his wrists and his ankles. He doesn't protest as I bundle him into the Hermès leather dog crate. He looks relieved if anything.

I was nervous about entering the US with my sister's unused passport. Worried the fingerprints might set off an alarm. But Immigration let me straight through.

'You know better than to ever come looking for me,' I say. 'Because you know what I'm capable of.'

In truth, if I kill him, his teams will come after me. I'll never stop looking over my shoulder. James has always kept his word. This is self-preservation, not mercy.

'I'm sparing your life. Full and final settlement. It's over.'

He nods his agreement.

I haven't decided what will happen to Bagby yet. The wise choice would be to leave him to self-destruct. I believe he will. But if I get bored I'll consider hastening his downfall. There are ways to attack a YouTube channel anonymously. Not trolling, not a single video to disgust his fans, but a campaign. A war.

Before I zip the leather dog crate shut I remove the 1969 Rolex Daytona Paul Newman watch from his wrist. I remember how much he paid for it. How rare it is.

The view from the plane is spectacular. Palm trees and white buildings.

I dress in James's clothes and I pull on his New York Yankees baseball cap. We're almost the same height and build. I put on his sunglasses. I strap on his Rolex.

As kids Molly and I would pretend to be each other. To shock our parents. To see what we could get away with at a friend's house. I'm not sure Molly knew I could research almost as efficiently as her. We weren't so different in that regard. The key to the pretence working effectively was always to believe in it yourself. Truly inhabit the role. It can be a thrill, actually. You have to *think* like the other person. I learned that from a retired undercover cop who lived for years as part of a motorcycle gang. His video taught me that to not let the mask slip, you must let go of your past self, albeit temporarily. You have to train yourself to think like the other person. I had to read my own FortressMail emails with fresh eyes. Molly's eyes. That search history trail was vitally important. I knew that if police looked into my digital records they'd find what Molly would have logically searched for. I thought like she would. I had to imagine every detail of what it was like for Molly to fly back to London. Implant those false memories. Even as kids, pretending, Molly and I both knew we had to fully commit.

The door opens, but the pilots stay in the cockpit as instructed.

Molly thought she knew everything about me, but she hardly knew me at all. I *know* I knew everything about her.

I wheel the dog crate containing The Man to the door and then I back away. The baggage handler retrieves it.

'Pleasant flight?' he says.

I nod from inside the cabin.

'Your car's waiting, sir.'

I wait for him to leave and then walk down the Gulfstream's steps, carrying only my leather portfolio case stuffed with used dollars. As I give the pilots the thumbs-up, I see my vintage Rolex glint in the equatorial sun. They see it, too.

I walk into my new life.

Imagine knowing a version of yourself exists in the world. A physical manifestation of all your worst traits and weaknesses. A constant reminder of what you could become.

The air is hot.

In time I'll bring my parents here and we'll live together in a modest house and enjoy a few modest years together. They'll be unencumbered from their debts and bad memories, most of which stem back to taking so much time to watch out for Molly. I think my parents want this new situation even though they'd be afraid to admit it. Mum will have joy in her life again. I'll never be a burden the way Molly was. I'll never put them through that.

We had three minutes together following my birth. Three perfect minutes. We'll have that again.

I climb into the back seat of the car and the dog box is taken to the terminal. I have my lighter in my pocket in case I need it.

We'll live out here, just me and my parents. Maybe I'll tell them Groot paid me off to keep my mouth shut.

They'll have time for me. We'll do things together. Share experiences.

Three ravens.

No extras.

No duplicates.

The perfect family.

Acknowledgements

I grew up as a shy, awkward kid in the midlands. I often felt like an alien observing another species. Watching, not participating. Trying to understand the kids around me. Trying to make sense of the world. Not much has changed. I never expected to be a writer. From an early age I found great comfort and escape in reading fiction. My family weren't readers. There were no books at home. But I was lucky. My mother would take me to a local mobile library truck and I'd borrow as many books as I could carry. She was busy and tired and I'll always be grateful to her for enabling me to discover so many imaginary worlds.

The shy British kid is now a forty-two-year old bearded man living semi off-grid in a moose forest in Sweden. Again, I never expected to be a writer – I didn't think it was an option available to someone like me. I was the first person in my family to stay in school past sixteen. The first to go to university. It wasn't until I was well into my thirties that I had the confidence to start writing. I was content until then to be a constant reader, and that part of my life is still central to who I am. A reader, first and foremost. A person addicted to the feeling of diving head-first into an immersive story. And so I'm thankful to the authors I have read. They have shaped my work. I owe them a lot.

Heartfelt thanks to Jo Dickinson at Hodder for taking a chance on me, and for helping me to improve each book. I'm indebted to Jenny Platt, Alice Morley, Sorcha Rose, Nick Sayers, Dominic Gribben and the whole team at Hodder. Extra thanks to my proofreaders and copyeditors who do an extraordinary job.

And when it comes to taking chances, I also want to thank my literary agent, Kate Burke at Blake Friedmann, for plucking my manuscript out of her slushpile years ago. Thanks also to Isobel Dixon, Conrad Williams, Julian Friedmann, James Pusey, Hana Murrell, Lizzy Attree, and the whole BF team.

I'm lucky to work with Emily Bestler at Atria/Emily Bestler Books in America. I'm grateful to her, and to Lara Jones, David Brown, Maudee Genao, and the whole Simon & Schuster team.

Thanks to all my international publishers and translators.

Thanks to <u>you</u> for taking the time to read this book. I appreciate it very much.

Finally, love and thanks to my wife and son. And my St Bernard. And my forest cat.

ORDER THE NEXT BOOK FROM WILL DEAN

THE LAST PASSENGER

My phone has no reception, something we've been told to expect from time to time out here, and my stomach feels uneasy. Maybe it's the motion of the waves or maybe it's the fact that Pete didn't leave a note or a text. He usually leaves a note with a heart.

I pull on jeans and a jumper and scrunch my hair on top of my head and take my key card and step out into the corridor.

Thirty seconds later it hits me.

All the other cabin doors are wedged open.

Every single one is unoccupied and unlocked.

My heart starts beating harder. I break out into a run. At the end of the long corridor I take a lift down to the Ocean Lobby.

There's nobody here.

My mouth is dry.

It's like I'm trapped on a runaway train.

No, this is worse.

The RMS Atlantica is steaming out into the ocean and I am the only person on board.

This was supposed to be the holiday of a lifetime for Cas. Now she just needs to survive.